Fleur McDonald has lived and worked on farms for much of her life. After growing up in the small town of Orroroo in South Australia, she went jillarooing, eventually co-owning an 8000-acre property in regional Western Australia.

Fleur likes to write about strong women overcoming adversity, drawing inspiration from her own experiences in rural Australia. Fleur currently lives in Esperance with her two children, an energetic kelpie and a Jack Russell terrier.

www.fleurmcdonald.com

FLEUR McDONALD

Where the River Runs

ALLEN&UNWIN
SYDNEY • MELBOURNE • AUCKLAND • LONDON

This edition published in 2019
First published in 2018

Allen & Unwin
83 Alexander Street
Crows Nest NSW 2065
Australia
Phone: (61 2) 8425 0100
Email: info@allenandunwin.com
Web: www.allenandunwin.com

A catalogue record for this
book is available from the
National Library of Australia

ISBN 978 1 76087 622 7

Set in Sabon LT Pro by Bookhouse, Sydney
Printed and bound in Australia by Griffin Press, part of Ovato

10 9 8 7 6 5 4 3 2

The paper in this book is FSC® certified.
FSC® promotes environmentally responsible,
socially beneficial and economically viable
management of the world's forests.

For you

'Music is the universal language of mankind.'
Henry Wadsworth Longfellow

Prologue

2001

'Chelsea, I've told you time and time again, it's your third finger, then thumb under, then fourth finger and thumb under for a double octave C major scale,' said Mrs Maher in a frustrated tone. 'I just seem to keep repeating myself. In fact, you might as well pack up for the day. You're not listening, once again.'

Thirteen-year-old Chelsea felt like screwing up her nose and crossing her eyes behind Mrs Maher's back, but since the piano teacher was sitting beside her and would probably see, she decided the punishment wouldn't be worth it. The old dragon would probably insist she practise scales for the rest of her life. Boring!

Two weeks ago she'd heard a Madonna song on the radio. It had been a live version, played only on the piano, and the simple melody had made Chelsea fall in love with it. Some of her friends had laughed, told her she was behind the times, but Lily hadn't. The two girls had spent hours dancing in front of the mirror, learning the words and singing at the tops of their voices.

Chelsea had tinkered on the piano, working out the notes and finally getting the tune for 'Crazy For You'. Of course, if she'd looked hard enough when she'd visited Adelaide with her family, there would have been a music shop that sold the sheet music, but Chelsea preferred to nut it out for herself. The sheet music would've meant she had to play the piece the way it was written. Working it out for herself meant she could play it exactly how she wanted to. Did it really matter if her technique wasn't perfect when she could touch the keys on the piano and make them sing sweeter than anyone in the school? The music theory was boring. She just wanted to play her own way, not the way she was told to, or expected to. Her Great-Grandfather Baxter had once told her she was unique, and Chelsea planned to keep it that way by rebelling against the rules.

Chelsea had heard Mrs Maher tell Mrs Granger, who was her English teacher: 'That Chelsea Taylor, she's the best student I've taught since I've been here. Very talented.'

'If you can keep her interested in the piano, you'll have done better than the rest of the teachers here,' Mrs Granger had responded. 'Chelsea lives in a world of her own. No focus at all, staring out the window or lost in her own thoughts most of the time. Frustrating, because she's really quite intelligent.'

2

'I'm not sure it's a world of her own,' Mrs Maher had countered. 'I don't think she likes to conform with the school rules so she does things her own way.'

The warm glow Chelsea had felt when she'd overheard the conversation started in her belly again. Well, until she remembered the last thing Mrs Maher had said. What would she know? Adults, even if they were right, didn't know anything about kids!

Instead of making a face at her piano teacher, she smiled and ran her fingers over the keys, causing a storm of notes to erupt, before settling into the beautiful and melodic chords of another Madonna song, 'Live To Tell'. She remembered the tune by heart. Learning to read music had always seemed a bore to her, especially when she knew she could remember the song easily. Perhaps not exactly as it was scored, but did that really matter? All the best musicians put their own spin on the music they played.

As her fingers ran across the keys, she imagined herself on stage in front of a packed audience at the Opera House, just like Richard Clayderman. Her Great-Grandfather Baxter had listened to the pianist and, although she'd never been to one of his concerts, she imagined what it must be like to play in front of a huge adoring audience.

Clayderman's music was continually played on the CD player she had saved up for, although neither of her parents could understand why she liked solo piano music when she could have been listening to good old country music like Slim Dusty or Kenny Rogers. Or even Anne Murray.

It wasn't that she didn't like the country scene; she loved all sorts of music.

'Music is putting a sound to your feelings,' her great-grandfather had always said. 'There is a piece of music for every emotion.'

Chelsea had always agreed with that, and it didn't matter to her if it was a modern pop song or a piece written hundreds of years ago. If she could feel what the music was saying, then she loved it. And the music helped calm her when she wanted to scream and yell at her mother, who had never understood her.

To her it was neither here nor there that the piano she was playing was slightly off key and an upright rather than a grand, with worn yellow ivories rather than glossy ones. She didn't hear anything but the music swirling up into the rafters of the concert hall and the applause afterwards.

'All right, all right, that's enough. I said pack up,' Mrs Maher snapped, bringing Chelsea abruptly back down to earth. 'Is your mother picking you up today?'

Chelsea's fingers itched to keep playing but she knew that tone. Reluctantly she took her hands away and placed them in her lap.

'I think so,' she sighed. 'I've got netball practice this afternoon.' She scowled at the thought of running around a court playing a game that held no interest for her. Gathering up her sheet music, she stuffed it into her bag. She hated netball and the after-school training. It meant time away from her horse, Pinto, and the piano. But her mother had been an A-grade goal defence and thought her daughter should be exactly like her.

Unfortunately, Chelsea was nothing like her mother, not in looks, stature or sporting ability, or in personality. Her mum was tall and willowy, which had helped her in playing a goal defence. Her shiny black hair was usually tied up in a ponytail and she kept fit playing sport and working on the farm. Chelsea was shorter, and a little heavier than she should be. Her hair was an uninteresting mousy brown like her dad's, but she had inherited his crazy-coloured eyes—sometimes brown, sometimes blue, depending on what she was wearing. Dale, her annoying older brother, said her eyes made her look like a madwoman. And, according to him, she looked even crazier when she was playing the piano.

'Get stuffed,' was her standard reply. Those words were exactly what she wanted to say to her mum when she dragged Chelsea to after-school practice and yelled advice from the sideline.

Wednesdays were a special kind of torture for Chelsea.

Mrs Maher broke into her grumpy thoughts about the afternoon's activities. 'Where's your practice book?'

Chelsea fished around in her schoolbag then brought out a tattered A4 notebook and handed it over, so Mrs Maher could write down all the boring scales and exercises she was supposed to do before next week's lesson—not that she did them often.

After a moment of scribbling, Mrs Maher handed it back to her, and Chelsea looked at what her next week's practice would be. To her surprise she saw the scrawly handwriting said: *Play. Play whatever you like, but make sure you play for at least two hours per day.* Chelsea blinked as the book was snapped shut with such force it sounded like a clap.

'I'll see you next week. Make you sure you practise everything I've written down.'

That was her standard line and Chelsea wanted to ask why she'd changed it from tedious chords, arpeggios and scales, but instead she shoved the book into her bag and hoisted it over her shoulder.

'See ya!' she threw over her shoulder as she rushed into the bright sunlight and heard a voice calling her.

'Chels! Have you finished?' Her best friend Lily Jackson was sitting underneath a large pepper tree. 'I've been waiting an age.'

'Yeah, I'm sure she kept me in there longer than normal. Got this idea I have to do everything perfectly.' She slung her bag down and pulled out her plastic lunchbox, hoping against hope that there was something left in there from yesterday. Her stomach had been rumbling ever since she'd realised she hadn't packed her lunch this morning. The curried egg sandwich would still be on the kitchen bench where she'd left it before she'd ridden her bike to the end of the driveway and caught the school bus. It was Dale's fault. He'd distracted her by teasing her about falling off Pinto yesterday and landing in a patch of bindi-eye prickles.

Yes! SAOs and Vegemite. They'd be soggy by now, but she didn't care. It was something to fill her stomach and distract her from the thought of netball practice.

'Did you forget your lunch again?' Lily asked.

'Uh-huh,' she answered around the crumbs.

Without saying anything more, Lily handed her half of her ham sandwich. 'You're always doing that!'

'Dale was teasing me, so it's not technically my fault this time. He distracted me.' Lily gave Chelsea a look which included raised eyebrows and disbelief at the 'not technically my fault' excuse. 'And then when I started riding my bike, I had all these notes running through my head. Tunes which would sound like rain if I played them, and I wanted to get to the school bus so I could write them down before I forgot.'

'And did you?'

'What?'

'Get it all written down before you forgot?'

'Yeah. I wanted to play it to her today,' Chelsea nodded towards the music room. 'But I knew she wouldn't listen to it. Or she'd tell me off: "You can't compose music when you don't understand the basics, Chelsea."' She imitated her teacher's snooty voice.

A horn tooted and both girls looked up as a mud-covered ute pulled up.

Chelsea sighed, then waved reluctantly. 'What is she doing here and why is she so embarrassing?' she muttered as her mother opened the ute door and walked towards them, pulling her hair back in a ponytail and tying it with the ever-present elastic tie she kept on her wrist. Dressed in jeans, knee-high boots and a red jumper, she looked like she'd stepped out of a fashion magazine. Lily had confided once she wished her mum was as trendy as her friend's.

Chelsea had been shocked. She'd never seen her mum in that light, but she supposed she was trendier than Mrs Jackson, who only wore one of two dresses to church every Sunday.

'Wow, she looks like she's stepped out of the *Cleo* magazine I've got hidden under my mattress so Mum can't find it,' Lily said, staring until Chelsea hit her arm gently.

'Wait until she starts yelling at you to make sure you've got a clear centre pass at netball. She won't look so trendy then!' She made a wide-eyed stare, imitating her mum as she called from the sidelines.

Lily giggled and shoved some more sandwich into her mouth.

'Hi, girls! Why aren't you out on the oval playing with all the other kids?'

'Because we never are, Mum,' Chelsea answered. 'We don't like sport.'

'Oh, rubbish,' Pip said, reaching up and tightening her hair tie. 'Everyone likes running around playing four square or dodge ball, don't they, Lily?'

'*We* don't,' Chelsea said emphatically. 'What are you doing here, Mum? I didn't think you were coming in until after school.'

'I'm here for a netball club meeting, and Mrs Maher rang to say she wanted to talk to me, so I thought I'd kill two birds with the one stone. Any idea why?'

Chelsea stopped chewing and looked up, fear trickling through her stomach. 'No. Have I done something wrong?'

'I don't know, have you? Better go and find out. I guess she'll be in the office. Coming?'

Reluctantly, Chelsea crammed the last of the sandwich in her mouth and grabbed her bag. What if Mrs Maher didn't want to teach her anymore? Sure, she didn't like the woman, but that would mean she wouldn't get to play during school hours and the piano was the only thing that kept her sane. After all, it wasn't like her mum understood her, because if she did, she wouldn't gently poke fun at her love of all the things that were important to her. Her horse, her music, the type of music she liked! Or push her to play sports all the time. Her mother didn't do that with Dale. She was always telling him how clever he was and how she was proud of the way he'd got the sheep in from the bottom paddock.

Her dad didn't really get her either. He loved music, but to him it was a form of relaxation rather than a real job, and she'd like to make playing the piano a real job, but she didn't really know how. Anyhow, her dad was always in the background saying encouraging things, rather than: 'Someone who knows how to pass the ball well doesn't just use their body weight, Chelsea. They use elbows and fingers. Come on Chels, I've shown you this before . . .'

What. Ever.

Chelsea gave Lily a rueful look as she got to her feet. 'See ya in class.'

'Good luck.'

'How did your lesson go today?' Pip asked as she hurried Chelsea towards the staffroom.

'Fine.'

'Did you remember to bring your sandshoes for netball training? We're going to be practising passing and ball handling. It'll be great to see how much you girls have improved since last week, with the new exercises. I've got a whole lot more to give you.' Pip stopped at the front office door and looked at her daughter.

Chelsea could read the excitement in her mother's face and felt a rush of annoyance. She hadn't done any training during the week, only played the piano and ridden Pinto. Why her mum had to be her netball coach, she did not know. Sighing, she followed her mother through the doorway and stood behind her, fidgeting while Pip gave the receptionist a warm grin and asked to see Mrs Maher.

When the piano teacher arrived, she put her hand up to stop Chelsea from following them into the staffroom. 'Wait here,' was all she said.

Chelsea crossed her eyes at Mrs Maher's back then slumped on a couch in the waiting room, her hand tapping in rhythm to the tune in her head.

Ten minutes passed before her mother came out, looking dazed and holding a shiny folder. She said to Chelsea, 'Mrs Maher thinks you're good enough to get a scholarship to the Conservatorium.'

Chapter 1

2018

Chelsea drove slowly through the small country town of Barker. Her home town was nestled at the base of the Flinders Ranges and had a population of only a few hundred people. Her eyes searched the streets to see what had changed in the past ten years. The trees that had been planted in the middle of the main street were green and lush, but the lawn beneath them was dry. So dry she'd probably cut the soles of her feet if she ran on it like she and Lily had in the middle of one night, the last summer she'd lived at home.

The town was quiet. The streets were empty and there was a total of three cars parked in front of the supermarket. The supermarket was the first change she noted. It used to be owned by Mrs Chapman; now it boasted the logo of the IGA chain.

The newsagency seemed the same, as did the post office across the road. There was a war memorial near the trees in the median strip, and her mouth pulled up in a half-smile as she remembered the night she'd stayed at Lily's place and they'd snuck out after midnight to roam the streets. They'd thought they were so adventurous and daring. Barker was as quiet and safe as a church. Ah, the naivety of youth! But the kids had forgotten that Barker was on the main road between Perth and Sydney so there were strangers passing through all the time. They had just never imagined anything untoward could happen in Barker. It was a sleepy town where nothing exciting took place.

Chelsea pulled into a spot next to one of the cars already parked in front of the supermarket. As she looked around, she realised that the chemist, where she'd always been given black jelly beans by old Mr Ford, had been replaced with a small café. Good, she might be able to get a decent coffee when she came into town. As Chelsea switched off the engine, she decided she would bet her last pay cheque that the cars parked in the street still wouldn't be locked and the keys would be in the ignitions. No one ever locked their cars in Barker. Even with the few changes on the main street.

'Mummy?'

The sleepy voice of her four-year-old daughter, Aria, startled her and she turned around to face the back seat. Her daughter's black curls were stuck to her head and her cheeks were flushed.

'Hello there,' she smiled. 'I thought we'd stop for an ice cream.'

'Are we at Papa's place yet?'

'No, this is the town where I went to school. Do you remember how I told you I had to catch the bus from the farm to school? Papa's place is a bit more of a drive yet.' She unclipped her seatbelt and opened the door. Unprepared for the blast of furnace-like heat, she gasped and slammed the door shut, before walking around to get Aria out of her car seat.

'It's boiling, Mummy,' Aria said, pushing her hair back from her face. She was hot and sweaty, but still did a couple of hops and a jump up onto the footpath.

'Summer in the Flinders Ranges is always hot, honey. I'd forgotten how hot.' She wiped her long, slim fingers across her brow and pushed her hair from her eyes. 'Come on, I think the airconditioner will be on inside the shop.' She pushed open the door and waited for Aria to go in first.

'Hello,' said the man behind the counter as she felt the first blast of refreshing cold air.

Chelsea tried to keep the look of shock from her face. Even though she'd realised Mrs Chapman probably wasn't running the supermarket any longer, she hadn't expected her to have been replaced by a man who looked like he came from the Middle East. This was Barker, after all, hardly a multicultural hub.

'Hello,' she said, gathering herself.

Walking around, she noticed a section dedicated to Middle Eastern and Asian cuisine that never would've been in stock if Mrs Chapman still owned the store. And very different to the chops and three veg that her mother used to dish up to her dad every night. She grabbed a few essentials then lifted Aria up so she could look into the freezer and choose an ice cream.

She put her items on the counter and the man rang up the purchases before putting them in a box. No plastic bags here. 'Where's Mrs Chapman?' she asked as she handed over a fifty-dollar note.

'Who?' the man gave her a confused glance.

'Mrs Chapman. The owner. Or doesn't she own the shop anymore?' She wondered how well he spoke English.

'Ah, Gloria,' he answered fluently, and Chelsea wanted to kick herself for making assumptions. 'She is no longer here. I bought the shop from her two years ago.'

'Right. Of course. I guess she'd be pretty old by now. Been a while since I was home.'

'You used to live here?'

Chelsea nodded and reached down to stop Aria pulling on her T-shirt, wanting her icy pole. 'Wait, honey.' Turning back to the man, she answered, 'Yeah, I'm Tom Taylor's daughter, Chelsea. Haven't been home in ten years. I guess a lot has changed.' Unwrapping the icy pole, she handed it to Aria and picked up the box.

'It is nice to meet you, Chelsea. And you too, little one. I am Amal. Enjoy your time being in your homeland.'

Giving him a curious smile, she guided Aria out the door. What did he mean, 'homeland'? How did he know she'd been away overseas?

'Let me just put this in the car and we'll go for a quick look around,' she said, placing the box on the back seat, then taking her daughter's hand.

They walked down the main street together, the heat rising from the pavement. Chelsea looked in each window in the hope of catching glimpses of people she knew—kids from school, or their parents. There was no one. How could the footpaths be empty with a few hundred people living in Barker?

At the end of the street they came to the butcher's shop and Chelsea wondered if she should get some steak for dinner tonight. Her dad always liked steak as a change from chops. Still, he might see it as a suck-up job.

The door opened and an old lady carrying a string bag stepped out onto the footpath. Something about the woman was familiar.

She glanced at Chelsea, then down at the little girl, and she stopped. 'Chelsea Taylor? Is that you?'

Chelsea couldn't place her, so she just nodded. 'Yes,' she added for good measure.

A look of disgust crossed the woman's face. 'Got a bit too big for your home town, did you? Well, it's about time you came back. Fancy, never turning up for your—' She broke off and shook her head. 'Well . . . I can't say that your father will be pleased to see you.' With that, she turned and stalked towards one of the four cars parked in the street.

Chelsea blinked, a sliver of anxiety running through her.

'Was that lady angry with you, Mummy?' The icy pole was now finished, and Chelsea could see Aria's hands were covered in a sticky mess.

'Let's go and clean up those hands and get going out to Papa's. What do you say?'

'But . . .'

'Aria, let's go.' Chelsea wanted to get off the street and away from prying eyes before anyone else could pass judgement on her. Was that what they thought of her now? Chelsea, the town darling, had become too big-headed for her home. She knew how a small town could have a person charged and guilty without any proper evidence, but the thought made her sad. If only they all knew . . .

A few minutes later they were back in her little red Ford Focus and heading towards the petrol station, which boasted three petrol pumps and the best takeaway in the area.

Chelsea's mouth dropped open as they drove by the site. It was gone. Actually, that wasn't strictly true. The shell of the building was still there, but the windows had been smashed in and the walls were covered with graffiti. There were empty spaces where the pumps had been. Where did people get their fuel from?

'Mummy, what are those bushes? They look really prickly.'

Chelsea ignored Aria's chatter from the back seat and concentrated on the road. Now she had left the town boundary, she still remembered to slow down as she went through the creek, which had an unexpectedly deep dip, and to keep an eye out for kangaroos near the grove of saltbush on the side of the road. Her dad had always said it was the best place for a roo to jump out and surprise them—especially since the roos were the same colour as the vegetation.

One kilometre out of town she saw the turn-off to the cemetery and lifted her foot off the accelerator.

Was her mother buried there? She didn't even know. Just as she hadn't known about the funeral. Or about her death. Until it was too late.

The lump that had threatened all day finally made its way to the middle of her throat and sat like a stone. She swallowed. It didn't move.

Tears were hovering too, but she couldn't cry in front of Aria. She had to be strong. Like she always had been. No tears, no emotion, no thinking about things that would make her feel overwhelmed by sadness. This was the reason Aria's father was never mentioned either.

'Mummy?' The high-pitched voice was now pleading. 'Mummy! You're not listening . . .'

'What?' The word came from Chelsea with such anger that Aria stopped talking and looked down at her hands, her lips trembling.

The cemetery was behind them now and Chelsea pushed her foot down and blew out a breath. 'I'm sorry, I'm sorry,' she soothed. 'Look, let's sing something. To take our mind off the trip. It's been such a long drive and you've been so good. I know it's hard being cooped up for hours. What would you like to sing? Your choice, honey.'

'One hundred green bottles!' Aria said, her voice triumphant, as though she'd been waiting the whole journey for this moment.

Chelsea closed her eyes briefly and sent a silent plea for patience, then started to sing.

Chapter 2

Scenes from Chelsea's childhood kept her company as she drove the dirt roads towards her parents' farm, Shandona.

Aria had drifted off to sleep at about the fifteenth green bottle and, by the twentieth, Chelsea knew she could stop singing without waking her.

As she passed through the deep creek lined with river red gums, she flicked on the local radio station she remembered listening to when growing up. More memories. She recognised some of the ads from years ago. Had no one thought to update them?

Ed Sheeran's 'Castle On The Hill' began playing, and goosebumps rippled over her skin as she listened to the words. He was singing about driving the roads home and how he couldn't wait to get there. Maybe he was singing about England, but the words still resonated with her in South Australia. The verse about Ed's friends started and it made her think of Lily. Did she still live in Barker? And what about Jason, or Kelly, or Shane?

She thought about the time a boy she'd known from primary school had smuggled a bottle of wine out of his parents' bar fridge and they'd sat on the edge of the reservoir, drinking under a star-studded sky. The moon had been nearly full and, if she closed her eyes, Chelsea could still see its reflection on the water. She had been home from the Conservatorium on summer holidays. The wine had been cold while her body was warm. That was the first time a boy had ever tried to kiss her. With her cheeks burning from the alcohol, she'd kissed him back. Kelly had told her later he had only done it as a dare. The hot flush of humiliation swept over her again, even after all this time.

Chelsea narrowed her eyes and focused on the road to banish the memory. She'd been in two minds about coming home. Part of her was pulled by some invisible force, a need to be where she grew up. To show Aria where she'd spent her childhood and to sit on the bank of the creek where she'd once played in the puddles. It was a place where she could breathe in the peace. The other part of her was saying there was nothing here for her anymore. Hadn't been for years. Why would she put herself through all the emotion of a homecoming when she didn't need to?

Rounding a corner, she saw the boundary fence of Shandona snaking its way down the rough hill onto the flood plain. She took her foot off the accelerator and she slowed down to take a better look. There had been an outcrop of trees on that hill when she'd been in primary school. The only stand of trees within a few miles. She'd wondered why they grew in that spot when there were no others around. One Sunday afternoon her Papa had slowly followed the winding track down to the flood plains. He and Gran had taken Chelsea for a drive after church to check the lambing ewes. It had been bitterly cold, but she'd still ridden on the back of the ute, enjoying the freezing wind against her face. One of those trees had caught her beanie and pulled it from her head and she'd called out to her Papa to stop. She'd watched her bright red beanie snared on a bare branch, waving in the wind, until he'd turned around and they'd gone back to pluck it from the tree. Her favourite beanie had been ruined. Gran had comforted her when they'd finally got back to the house and promised to knit her another one. 'You'll need something to keep your ears warm when you're riding your horse,' she'd said.

But Gran had died before she'd been able to finish knitting the new one. She'd gone to bed one night and not woken up the next day.

Chelsea hoped the half-knitted red beanie was still in the bottom drawer of her bedside table. She'd put it there after her gran's funeral so she'd always have part of her close by.

Driving slowly, Chelsea noticed changes to the road—it was now smooth and well cared for, not the potholed, two-wheel track it had been before the council had taken over the management of it. It was the opposite when it came to the boundary fences of Shandona: they were sagging and the wires were a combination of rusty and new.

It looked as if someone without much money had tried to patch them the best they could.

The land they enclosed was bare, save for scrubby bushes scattered here and there. On one side of the road, the paddock contained hundreds of emus—it looked as if they were being farmed, but she knew better. The country was in the grip of a drought and the emus would be looking for any skerrick of grass they could find.

But the rivers, her favourite places, although dry and devoid of grass on the banks, looked just the same as they had when she used to ride Pinto through them. The beds were still filled with stones and river sand; the trees, hundreds of years old, towered overhead as though they were the rivers' guardians.

The road curved sharply, and there was a turn-off to the homestead just in front of her. She saw the white forty-four gallon drum posing as a mailbox, then the cattle grid. After she'd bumped across the grid, there was a short drive to the dam on her left and then she turned through the gates of Shandona for the first time in ten years.

When Chelsea saw the house, her breath caught in her throat. The raised voices of the past screamed at her.

'You won't amount to anything by following that path!' her mum had yelled.

'After everything we've done for you, this is how you repay us?'

And the pleading—'Why?'—from a different time, after Dale had died.

With a deep breath, she pulled her little car—her jelly-bean car, her friend Tori had called it—underneath the large gumtree on the corner of the disused tennis court and shut off the engine.

'Mummy?'

Chelsea turned in her seat. 'We're here, honey. Ready to get out and meet Papa?'

Aria's deep brown eyes were serious. 'Yes.'

'Okay, then let's go.' She unclipped her seat belt and got out, this time ready for the heat. The galahs, perched in the tree above her, rose with screeching protest as the noise of the door slamming echoed around the empty yard. Chelsea hadn't even reached Aria's door before they settled straight back down into the tree again.

As she helped Aria out of the car she couldn't keep her eyes still. The old meathouse that stood in the middle of the yard looked like it was derelict and disused, but the overseer's house seemed well tended. The gardens were neat and tidy and she could tell the walls, although covered in a thin film of ever-present dust, were newly painted. This house was where she had lived with her parents until her grandfather had retired and moved to Adelaide, leaving them the main house. She wondered if the kitchen walls were still painted the same pale blue.

Looking at her old home, she assumed there must be someone living there. A grey ute was parked out the front, and there were chooks in the hen house, along with a pile of logs on the verandah. Not that whoever was living there now would be needing them in the middle of summer, she thought. Her dad must have employed a workman.

'Come on.' She took Aria's hand more for her own comfort than her daughter's and started to cross the gravel yard. She kept her eyes peeled for snakes out of an old habit she thought she'd long since forgotten.

Her family had moved into the main house when she was eight, the year Gran had died. Leo had decided he didn't want to farm without his wife and that decision had stopped the arguments between Leo and Tom about succession. Tom, at forty-one, had more than enough experience to run Shandona on his own.

The pathway leading to the main entrance was slate and wound its way between large, free-flowing plumbago bushes, which seemed to be planted in the ground but had been allowed to grow wild. They had to push it out of their way as they walked. On the other side of the path was a stone building that had been her dad's schoolroom when he was a kid. Shandona was too far from Barker for Tom to attend school so, along with School of the Air, Leo and Evelyn had employed a governess to help educate their son, before sending him to boarding school in year eight. The last time she'd peeked into the disused room, the old desks and faded times-table charts, long since forgotten, had still been on the wall.

The laundry was next to the schoolroom and Chelsea wondered whether the twin-tub washing machine her mum had used was still there. Chelsea knew she'd kept it because it didn't use very much water, but it had always seemed like a lot of extra work to her.

Pip had loved maintaining a tidy and organised house. And a nice garden.

As well as forcing you to play netball and not understanding you, a tiny voice in her head told her.

Shush!

The house was built from stone and had an enclosed verandah on one side, which had always been called the sunroom. Its louvred windows were open and dusty— something that would never have happened when Pip was alive. Chelsea's stomach constricted. The temperature gauge that had always hung just outside the door was still there.

Everything seemed the same, but it wasn't. The house didn't have the same loved feel as it had the last time she'd been here, and what she was seeing made her realise it was really true, her mum was gone. Swallowing hard, she blinked, hoping to see her mum raking the leaves from the lawn or walking back to the house from the shearing shed.

There was nothing, except an old border collie sleeping at the end of a chain near the laundry door. As they pushed past him he sat up and gave a sharp bark. Aria squealed and made sure Chelsea was between them.

'It's okay,' Chelsea told her. 'He'll be for chasing the sheep, and warning of visitors. He won't hurt you.' She realised Aria had never seen a border collie before. There had always been dogs when Chelsea had been living at home. Hers and her daughter's childhoods were very different.

'Hello? Dad?' She knocked on the screen door and pushed it open. The dusty door squeaked and she called out again.

'Papa?' Aria copied her mother and pushed in front of her.

'No, Aria.' Chelsea grabbed her shoulder gently and pulled her back. 'You can't go into other people's houses if they're not home.'

'But he must be. He lives here,' Aria said frowning. 'I want to see him!'

'Maybe he doesn't expect us yet. Perhaps he's still out in the paddock. I didn't see his ute here when we pulled up.' Truth was, after all this time there could have been ten utes parked out the front and she wouldn't have known which one was her father's. She tried again. 'Dad?'

There was a crash from deep inside the house, then: 'Hold on!'

Chelsea recognised her father's deep gravelly voice and instinctively held Aria's hand tighter. She hadn't realised she was so nervous about seeing him after all this time. Of course, the lady she'd recognised but whose name she couldn't remember, and who'd warned her father wouldn't be pleased to see her, had made her even more anxious.

'Who is it?'

The noise of boots on the wooden floorboards echoed through the large house, but they weren't her father's normal footsteps. It sounded as if he was limping.

'It's me, Dad. Chelsea.' She paused. 'And Aria.'

'Chelsea?' His tone went up in surprise and the foot-steps stopped.

Then started again.

'What are you doing here?' he asked, appearing in the doorway.

As she saw him Chelsea sucked in a breath. This wasn't her dad. Stubble covered his chin and cheeks, and his eyes were sunken. His shirt hung loosely from his thin frame. He was nothing like the jovial, heavy-set man he'd been ten years ago. Chelsea wasn't sure that he could have shrunk in the years she'd been gone, but it certainly looked like he had. His hair, which had been the same mousy brown as her own, was now grey, and he had a bewildered look on his face.

Clearly he'd taken her mother's death hard. *Of course he has,* that little voice told her. *On top of Dale's death as well. Don't forget you haven't been here to support him either. He's been alone.*

'Dad.' The words felt like they were stuck in her throat.

'Who are you?' He looked down at Aria, who was standing next to Chelsea, her eyes wide.

Shaking off her mother's hand, she took a step forwards and smiled up at her grandfather. 'I'm Aria and you're my Papa.' She opened her arms and ran to give him a hug.

Startled, Tom's eyes flew to Chelsea. 'You've got a daughter?' he managed to ask before Aria connected with his legs and threw her arms around them. His hands came down on her head and he touched her lightly on the crown, before looking back up at Chelsea.

Cold fear dripped through her. 'I've told you about Aria, Dad,' she said softly. 'I wrote to you and Mum when she was born overseas. I sent photos too.' She paused. 'And I told you about her on the phone, when I rang to say we were coming for Christmas.'

'Christmas?' Then recognition flashed across his face and something seemed to shift inside him. 'Of course you did. Although I don't know why you bothered after all this time!' He focused on Aria, 'Hello, Aria, aren't you a sight for sore eyes. Now you come into the kitchen and tell your Papa all about your trip up to Shandona. Was it a long drive?' He took her hand and led her through to the kitchen where he opened the fridge door and offered her a cold drink of cordial.

Chelsea followed, a lump of anxiety in the pit of her stomach. She was grateful Aria hadn't noticed her reaction and was chatting happily away.

'I'd forgotten you were coming,' her father admitted, his initial anger apparently gone, his normal tone back. He took the empty glass from Aria and lifted her down from the bench where she'd been sitting. 'You can see it's pretty dry. We've been busy. Feeding the sheep and keeping everything alive. I haven't made up your beds or got enough food.' He looked distressed. 'Maybe . . .'

'It's fine, Dad. We brought some supplies with us and I can easily make up the beds.'

Tom looked around vaguely. 'I guess there are spare sheets somewhere. Your mother . . .' His voice trailed off then, without warning, the angry expression flashed across his face again. Chelsea braced for the onslaught.

'Hello? Tom, it's me, Cal.' The screen door slammed, and a silhouette of a man wearing an Akubra appeared in the doorway, stopping any verbal attack from her father that might have followed.

'Cal, how are you, mate? Meet my daughter Chelsea. And this little one is, um . . .' Tom paused.

'I'm Aria.'

'Well, hello there, Aria,' Cal said, squatting down and holding out his hand. 'I'm Cal, which is short for Callum. How do you do?'

Aria giggled then held out her own small hand and said shyly, 'Hello. Are you a real cowboy?'

Cal snorted. 'Nope. No cows out here, and I ride a motorbike. My hat is to keep the sun off my face so I don't get burnt.' He stood up and looked at Chelsea. 'Nice to meet you.'

He didn't smile or hold out his hand and Chelsea got the distinct impression he was not happy to see her. Apparently the nameless lady in town wasn't the only one.

'Nice to meet you too,' she answered, twisting her fingers behind her back. 'You work here?'

'Yep. I do.'

Chelsea nodded. That explained the tidy overseer's cottage.

'Be lost without him,' Tom said.

'That's great,' she said, then wanted to kick herself. What was great about it? Her dad needed help?

Cal turned and focused on Tom. 'The tank at the back of the shearing shed is leaking,' he said. 'Reckon it's just about buggered. We can get the bloke to come back and poly-weld it, but because it's the main tank, I think we should order a new one. You right for me to give RuralCorp a call to order a newbie?'

'Damn, I was hoping it would hold. I noticed a split in it a couple of days ago.' Tom sighed. 'No point in ginning around with poly-welding it. Get a new one, but get a different brand. That's the second one we've had that's split down the join.'

'Sure thing. Right, I'll be on my way. Do you need anything in town?'

'Can you pick me up another script? I phoned the order in this morning.'

Chelsea wondered what the medication was for. Depression maybe? That could explain the way her father was looking. She imagined living here, just one person rattling around in a house that could've held six people. It would have to be lonely.

Cal nodded. 'I'll drop it in after tennis.'

'Thanks, mate. Have a good game.'

The room was silent after Cal left and Tom looked around as if unsure what to do.

'Which rooms can we sleep in?' Chelsea finally asked. 'I'll go and set them up.'

'The top two. Think the bathroom up there works okay. Well, it did when your mother was alive. I haven't had any need to go up there since then.'

'Thanks. I'll get our bags.' She felt like she was talking to a stranger. But what more could she expect? She hadn't visited since she was twenty and her parents hadn't tried to see her either. Chelsea had hoped her mother would come when Aria was born, but she'd been born overseas, and by the time she'd returned to Australia, Chelsea's circumstances had changed ... and life had continued without her parents in it.

She'd been left to cope by herself.

Anger swelled up in her as she remembered the endless nights rocking Aria to sleep, the pain of the birth which lingered for months afterwards, the silence from her mother. All in a foreign country. Well, her dad might have cause to be pissed off with her, but she had a good reason to return the feeling. Maybe coming back here wasn't going to be the therapy she needed. Perhaps it would only unsettle her and make her angry again.

Chapter 3

'Phone call for you, Dave.' Jack waved the phone to get Dave's attention then put it down in the cradle.

'Line?' Dave asked, looking at the three flashing red lights on the switchboard. Three? Unheard of in the quiet town of Barker. 'Who else is calling in?'

'Line two. Joan's on the other one.'

'Who's the third? I didn't know we had that many lines into the station.' He picked up the phone and punched at line two. 'Burrows.'

The silence hissed down the line and Dave was about to hang up when he heard a noise.

'Hello, this is Detective Dave Burrows, can I help you with something?' There was a sniff and Dave realised the caller was crying.

'I'd like to be able to help you,' he said gently.

'Dave, it's Mandy.' There was a pause. 'Your sister-in-law.'

Dave sucked in a breath. 'Mandy? What's wrong?' His voice held a hint of urgency. The fact she was crying could only mean bad news. He wasn't sure when he'd last spoken to Mandy. Maybe a year ago, when his father had died. Maybe his mum . . . No, he didn't want to think about his mum dying too.

'It's Dean,' she said. 'He's had an accident on the farm.'

Dave's heart slowed and he waited for more information. It wasn't forthcoming.

'What type of accident?'

'He was fencing. Using the digger to drill pilot holes. The auger caught his shirt and dragged him into the auger. He . . . Dean, uh . . .' A fresh round of sobbing started.

Visualising the accident, Dave saw the drill going around and around and around. Once it caught hold of something, it would continue to pull in whatever it had caught, whether it was dirt, hair or an arm. He could hear his brother's screams, the frantic attempts to flick the lever to throw the machine out of gear and stop it from turning.

Dave could smell the blood.

'Is, ah, is he alive, Mandy?'

Her breath came out in a rush. 'At the moment, he is, but he's lost so much blood. They don't think they're going to be able to reattach his arm. He's had two blood transfusions . . . The RFDS came. After the ambulance . . .'

'And the kids, where are they? Are they okay?'

'Yeah, yep. They're fine. They're here with me at the hospital.'

'Okay.' Dave tried to keep his tone calm. 'And Mum?'

'She's here too. Dean's still in surgery, so we won't know too much until afterwards.'

Dave thought about the farm and the timing of the accident. Bad timing—still, was there ever a good time? Of course not. But it was summer, and surely Dean should have been harvesting, not fencing? And there would be animals to feed and troughs to check.

'Do you need me to come and help?' he asked. 'Where are you up to with the harvest?'

'I really don't know, Dave.' Despair overtook her voice. 'I haven't had anything to do with the farm for the past six months.'

Tapping his pen on the desk, Dave thought about how to respond. 'Oh. Why's that?'

'Dean and I have separated.'

There was a long pause while Dave processed that piece of news. Why in God's name hadn't someone told him? Surely his mum would have.

'I'm so sorry, Mandy. I had no idea.'

'No, we kept it quiet. That was the deal we made. I'm still living in the house in the spare room. Just for a time.'

'What? Why are you doing that?' Dave was astounded.

'I don't hate him, Dave! And he doesn't hate me. The farm can't afford to pay me out at the moment, so we live our own lives, but still under the same roof. It's working for the time being. Anyway, I didn't ring to talk about that, but I can't really tell you what's going on farm-wise.'

'Do you need help over there?' Dave asked again. He was loath to go back. He hadn't been there since he'd left at the age of twenty-three. And the communication he'd had with his two brothers since had been sporadic at best. He talked to his mum about once a month, and she usually reported the family goings-on, although she'd clearly failed in this case. But he'd never felt the need to talk to his brothers regularly, not since they hadn't stood up for him when his father had kicked him off the farm.

He knew what Kim would want him to do. Go home. See them all. Let bygones be bygones. She'd wanted him to do that the whole time they'd been together. He was resistant. He could still hear the words his father had shouted at him: 'The quicker I'm rid of you, the better off we'll be!' It didn't matter that his father was dead. The memories were still there and they hurt. Wind Valley Farm wasn't a place he wanted to visit.

Getting away from Barker in the lead-up to Christmas would be tricky too. Most police officers didn't get leave at this time of the year because people seemed to turn into idiots during the holiday season. Drink-driving and speeding were the two biggest problems, but occasionally some really bad eggs would turn up. Two years ago they'd had a drug dealer book into the caravan park and start selling. It was only after the hospital had reported two ODs—not deaths, thankfully, but still requiring life-saving stomach pumping—they'd realised what was going on and arrested the dealer.

But family was family. Even if they were a dysfunctional one. He would go if he was needed, but he wouldn't rush there just yet. His heart gave an extra quick beat at the possibility of not seeing Dean again, before he refocused and put his policeman's shield around his emotions while he listened to Mandy's answer.

'I don't know. Jake's able to do a lot of things.'

'How old is Jake now?' Dave felt awful he didn't know. If Kim had been here she would've been able to slip him a note that said thirteen, or twenty-two, or whatever the hell he was. She'd been the one sending birthday cards and presents on his behalf.

'Twenty-three. And he's been working here for the past two years, but it's such a big job for someone so young.'

'What about Adam? Can he help out?' Last he'd heard, his middle brother was working in shearing teams. Adam's marriage, the one they had all thought would last, hadn't. He'd hit the bottle fairly hard after Tiffany had left him, taking the kids with her. Lost his savings and the will to live, according to his mum.

'I haven't rung him yet. Just wanted to let you know what was going on first.'

'Is Mum there? Can you put her on?'

'I'll get her to call you. She's with Jake and Christy at the moment.'

Dave racked his brains to remember who was the eldest child—Jake, he was sure of it. 'What's Christy doing now?' he asked.

'She's in her second year of Farm Management at uni.'

'Okay, good. Good.' He was talking to himself more than Mandy. If there were two kids who had an interest in farming, it would make things much easier for Dean when he came home. If he came home. Dave pressed his lips together as he thought about that. Losing his brother was more than a sobering thought. 'Let me know when there's more news, okay. And, Mandy, anything you need, make sure you call.'

'Sure. Thanks, Dave.'

Dave hung up the phone slowly, his mind racing. A brother who'd hopefully lose his arm rather than his life, a marriage break-up he hadn't been aware of, a possible return to the farm he hadn't set foot on since 1990. He crossed his arms. He hadn't returned when his father had died, citing distance, but he wasn't sure how he'd be able to avoid it now if Dean needed help. Even after all this time, he could still feel the sting of his father's betrayal in shutting him out of the business. He'd forced Dave to leave Wind Valley Farm, even though he'd known that all Dave had ever wanted was to farm that piece of land with his brothers. It had hurt him terribly that neither Dean nor Adam had quashed his dad's heavy-handed tactics. His mum had tried but she'd been beaten down, whether by words or fists, he'd never been quite sure.

Gradually their father's bitterness had worn away at all of the brothers. Adam and Tiffany had left to try farming with her family. When that hadn't worked out, they'd borrowed money and bought their own place. Bad seasons, low grain prices and high interest rates had seen them go under quickly. According to his mother's letters, Tiffany had packed up one night and disappeared with the children. The last time Adam had heard from her was when he'd received the divorce papers. Adam had been desperate to contact his children, but continually trying and failing had chipped away at him and the bottle had finally taken him.

In the end it had come down to Dean, who had given his father an ultimatum: let him take over the reins or he would leave too. At seventy-odd, Sam had had no choice. He hadn't been able to afford for Dean to leave; he'd needed someone to do all the physical work.

Kim had said more than once that it was incredible how much bitterness and resentment could brew in one family. The brothers couldn't be more distant now, in either geography or relationship.

Dave realised he could smell something and looked up. Kim was standing in the doorway, holding a container. He broke into a smile.

'I thought I smelled you.'

'What?' Kim sounded indignant. 'You won't get any quiche if you carry on like that. And it's your favourite, fresh out of the oven.'

'I wasn't meaning it in a bad way, as you well know. I could smell your perfume.'

Kim stared at him, a small grin curving up one side of her face. 'My perfume? I don't wear perfume.'

'Yeah, you do. Your cooking.'

She laughed and came into the room, placing the container on his desk. 'You're looking very solemn.' She leaned down and gave him a kiss.

'Will you two just get a room!' Jack yelled from the outer office.

Kim giggled against Dave's lips and he pulled away.

'You're just jealous!' he called back.

This was their standard banter now.

Jack appeared in the doorway. 'No, I'm not. How are you, Kim? That's a nice-looking cheese and tomato quiche. Nice golden crust.'

'Hungry, are you, Jack?' Kim asked.

'Always,' he answered.

'We're going to have to find a nice woman to look after you,' Kim said as she cut a large piece and handed it to him, along with a paper napkin.

'Nothing on offer here in Barker. Thanks. That looks magic.'

'What about some of the online dating agencies?' Kim asked. 'I've heard of people having success with those.'

'Not for me, thanks, Kim.' Jack started to walk back to his desk. 'All sorts of crazies online. Anyway, I've got you to cook for me. And I don't have to put up with any of the crap that goes with having a woman. Best of both worlds.'

Kim blinked and turned to look at Jack through the glass window.

He was grinning.

'He's winding you up, sweetie,' Dave said, resting his hands on her hips and giving her a gentle squeeze.

Kim turned back to Dave. 'What were you looking so worried about when I first arrived?'

He gave her a summary of the phone call.

'How awful!' Kim's voice was full of sympathy. 'What can we do to help?'

Dave smiled, knowing that would be her response. 'I'm not sure. It's not a good time for me to go on leave, but it's their busiest period of the year. I'd have to get special permission to go. I guess we'll just need to see how things play out.'

'But, honey, you need to go over there and make sure they're all okay. What if he dies? You can't not go!'

Tapping on his desk for a moment, Dave thought about it a little more. She'd just verbalised everything he was thinking. Then he shook his head. 'No, not at this stage,' he said finally. 'I don't think I need to go back unless I'm asked to. So, what are you doing for the rest of the day now you've fed Jack?' He closed the conversation before Kim could say anything else.

'I'm on my way to the roadhouse. Couple of the girls have called in sick. Bit of a bugger because I'm behind in cooking the meals for Catering Angels. I've heard that there are three older men whose wives are in hospital, so I wanted to go and see them and offer them the service.'

Two years ago Kim had started her own catering service for people who were unable to look after themselves while their loved ones were in hospital. Her first customer had been Fiona Forrest after her husband had been killed. The business had grown exponentially since then and now she had clients all over the shire.

'Late night for you then?' he asked, rubbing her shoulders. 'Want me to cook tea?'

'I'd like to be home by six if the night shift doesn't call in sick. Let's hope the summer flu hasn't hit them as well!' She turned around and gave him a kiss. 'See you tonight.'

As Kim left the phone rang again, and Dave looked at it before answering, hoping that it wasn't any more bad news.

'Dave, it's Kelly from over at the Giftory. I've just had a shoplifter.'

'Do you know who it was?' asked Dave, standing up and reaching for his hat.

'No, not a local. I've got the video footage and I'm sure they left in a blue sedan.'

'I'll be right there.'

Chapter 4

Dinner at Shandona on Chelsea and Aria's first night was a silent affair.

Except for Aria chatting away as if nothing was wrong, there was only the clink of cutlery and the occasional dog bark outside.

That was the good thing about kids, Chelsea thought as she pulled the covers over her sleeping daughter's shoulders and listened to the sound of thunder rumbling around the sky. They didn't always pick up on the vibes that adults were putting out.

The silence had given her time to observe her father; he had aged dramatically in the ten years she'd been gone. She'd come to the conclusion he was a very old sixty-three. The way he moved around you'd be forgiven for thinking he was in his eighties.

Standing at the window now, she looked out into the blackness. Storm clouds had scurried over the hills late in the afternoon, a mixture of vivid white and inky volcano-looking clouds that blacked out the sun and cooled the landscape with their shade.

The noise of the birds and animals had stilled, making the atmosphere crackle with anticipation. The first sound of thunder had come from behind the ranges, but it hadn't taken long to move across and sit right over the house.

Aria had never heard thunder like it, nor seen rain so heavy. Nor smelled the intoxicating aroma of rain on dry earth. They'd both sat watching at the window, mesmerised, and Chelsea had told her daughter stories of storms she remembered from when she was a child—how the rivers ran just with a trickle at first, how she'd raced in front of the water as it first started to flow down the riverbed. Then later how fast and deep the water would be, how noisy! And when the river had stopped running, how she'd played in the puddles left behind.

Before the rain had become very heavy, her father had retired to his room, saying his ankle was still sore from the fall he'd had in the sheep yards last week. Chelsea had offered to look at it for him, perhaps strap it, but he'd declined and limped into his bedroom. He seemed to spend a lot of time in there.

Chelsea had wondered if he'd done that so he wouldn't have to make small talk with her. Even in the short time she'd been home, she could feel a change in Tom—as if he didn't fully concentrate or wasn't interested. She couldn't put her finger on what was going on with him.

Lightning split the sky again, illuminating the creek and gumtrees with an eerie white light. The landscape was familiar yet unrecognisable to her. The stark purple soil was devoid of any feed, and the trees and bushes looked brittle. She knew the soil would erode with the force of the water flowing down the hills.

She hoped the stock had shelter—trees and bushy groves to nestle among. The storm after the heat this morning, along with a lack of feed, wouldn't make tonight very comfortable for them.

Even though she hadn't seen any of the stock her father had talked about, the signs they were being hand-fed were there. The ute had a sheep feeder hooked up behind it and there was an auger in the silo ready to pump the grain into the feeder so Cal could trail-feed the sheep.

She'd been glad to hear the first few drops of rain turn into a steady stream. Even her dad had finally smiled, for the first time since Cal had left.

'Rivers will be running by morning,' he had said by way of goodnight. 'I hope you're prepared to be stranded here for a while.' He paused. 'Still, they probably won't take long to go down. Been so dry for so long, the moisture'll disappear into the soil pretty quick.'

From her childhood, Chelsea knew the rivers were never uncrossable for long—a day or two at the most. And it wasn't as if she had anywhere else to go, although she felt uncomfortable and uneasy, as if she were waiting for something to happen. For her dad to blow up. For the memories to overtake her. For tears and anger and resentment to build to breaking point.

Then what would happen?

When the lightning struck again, she could see water in the bottom of the creek.

'Water sheets off the hills around here,' her father had said when she was young. She'd asked him why the rivers ran so quickly and easily—even when there had only been a small amount of rain. 'It's that heavy type of soil so the water doesn't soak in, just runs off. Great for dams but there's got to be a fair bit of rain to really wet the earth.'

As she walked through the house, pinpricks of goosebumps ran across her skin. The rain on the dry ground smelled beautiful, familiar, and she loved it.

She pulled opened the door and went out onto the verandah. The air was still hovering between being warm and quite cool. She knew instinctively that if it wasn't raining tomorrow, it would be sultry. Maybe the storms would build up tomorrow afternoon and deliver more rain.

Even after being away for so long, she didn't need to be told this country needed a good drenching. Between the kangaroos, which looked like they were in plague proportions, and the emus, there was very little feed for the stock.

'It has rained so little this year, we only have the core ewes left. Nothing more. Country can't handle them,' her father had said when she'd commented on the number of emus she'd seen driving in.

Drought, even though it was an emotional subject, was a safe topic and Chelsea had listened to Tom talk, picking up the farming language as if she'd never been away. He hadn't asked about her music, or her career, or who Aria's father was. The little that had been said was all about the farm. Safe talk.

She didn't mind; perhaps neither of them was ready for the conversations she knew they would have to have.

Chelsea held her hand out and jumped as the drops fell on her hot skin. The healing rain didn't seem like it was going to let up tonight and for that she was grateful. She pulled up a chair and sat with her legs tucked up underneath her, enjoying the sound of nature's music.

❧

A noise outside her bedroom window woke Chelsea and it only took a few seconds to realise her heart was pounding hard. Confused, she tried to work out what was going on. Then she heard it again: *bang, bang, bang!*

'Dale.' She muttered her brother's name and jumped out of bed. Overcome with memories, she felt her chest constrict and her breathing become ragged. Then she heard Cal's voice.

'Hello? Tom, you around? I need the phone. Tom?' Cal's tone was urgent and Tom didn't answer. Thank God it wasn't the police as her body had been telling her a moment ago. She could see sunlight filtering in through the slim gap in the curtains. It was morning and she must've overslept. Chelsea threw on her dressing gown and went out to greet him.

'Hi, Cal, come in. I'm not sure where Dad is.'

'I just need the phone,' Cal answered, taking off his hat as he stepped inside. 'I've got a problem.'

'Use Dad's office. I'm sure that'll be okay. I'll check his bedroom and see if he's in there.'

She went through the passageway and called out: 'Dad? Dad, are you there? Cal is looking for you.' The house remained silent.

A trickle of alarm ran through her as she looked at the clock on the sitting-room wall and saw it was past ten.

Aria!

She ran to her daughter's bedroom and found the bed empty.

'Breathe,' she muttered to herself. 'They'll be somewhere together.'

Heading back to the kitchen, she searched the bench for a note but found nothing. She looked around frantically for a two-way she could call on. Nothing. She'd ask Cal.

She could hear the final piece of the conversation: 'Yeah, no worries, Dave. Cheers, mate. See you soon.'

'Dad's not here and neither's Aria,' she said, trying not to sound panicked.

'Check the garage,' he instructed. 'If the ute isn't there, he'll probably be out checking the fence lines for damage.'

'Do you have a radio you can call him on? Or a phone?'

'Mobiles don't work out here.'

Shit, she knew that. Hers hadn't rung since she'd been here. It hadn't bothered her.

She ran outside and felt the rain on her skin. How nice it hadn't stopped, but now it was a slow, misty sprinkling.

Yanking open the sliding door into the garage, she saw it was empty and her heart rate started to slow down. Cal was right. They'd be out looking at dams or fences or stock. Tom had taken Aria for a short drive to see the sheep yesterday and she'd loved it, asking to go again as soon as they could.

Yes, that was where they'd be.

She started to jog back and saw Cal getting out of his ute. He must have changed his motorbike for the ute because of the rain, she thought.

'I've called him,' he said. 'Didn't answer.'

'The ute isn't there, so you must be right.'

'Get dressed and we'll go for a look.'

He sounded casual enough, but Chelsea picked up an underlying tightness in his voice. 'Is there reason to be worried?' she asked.

Cal shrugged. 'I wouldn't have thought so but it has been raining. They might be bogged and need a pull.'

Chelsea suddenly realised she was still wearing her dressing gown and her face flamed red. 'Late night,' she stuttered. 'Be right back.' The look on Cal's face told her he wasn't impressed.

Why would he be? He'd probably been working since it was light and here she was sleeping in until halfway through the day! He wouldn't have understood that ten in the morning had once been early for her. Her concerts had rarely finished before eleven and then she'd had to get home and wind down. Sleep often hadn't come until the early hours of the morning.

Throwing on a pair of jeans and a T-shirt, she tossed her head, pretending not to care what Cal thought. Truth was, she did, because lately she cared what everyone thought of her. Four years ago people's opinions of her would have barely registered. But when the conductors had started to shun her, she'd realised her careless attitude had hurt her greatly. Now she cared.

Pushing all those thoughts aside, she quickly combed her hair and pulled it up into a ponytail, fastening it with an elastic band before running out the door.

'Sorry,' she said, getting into the ute.

'No matter,' Cal said as he started the engine.

'Where are we going?' she asked.

'I reckon he'll be over near the reserve,' Cal answered. 'Now I think about it, I'm sure I saw fresh tracks there when I went to get the pump earlier this morning.' He stopped talking while he put the ute into gear and took off, the wheels spinning for a couple of seconds on the wet ground. 'The fences tend to get washed away from there with the smallest amount of rain, because they run through a deep creek. We've got one mob of ewes up there and another in the next paddock. He won't want them boxed up.' He glanced over at her. 'Getting mixed up together,' he clarified.

Chelsea straightened and lifted her chin. 'I know what boxed up means.' She stared out the window and watched the drenched countryside pass by. The trees had been washed clean from all the dust, and instead of being coated in purple, the leaves were now a vivid green. Puddles had formed on the roads, and out in the paddocks there seemed to be a tinge of green already forming. The grass would grow quickly now, she knew, because the ground was warm.

They bounced over the two-wheel track in silence.

'How long have you worked for Dad?' Chelsea finally asked, feeling the need to fill the silence.

'Four years this Christmas,' Cal answered.

'Really?' Chelsea wanted to fold into herself. That probably meant he knew everything about her. He'd been working for her dad since Aria had been born. He'd been here when her mother had died. He'd know about Dale. And he'd know Chelsea hadn't returned for her mother's funeral.

'Do you like it?'

'I love it,' Cal replied.

'You didn't say why you needed the phone.'

Cal yanked on the steering wheel and turned down a side track to where the road was covered by water. 'Look there.' He pointed to the river. Muddy brown water was flowing strongly, gurgling and splashing around the base of tree trunks and up to the edge of the bank. And in the middle of the crossing was a white ute.

'Geez!' Chelsea exploded as she saw Aria sitting on the roof and her father standing in the middle of the stream. 'What's he doing?' She leaned forwards and peered through the rain-splattered windscreen.

Not answering straightaway, Cal continued to watch.

'There,' he finally said, pointing. 'Ewe caught in the fence. She'll be too heavy for him to lift.' He parked and pulled out a pair of rubber boots from behind the seat. He ripped off his Rossi boots and pulled on the rubber ones. Within a few moments he was wading through the water to help her dad.

'Aria, don't move from there, honey!' Chelsea knew the water wasn't flowing fast enough for the ute to be swept away, but her daughter couldn't swim. What if she fell from the roof? She had a sudden image of her daughter falling into the swirling waters and disappearing. A mixture of fear and anger swept over her. How dare her father put her daughter in such a dangerous situation!

Aria heard Chelsea call and swung around, her face alive with delight. Her hair was wet and pushed back from her face while her cheeks were red from the cold water. 'Fun, Mummy!' she called above the noise of the water.

'Oh, you think, do you?' Chelsea muttered, trying not to show she was concerned. She plastered a smile on her face. 'That's good. But don't move until Papa gets back there, okay?'

Aria waved and went back to watching Tom and Cal untangle the ewe and, finally, lift the water-laden animal onto the back of the ute.

Once she was made secure, Tom held out his arms to Aria and she scrambled forwards. Chelsea held her breath as Tom lifted her into the front seat. Climbing in next to her, he reversed the ute close to where Cal was parked.

Only moments later, both her father and daughter were safely on dry ground. It was then and only then that Chelsea felt as if she could breathe again.

'I gotta go,' Cal said. 'Got to meet Dave Burrows up on the road.'

'Thanks for your help, son,' Tom said. 'Appreciate it. Wouldn't have got that soggy old girl up on the back without your help. I'll take her back to the mob. Hopefully she'll dry out quick and be back on her feet.'

'No worries but, Tom, we've got a problem.' He glanced at Chelsea as if he didn't want to talk in front of her.

Chelsea crossed her arms and stared at him. She was still angry with her father and she could be angry with Cal too if she needed to.

'What's that?'

'Well, this Dave Burrows, he's the local copper.'

Tom squinted. 'What are you meetin' him for?'

Aria chose that moment to try to open the ute door and clamber back inside. 'Mummy, I'm cold.'

Chelsea, torn between wanting to hear more and helping her daughter, took off her rain jacket and beckoned Aria to come over to her.

'There's a problem up in Beckers paddock,' Cal said in a low voice. 'I went there first thing this morning. That pump we've been using, it's on the edge of the well and the well is in the middle of the river.'

'Yeah?'

'The water's come hammering down one side of the hill and washed a heap of soil away. Gouged out a deep crevice.'

'Bugger it,' Tom said. 'Have to get the front-end loader over and fill it in. That's the only problem with this rain. Came down a bit too hard and fast.'

Cal shook his head. 'That's not the worst of it. Where the dirt's been washed away, I can see something's been buried.'

'Buried?' Tom stilled and looked over at Cal.

'A skeleton. I'm sure it's human.'

Chapter 5

Dave parked his four-wheel drive under a tree and looked through the curtain of drizzling rain. This wet weather hadn't been forecast and it was unusual for the rain to continue after the storms had passed. Still, by all accounts it would be dry tomorrow. Then the humidity would kick in and everyone would be wishing the rain hadn't arrived, and Kim would be complaining about how frizzy her normally curly hair was.

'Fun,' he commented, before sighing and opening the door.

'Better than sitting at the station doing nothing,' Jack answered, reaching into the back and pulling out the waterproof camera. 'I bet the remains aren't human, though.'

'This Cal was very sure they were.'

'If I had a dollar for every time I've been involved in a skeletal discovery the finder claimed was human, I wouldn't be working here—I'd be lying next to a pool in Hawaii!'

Dave laughed. 'Well, mate, there's a first time for everything. Come on.'

They shrugged into their rain jackets and rubber boots and got out of the wagon, then walked quickly towards the two men who were waiting for them at the base of the hill.

'G'day, I'm Dave Burrows,' Dave said, holding out his hand when he was close enough.

'Cal,' the younger one said, 'and this is my boss, Tom Taylor.'

'You were the one who called it in?' Dave asked Cal after shaking hands with Tom.

He nodded.

'What were you doing down here in the rain? Not a great day for checking the stock,' Jack said.

'It's probably the best day for checking the stock,' Tom corrected him. 'Big rain after a hot spell, the temperature drops and that's when you lose sheep. Especially if they're a bit hungry.'

'Have you lost any?' Dave moved forwards and peered at the base of the tree. He could see deep erosion from where the water had rushed down the hill.

'Not that I've found,' Tom replied. 'But I haven't got far yet. Saved a couple who'd got tangled in fences. Most of them are in paddocks with good shelter but always gotta keep an eye on them.'

'Well, let's hope they're all okay. So, what were you doing out here, Cal?'

'I came to get the pump from the well. Wasn't sure how high the water'd be running and didn't want to lose it. Was on top of the wall. Over there.' He pointed, and through the rainy haze Dave could just make out a red pump.

Wiping the water away from his eyes, he turned back to Cal. 'How'd you find this? It's away from river.' He indicated to the washed-away section where he could see the glimpse of white within the deep purple soil.

'Mate, you can see how much erosion there is here. I went over to take a closer look. See how bad it was. See how hard it was going to be to fix—or if I could get the front-end loader in now and start to divert the water away from where's it tracked so it doesn't get any worse. Better to act on this type of erosion at once rather than wait until the water has stopped running.'

'Did you know what it was straightaway?'

'Nah, took me a little while to work it out. First up, all I saw was white—or grey. But it stood out against the dirt. Then I realised they were bones and just thought it was a dead sheep or roo or something. But the skull. It didn't look right. Walked a bit closer, realised it looked human.'

Jack pulled on a pair of gloves. 'Seen human remains before?' he asked.

'Only on TV.'

'Better have a look,' Dave said. 'Did you get close?'

'Only within a couple of metres. When I realised what it was, I knew enough to stay away.'

Dave glanced around, getting a feel for the country. The river was settled deep within two lines of hills, one to the north and the other to the south. A public road, running along the edge of the river, snaked its way through the middle. He could see where the water had gouged out a deep crack down the side of the hill and run in a zigzag across the country until it reached the low ground. The height of the hills made it easy for water to run hard and fast when there was a heavy downpour. Looking up, he realised that to the west the cloud was clearing; there was a glimpse of blue among the heavy grey clouds. If this was a grave, the person buried here was in a picturesque and peaceful spot.

Jack was already standing over the bones and examining them. Dave asked Cal and Tom to stay where they were for the moment and walked over too.

'You won't believe this,' Jack said in a low voice.

'They're human?'

'They bloody are! Look here.' He pointed to the rounded skull which was lying face-down in the soil. 'See the curve? And here's the start of the spine,' he continued. 'And before you say anything, there're no monkeys or chimps around here, so I'm not making an assumption!'

Dave nodded. When he had first arrived in Barker and started investigating a carjacking, he'd kept making the comment that assumptions weren't part of detective work. His junior officer had never let him forget it. 'Good to know I have taught you something!' There was humour in his voice.

Squatting down, he looked into the grave. There was water pooling in the hole and trickling out to the creek below. Although he could only see the base of the skull and a small amount of the spine, he had to agree with Jack.

The parts he could see were encrusted with the deep purple soil, and there seemed to be a decaying hessian bag, which perhaps the body had been wrapped in.

'Right, we'll need to get forensics up here. Tell 'em it's wet and soggy. I'll get the camera.'

Together they walked back to the two waiting men.

'Unfortunately, you were correct, Cal,' Dave said when they got closer. 'They are human remains. We're going to have to cordon off the area and get a forensics team up here to excavate the skeleton.'

Tom stared at him. 'Has it been there long?'

'We're going to have to wait until the examination has been done. There's no way I can answer that.'

'But . . .' The older man looked bewildered. 'Do you mean to say that a person has been lying there for months and no one has known? Why would they have been buried there? Is this going to be part of a murder investigation?'

'I certainly can't tell you whether their demise was the result of murder or natural causes. We'll need to look at everything much more closely. Working this out will take time. And people who know what they're doing. We'll call them in and get started on it as soon as we can.'

Cal kicked at the ground with a scuffed boot and scratched his head. Dave recognised all the signs; he was uncomfortable. He turned to him.

'How long have you worked here, Cal?'

'Four years this Christmas.'

'How'd you get the job?'

'Hang on,' Tom interjected. 'Are you questioning him? Doesn't he get a lawyer or something?'

'S'all right,' Cal said, turning to Tom. 'They gotta do what they gotta do. I'm more worried about how this is going to hold up the dam digging we had planned.' He turned back to Dave. 'I got the job after Tom advertised in the *Stock Journal*. Been over in the west working on a cattle station out of Broome and wanted to get back a bit closer to home. My olds live in Port Pirie and are not getting any younger.'

'I tell you what,' Dave said. 'Why don't you blokes go back to the house and get dry. We'll do what we have to do here and be back to catch up with you both. Hopefully by the time the forensic team arrives, the rain will have cleared and the conditions will be easier to work in.'

'Good-o,' Tom said and walked towards his ute without a backward glance.

Dave noticed Cal was slower to walk away and kept glancing towards the site.

When the men had driven off, Dave got out the camera and started to take photos of the skeleton in situ while Jack put up a tent to cover the remains.

'No point in getting the crime scene tape out here, I don't reckon,' Dave said. 'The tent cover will be attraction enough. How long before the team get here?'

'Probably three hours. They're coming from Port Augusta, not Adelaide.'

'Well, that's good news. Won't have to hang around here too long.'

'I don't suppose it'll be you anyway, will it?'

'What'd you mean?'

'You'll go back and talk to them and I'll stay here keeping the silent witness company.'

Dave grunted. 'Maybe.'

They worked in silence for a while, Jack fastening and securing the tent, while Dave shot photos from every conceivable angle.

'Hey, Dave, look at this.' Jack pointed to a spot a little way from the body. 'What do you think this is?'

Dave crouched down and looked carefully, before putting on another set of gloves and carefully scraping away a small amount of soil.

'What do you think it is?' Jack asked, getting out a flashlight to brighten the area.

'Hmm. Maybe a box of some sort.' Dave gently scraped the dirt away to reveal a dark wooden corner.

They looked at each other.

'This scene just got a bit more interesting.'

Dave nodded and snapped a few more photos. 'Better leave this to the experts. Don't want to bugger that up in any way. Might be important information in it.'

'How long do you think they've been there?' Jack asked as he finished his task.

'Hard to say. I don't think I've seen one like this. I've always told you not to make assumptions.' He glanced up and grinned. 'Don't make me make them.'

'Did you see Cal's reaction?'

'Mmm. Might be a bit unsettled because he found the remains, that's all. He's probably never seen anything like this before.'

Both men stood at the side of the grave and looked in as they talked. Now that the tent was up, the water was soaking into the ground.

'Wonder what the story is,' Jack said quietly. 'But it's a proper skeleton all right.'

'We don't know that! Got no idea what it might look like underneath the dirt. We can only see that small part of the skull which, yeah, is clean and devoid of any flesh, but the rest of the body mightn't be like that.' Dave clapped Jack on the shoulder. 'We don't know, so no point in speculating. We'll have to be patient. Come on, let's go and talk to those blokes. I'll zip this up and secure it, so no one can get in.'

They went outside and Dave zipped up the tent flaps while Jack got out the tape and stuck it over the zip, then looked at his work.

'A passer-by will probably think this is a cover for a pump or something,' Jack said.

'Hope so.'

❧

'Cup of tea?' Tom asked as the two policemen sat down at the kitchen table. They'd left their wet rain jackets rolled up in the back of the car to be hung out when they got home and their muddy boots at the door.

'I'll get the tea,' the woman in the kitchen offered.

'I'm fine,' Tom replied, his tone hard.

She raised her eyebrows and backed out of the kitchen. Dave watched them closely; there was clearly some animosity between father and daughter and he wondered why. Then he caught himself.

'Your daughter?' he asked, tilting his head towards the door she'd disappeared through.

'Yes. Chelsea.'

One-word answers. Excellent.

For a moment his mind flew to his ex-wife, who had always been an expert on one-word answers. Then he shook himself, surprised. He hadn't thought of Melinda in years. Maybe it was the phone call from Mandy that had dredged up the past. He briefly wondered how his brother was doing and then focused on Cal, who was sitting at the end of the table picking at his fingers.

'How much rain was there?' Dave asked.

'One and a half inches,' Cal answered, looking up.

'Just over thirty-eight.' Dave did the conversion in his head. 'Nice. I know it's not the best time of the year, but it was needed.'

'It'll be fantastic for the dams,' Cal agreed. 'There probably won't be too much feed turn up from it. Actually, that's wrong. The feed will spring out of the ground, but the heat will burn the seedlings before they get the opportunity to adjust. It'll get hot as soon as this cloud disappears.'

'And humid,' Tom put in as he filled the kettle and switched it on. 'We'll have to watch the sheep for flies, Cal.'

'How many sheep do you run?' Jack asked.

Dave nodded approvingly to himself. Jack had come to understand that detectives needed to connect with people to gain their trust. People would never talk to someone who they didn't. They might give the basic information, but nothing more.

'Three thousand. Shandona is only small compared to a lot of the stations around here, thirty-five square miles. Carrying capacity is dependent on the season.'

'Thirty-five square miles? What's that in hectares?'

'Close enough to nine thousand.'

'And you're the only farmhand who works here?'

He nodded.

'Couldn't do without him,' Tom said as he put the pot of tea on the table and went back to the bench for the cups.

The sound of little feet running on floorboards echoed through the house and a young girl appeared, her hair damp. 'Papa! Can I have a cup of tea too, Papa?'

'Aria!' Chelsea followed her, a towel in her hand. 'Leave Papa be, he's busy.'

'Never too busy for you, my dear,' Tom said with a smile. 'But this is grown-up talk. How about you take these cups over, and once these nice men have left, you and I can take a thermos and some sandwiches out into the paddock and check the sheep?'

'Okay.' She reached up for the cups and took them across to the table where Dave leaned down to take them. Chelsea disappeared again while Aria helped her grandfather.

'Thanks, missy. What's your name?'

'Aria,' she said shyly.

'Well, Miss Aria, are you up here visiting your pop?'

She nodded her head vigorously. 'It's my first time here.'

'Wow, your first time? You must be having fun. Tell me, how old are you?'

Aria held up four fingers.

'Four?'

Nodding, she went back and stood next to Tom.

'And we're having fun aren't we, Aria?' Tom said.

'Yes.'

'Now you run along and find Mum, there's a good girl. I'll come and get you soon.'

'Always nice to have family visit,' Dave said as he poured himself a cup of tea, hoping to get to the bottom of why the relationship between father and daughter seemed so strained when Tom was clearly besotted with his granddaughter.

'How long are you going to be in my paddock for?' Tom asked.

Dave leaned back in his chair and looked at him. He didn't seem like a man who was pleased to have his family visit. Or at least his daughter. 'That's a bit like the eternal question, "How long is a piece of string?". Forensics should be here in—' he looked at his watch—'about an hour and a half. They'll have to process the scene. Get the bones out of the ground, account for them all, then we'll have to sift through the soil to make sure we haven't missed anything.'

'Like what?'

'Anything really. Extra bones that don't match the skeleton. Personal belongings, any indication as to whether it was a natural death or not. It's going to take a few days at least.'

Tom was beginning to look worried.

Cal leaned forwards and drew the sugar bowl over. 'That's okay,' he said more to Tom than anyone else. 'I've been thinking. The dozer can start on the other end of the place.'

'I don't know . . .'

'It'll be okay, Tom,' Cal said, and took a sip of his tea.

Chapter 6

'Where to now?' Jack asked, climbing into the passenger seat and reaching for his seat belt.

'Back to the site, I think. We'll give forensics a welcome and brief them, then leave them to it. Good thing they could come so quick.'

'They'd just finished up something in Port Augusta, so they were right to leave once they got the last of their team back from the scene.' Jack wound the window down a fraction to stop the windscreen from fogging up. 'Strange feeling in the house,' he commented as they drove past the dam.

Dave didn't say anything. He was too busy himself thinking about the things that hadn't seemed right: strained relationship with daughter; a workman who seemed more like a son; a boss who disappeared within himself when the conversation became stressful or pressured.

'Did you take any notes?' he finally asked Jack.

'A few.' He opened his notepad. 'None of them know of any missing persons from around the area. No family members missing, nothing in the history of the place that indicates there should be a buried body here.' He paused. 'It could be anyone! Someone who died in the Depression or something. I mean, there have to be bodies buried everywhere out here, don't there?'

Dave laughed and flicked on his blinker to turn out onto the main road. He drove carefully. The roads were still oily from the rain. He was glad it had cleared up—drying conditions would be much easier to work in than wet.

'I'm sure there aren't bodies everywhere! Well, I'd bloody hope not. Still, in the early years many people died natural deaths and were buried in graves out in the bush. There wasn't always time to get them to a cemetery, especially if they died in the middle of summer. People had to make do. But then again, it could be the remains of someone who has only been there for ten or so years, and even though that makes it a cold case, it still needs investigating. Alternatively, it could be someone who was buried recently. We've really got no idea.'

'Except we know that it wasn't a short time ago.' Jack glanced over at Dave. 'There's no flesh.'

'I know, I know. That box is intriguing me.' He tapped the steering wheel as was his habit when he was thinking. 'Trouble is, if the remains are old, we're going to have trouble investigating. Depending on the age of the bones obviously. I'm mean, if they're fifty years old, is it in the public interest to excavate them? Can we make an arrest? Maybe not. We might be tying up money and resources for no outcome. If they're twenty years old, we've got cause to investigate. Guess we'll just have to wait and see what the forensics crew say.'

As Dave drove, he noticed there were kangaroos still huddled under the trees for shelter. A large mob of emus was out grazing on the side of a hill and they walked slowly, their heads down, looking for food. It seemed as if the whole hill was moving.

'Pity we didn't get this rain in the growing season,' Dave said. 'Would've made the farmers' lives much easier.'

Jack's phone dinged with a phone message. 'Hell!' He jumped. 'Bloody internet connection,' he said, digging into his pocket. 'Never works when you want it to, then scares the shit out of you when you least expect it!'

Dave grinned. 'Just keeping you on your toes.'

He listened to the message and said, 'It's the council wanting to know if we're going to authorise the roadblocks for the Christmas pageant.'

'Of course. We always do. When is it?'

'Next Sunday evening. When's that? Five days' time.'

'Bloody hell, when's Christmas? Tuesday?'

'Yup.'

'I haven't got Kim a Christmas present yet. She's so hard to buy for,' Dave sighed as he pulled up at the crime scene and switched off the engine.

'Funny, she says the same about you.'

Dave harrumphed. 'Can you get the crew on the radio and find out how far away they are? I'll check the scene.'

The rain had stopped but the slope below the remains was still slippery. As he suspected, the tape hadn't been touched. A flock of galahs rose overhead, screeching as they soared into the grey-blue sky. The birds settled in another tree and started stripping the leaves. The sound of twigs cracking and the low murmur of galahs as they talked to each other filled Dave with pleasure. He wondered if whoever was buried here had enjoyed the galahs, or if, like many farmers, they had found them annoying and destructive.

How had this person died, and why did they end up here? At least one other person must know about the death, because the body had been buried. And how long had the body been in the ground?

He knew he'd get some answers soon enough, but he couldn't help turning the questions over in his mind. As a detective, he'd had to learn the art of patience; sometimes it took weeks for results and information to come through, though it never stopped him from thinking about or querying the crime scene or investigation.

The sound of an engine overtook the birds and he turned to see a white government-issued van heading towards them, with another car following. Looked like the whole forensics team had come out.

Dave took one final glance at the tent and went down to meet them.

As he watched the team leader, Michael Finlay, give the nod for the body bag to be shifted, Dave stood with his hands in his pockets, waiting to talk to him.

It was two days after the discovery of the grave and, after much painstaking work, the remains were heading back to the lab in Adelaide; soon there would finally be some information. John Gardner and Tim Dunston, the evidence recorders and custodians of the site, would stay and finish sifting through the soil, but the bulk of the work was done.

'There we have it, Dave,' Finlay said, walking towards him and taking off his gloves before wiping the sweat from his brow. 'All done. We should have something to report just after Christmas. So long as the coroner doesn't get inundated with suicides. It's that time of the year, I'm afraid. God, the humidity is awful, how do you stand it?'

Dave nodded in agreement. 'It's not something we get up here very often. More the dry heat and really hot days during summer. But, as you can tell, we had rain yesterday, and as soon as the sun comes out, things get a bit sticky. This is quite unusual.'

'I'd hope so. Anyone would think we were in the middle of the tropics!' He mopped his brow again and looked up at the sky, which was dotted with fluffy white clouds. 'Bit of breeze would be nice.'

'We probably won't get any among the hills here. You'd better get your car running and the aircon on,' Dave grinned, then changed the subject. 'Can you tell me anything about the bones yet? Just something to get me started on looking for a missing person?'

'The pelvis and jawbone are consistent with the bones being male, but that's all I'm telling you. You know better than to ask a lowly team leader to make a comment! But off the record and very much between you and me, in my experience . . .' He scratched his cheek and grimaced a little. 'I'd be lying if I said I could give you an accurate estimation of how long the bones have been in the ground, but I can see they are brittle and there is no flesh remaining on them at all, which puts them in the fifty years plus range. We'll have to wait for the science before we can confirm that, though.'

'Long time.'

'Sure is. And you know what everyone thinks about tying up money and resources. I doubt they'll see this as a priority. The bones will need close examination to determine cause of death, but the skull had a fracture in it. Now what role that played in the death, you'll have to wait and see what the crew at the morgue say. Of course it might just be that the bones can't tell you anything. If it was a heart attack, say, or a stabbing and the knife didn't touch the bones . . . The bones can only tell us what's happened to them. But of course a veteran of your experience already knows that, Dave.'

The familiar thrill began to trickle through the detective. This could possibly be a murder! And one so old would test his skills. He knew that even if the powers that be in Adelaide weren't too keen to spend time on it, he'd be pushing to do so.

'The wooden box is certainly the worse for wear, which is another indicator that the remains have been there for a long time. We did find this underneath the bones.' Finlay reached into his pocket and handed Dave an evidence bag.

Holding it up to the sunlight, Dave studied the gold brooch within the clear plastic: two roses with long stems, a twisted gold rope holding the stems together and what looked like diamonds in the centre of the roses. He'd never seen anything like it before.

He got out his phone and took a few photos, thinking he might be able to track down the owner of the brooch by showing it to people. 'Wonder if this was an heirloom,' he mused out loud.

'It's beautiful, whatever it is,' Finlay answered. 'And I'd think it was worth a small fortune. I don't know much about antiques, but this is certainly one. I suspect if you find the owner of this, you'll have a very good chance of IDing your John Doe.'

'I agree.' Dave handed it back to him. 'I'll start there. Make a few local enquiries. Hopefully someone will recognise it.' He looked around then said to Finlay, 'Well, thanks. I know it's been a hard slog. Appreciate the time you've put in. Have a safe trip back to Adelaide.'

They shook hands. Dave couldn't wait to get back to the office and start researching the brooch. His gut told him that there was something very special about that piece of jewellery.

And Dave always listened to his gut.

Pulling up at the front of Shandona's homestead, Dave heard the dog bark before he saw the border collie shoot out from under the plumbago bush and bark at his tyres twice, before heading back to the shade of the leaves.

'Steady there, old dog,' he said as he wound the window down to keep the car from overheating while he was inside.

His knock on the front door echoed loudly through the old house. He heard a woman's voice call, 'Hang on!'

Taking out his phone, he pulled the photo of the brooch up on the screen.

'Hello.' Chelsea stood in the doorway, dressed in shorts and a T-shirt that were covered in dirt.

'You look like you've been working hard,' he observed.

'Been cleaning out the kitchen cupboards. I don't think they've been done since Mum died,' she answered. 'And you look like you've been playing in the mud!'

'It's certainly a bit of a slippery slope up on the hill. The dirt cakes onto the bottom of your boots. I think I'm about three inches taller than usual!'

'The joys of our sticky purple dirt.'

'That's it. Can I come in?'

'Oh, sorry, where are my manners? The kitchen is a bit of a tip, but I'll put the kettle on.'

Dave took off his boots and followed her inside, saying, 'No, no, that's fine, I won't hold you up for long. How long has it been since your mum passed?'

'Mmm, two and a bit years now.'

'Your dad lives here by himself?'

'Yeah. I'm just here for a visit.'

'Where are you from?'

'Until recently, here and there really. I used to travel a lot with my work. I'm a—' she paused—'was a concert pianist. I have an apartment in Sydney, but I've been staying in Adelaide for work.'

Dave paused. 'A concert pianist? That sounds like a fascinating career. How did you become a pianist?'

'That's an interesting question really,' she answered, crossing her arms. 'Have a seat.'

Dave took a chair at the table and waited. Pulling out a chair too, Chelsea sat and chewed at her bottom lip before answering.

'I won a scholarship to attend the Conservatorium in Adelaide when I was thirteen. By that age I was a little late to the party—most of those kids had been playing seriously since they were four or five. Sometimes even younger. They lost their childhood by doing that, so in one way, even though I was behind, at least I got to have fun when I was small. I loved the piano . . . Ah, maybe it was the music rather than the instrument. I think I loved music.

'Anyway, Mum said it was a great opportunity for me, so I moved to Adelaide at thirteen, but by the time I got there I had some bad habits—or at least what the teachers called bad habits—technical idiosyncrasies, so I had to work a lot harder than the other students. And I did. I worked my heart out. It all paid off when I was offered a job with the Adelaide Symphony Orchestra.'

'Sounds glamorous.'

Chelsea gave a snort and shook her head. 'If your idea of glamour is practising until your fingers and hands ache, if you like conductors yelling at you and never having a social life, then, yes, it was a glamorous life.'

'Bit like being a detective,' Dave said. 'Everyone thinks the job is all about shoot-outs and running after criminals, when most of the work is done behind a desk researching and gathering information.'

'Exactly! Anyway, from there I worked with the Sydney Symphony Orchestra—of course, that's scary enough in itself. Sometimes you only get a week's notice and you have to learn a whole score in such a small amount of time.' She shook her head with a rueful smile. 'It's certainly a 24/7 job—late nights and long days practising. But that's where the passion and love of it has to come in because I'm sure no one in their right mind would go through what we go through if they didn't absolutely love it. You've got to have a hunger ... a desire to achieve.' Her voice became more urgent as she talked, and Dave could see the fire ignite inside her.

'Is it the adrenalin of the performance that you love?' Dave asked.

'Yeah, that's part of it,' she paused, thinking. 'One of my professors said that to be a professional you've got to be fearless—never doubt your own ability. That can get wearing because there are always times when you do. Doubt yourself, I mean. Sometimes another pianist will get brought in when you were sure you had the job.'

She shrugged. 'But he also said it was about hard work, passion and a good dollop of luck.'

'You obviously had all of those,' Dave said.

Chelsea was silent for a while, seemingly lost in memories. Then she looked over at him. 'Yeah, I guess I did.' She paused. 'Are you sure you don't want a cup of tea?'

Dave sensed she didn't want to talk about herself anymore, so he said, 'I really came to see your dad, but I guess he isn't here.'

'No, he and Aria are out somewhere.'

'Ah, the fun of being a grandparent.' He glanced around at the cooking equipment and crockery piled on every available surface. 'Big job?'

'Yeah. Trying to help out a bit while I'm here. Don't think Dad will notice, but I'll feel good if I leave the place in better shape than I found it. So, what did you need Dad for?'

'I was going to tell him that we'll only be here another two days at the most. Probably less. We're just tidying up the site and making sure nothing has been missed. As soon as we've done that, we'll be out of your hair.'

'I'll let him know.' Chelsea frowned. 'Do you know who it is?'

'No, not yet. It'll take a while to get the reports from Adelaide but then hopefully we'll have more of an idea when the person died and how. That'll be the starting point.'

Chelsea got up and went to the window. She stood looking out, her arms crossed over her chest. 'You know, I used to ride my horse all through that area when I was a kid. I'd pack a saddlebag with sandwiches and take a water bottle and disappear for the whole day. Pinto and I, we'd follow the creeks and pretend we were explorers. The only people to ever set foot here. Wouldn't it be strange if that grave had been there all the while and we never knew it existed . . .' Her voice trailed off.

'Tell me,' Dave got up and walked over to her, holding up his phone. 'Have you ever seen this brooch before?'

Chelsea reached out and took the phone. 'God, that's beautiful. Unique. Did you find it with the body?' She looked up at him, her eyes wide.

'It was found at the scene.'

'Stunning. Even though it's filthy.' She used her thumb and forefinger to enlarge the picture. 'But no,' she finally said. 'No, I haven't seen anything like that.'

'Not in photos of old relatives?' Dave prompted.

Shaking her head slowly, she seemed to be reaching for a memory, but again she said no.

'Well, if you come across anything, will you let me know? Maybe you could have a look through old photo albums if you have any.'

'Of course.' She smiled. 'Perhaps my new career could be in detecting?'

Dave laughed. 'I'm sure you'd find some similarities between your old career and the new one.' He turned to go. 'Oh, one last thing, did you ever hear of any family members who have gone missing or who were just never heard from again?'

A look of curiosity passed over her face, and Dave could see her brain was racing. 'Are you looking for skeletons in the closet, Detective? I thought you would've had enough skeletons on your hands at the moment!'

'Yeah, I suppose it sounds a little like that,' he said with a grin. 'But I have to ask. Old stories of lost relatives, people who wandered off into the bush and never came home? That sort of thing.'

'I don't know of anything like that, sorry. I'd love to be able to solve the mystery for you straightaway.'

'If you think of anything, please let me know.'

'I will.'

He handed her a card. 'Can you have Tom call me when he comes back in?'

Chapter 7

'Now see this here, Aria.' Tom bent down and pointed to a tiny seedling pushing its way through the ground. The rains had caused the country to burst into bloom as they always did, but he knew it wouldn't last. The first forty-degree day would see these baby shoots wither and die.

'What's that one called, Papa?'

'This is windmill grass. You can't see it now, but the flower looks like a windmill. I'll show you some photos when we get home. Like the windmill down at the house dam.'

'Do they go round and round like windmills too?'

'Only when they're not attached to the plant. Your mum, when she was little, liked twirling them in between her fingers. Your uncle did too.' He paused as he thought of Dale, which he did every day.

'Who's my uncle?' Aria asked, looking up at him.

Tom looked down at her and cleared his throat. Her eyes were so dark, they were almost black. Dark pools of deep brown, and as he gazed into them he thought there was something different about this little girl. She was calm and thought carefully about what she said. 'Considered', Pip would have called her. But could you call a four-year-old 'considered'? That confused Tom and a familiar trickle of fear started to drip into in his stomach. He'd heard Chelsea call her an 'old soul' but he didn't really know what that meant.

Aria's dark hair was pulled back into a ponytail and the look on her face gave him a strange unsettled feeling. He wasn't sure why. She didn't look like either Dale or Chelsea, so she must resemble her father. But who was he? Tom realised he'd never asked Chelsea who Aria's father was. Clearly he had nothing to do with raising her because neither Aria nor Chelsea spoke of him.

'Papa?'

He hadn't answered her question. Clearing his throat, he shook his head. 'Oh, it's a long story, Aria.' He looked out across the paddock, the familiar ache in his chest threatening to overwhelm him. 'Long story,' he repeated.

'How—' Aria started to ask, but he shook his head once more. She seemed to understand and stopped asking.

Tom straightened up and looked out across Shandona. 'We're going to have to keep an eye on the sheep for flies now it's rained.'

'Why?'

'So they don't hurt the sheep.'

Aria looked puzzled and finally said, 'Flies are small. They can't hurt sheep, Papa!'

Tom started to laugh, but Aria was still frowning as she said, 'They fly in the air!'

'You're right! But they always have to land somewhere.' He started to explain how flies caused maggots in the wet wool and, if left untreated, would burrow through the skin of the sheep until they died. But then he saw the look on her face and stopped. 'Yeah, it sounds a bit yucky, doesn't it? Anyway, we will have to watch them to make sure they stay healthy.'

Looking around, he tried to think of something to change the subject. His mind was blank. 'Ah.' His eyes fell on the thermos he'd made before they'd left the house. 'How about we have a cup of tea?'

'Yes, please, I'm thirsty,' Aria said.

'Right, I've got a special spot in the creek up here, where we can go and sit. Jump back in the ute, love.'

Tom went around to the driver's side and got in, trying to get his bearings. He knew the picnic spot he and Pip used to go to when the kids were little was close by, but he couldn't quite remember where it was. Again there was that fear. Fear he was going mad or losing his mind. This wasn't the first time it'd happened.

That first time, Tom had been droving a mob of sheep back to the paddock after crutching. Somehow he'd forgotten where the gates were in each paddock and had ended up driving them along the fences of the thousand-acre paddock, looking for an opening. When Cal had come to find him, it had been nearly dark and he'd been angry with himself. And embarrassed. But he'd covered up what had happened, telling Cal that the sheep had broken away and it had been hard to mob them all together again, with the terrain being so rocky and rough.

He was pretty sure Cal hadn't believed him.

Then there was the time he'd been driving into Barker to pick up something from RuralCorp. He'd got halfway into town and forgotten what he was going in for. He hadn't taken a list with him, so he'd had to call Cal on the two-way and ask. That could have been put down to having too much on his mind; after all, he could remember Pip telling him that if she forgot her shopping list when she went into town, she'd never remember to get everything on it. But there'd been something in the look Cal had given him when he'd returned home to Shandona that had made Tom feel as if there were more to the incident than just forgetting what was on the list.

'Papa?' Aria's voice broke into his memories.

'Yeah?' The gumtrees all looked the same to him here. *Think, Tom!* he told himself.

'Are we going?'

'Sure are.' He shoved the ute into gear. Somewhere a little voice inside his head told him it wouldn't matter if he didn't find the exact spot. Aria wouldn't know because she'd never been there before.

Ha! He scoffed at his thought process. That didn't come into it! *He* would know. *He* would know if he wasn't in the right place and *he* should know where the old picnic spot was. He wasn't old or senile. Was he? When he'd looked in the mirror this morning, he'd got a fright at the number of grey hairs that had appeared from nowhere. Avoiding the mirror had become his speciality since Pip had died.

Driving slowly along the edge of the creek, he looked for any familiar signs. What had been so special about the spot? Dale had liked to play in the old ruins near the edge of the creek and Chelsea had ... The memory was just out of his reach. Tom squinted.

'Come on,' he coaxed himself. 'Come on.'

'What?'

Tom glanced over at the little girl in the passenger's seat. Dark eyes, dark hair ... He must have spoken out loud. 'Pardon,' he automatically corrected her.

'Papa?'

'Aria.' He breathed her name and tried to commit it to memory. 'Aria.' Somehow the murky haze lifted, and he realised that his granddaughter was looking at him strangely. 'Well, bugger me dead,' he said with a smile. 'Look where I'm driving! Completely in the wrong direction. Now, how about we take a left here ...' He turned the steering wheel and took the ute along a different track. 'If we wind our way along the edge of the creek for about two miles, I reckon, Aria, we'll be in the right place.'

As he drove, again he tried to bat down the fear. Why did these little blanks keep happening? What was wrong with him? Did he have a brain tumour? Didn't you get headaches with a brain tumour? He hadn't had any headaches.

'Look, see those white birds high up in the tree?' He began to tell her a story about the corellas and how one old bird used to fly higher than the others. It was the same story he had told his own kids at bedtime.

'But why?' she asked, craning her neck to see the birds.

'Well, he thought if he flew higher he would see more. Get more grubs and insects. Birds have very good eyesight, you know. This old bird, he liked his food. And if he was higher than the others he could keep a watch for enemies as well. But there's a really important lesson in this story, love,' he told her. 'Old bird forgot that even though he might see more from a higher spot, it would take him longer to get to the ground and the other birds could reach the grubs and insects before he did. So he grew old and skinny, because all the others were flying lower than he was. But he liked being high and feeling free. Slowly and slowly, he grew weaker and weaker, until finally he couldn't fly higher anymore. It was then he realised that if he flew at the same height as all the other birds, then he would be able to get to food more easily.'

Aria didn't answer, only frowned and looked through the windscreen up at the sky, as if trying to see if there was one higher than the others.

'Sometimes you need to do things the easy way,' he said. 'Be the same.'

'Mum says being the same isn't good.'

'And look where that got her,' he snapped before he could stop himself. He took a breath and pulled the ute to a halt. 'Sorry, Aria, love, I didn't mean that. And, yeah, your mum is right in some ways. Now, look, here we are. See that old ruin over there?'

Aria nodded.

'Well, that was built by my granddad. He was your great-*great*-granddad. His name was Baxter. He used it as a shepherd's hut. Somewhere to sleep and eat when he was out watching the sheep or mustering.'

'It's falling down.'

'Mmm, it has been for a while. It's a good place to play. Do you think you could serve me a cup of tea in there?'

A smile lit up Aria's face. 'Yes. I'm a very good tea pourer.' She opened the ute door and slid out onto the ground, before walking unsteadily across the stony ground. 'These trees are very tall, Papa!' she called back to him.

Tom reached into the back of the ute and grabbed the esky and thermos. 'How tall do you think they are?'

Aria stopped and looked up. He smiled as she almost tipped over backwards, trying to see their tops.

'Maybe . . . as tall as the sky!'

'Nearly, but not quite. Maybe about forty-five to fifty metres, but they live a very long time.'

'How long?'

'Sometimes five hundred years. That's much longer than you and I.' He could see her grappling to understand and realised it was a bit hard to explain. 'Put it this way. These trees were here, looking just like they do now, when my granddad, Baxter, built this cottage.' He pushed open the wooden door of the tiny two-roomed ruin and checked inside before letting Aria in. The roof had completely gone and some of the walls, which had been built with stones and mud, had started to crumble, but it was still an adventure for Aria.

He sat himself down on some fallen stones and wiggled to get comfortable, while Aria unpacked the cups.

'Papa?'

'Hmm?'

'It won't open. Can you help?' She held the thermos out to him.

As he looked across at her a bubble of emotion welled in his chest and for some strange reason his eyes felt hot. He, Tom Taylor, didn't cry! He hadn't cried when Dale had died, and he hadn't cried when he had stood alone next to Pip's grave. How could one small action from a little girl have such an effect on him?

'Course I can,' he said gruffly. Twisting the top, he handed it back, then watched Aria pour the tea and set out the food that Chelsea had made yesterday.

When Tom had come in the previous afternoon, he'd stopped short at the smell permeating the house. For a moment he'd forgotten Pip was dead, because no one else made her beef stew the way she did. Turned out Chelsea had found Pip's recipe book and they'd had all the ingredients. The red pot Pip had loved had been sitting on the stove bubbling, the way it had when she'd been alive. And on the bench a banana cake had been cooling. Aria had been standing on a stool, mixing the coffee icing to go on top.

Banana cake had always been his favourite.

Tom now realised he should've thanked Chelsea for cooking, rather than grunting at her as he walked through the kitchen. He hadn't, however, been able to stop himself from pausing at the stove and lifting the lid. That's when he'd had to leave the room. All the memories were pushing too close to the surface and he'd been frightened he might lose control.

'Cheers, Papa!' Aria raised her cup to him and, as he pulled away from his thoughts, he saw she'd eaten a piece of banana cake and still had icing on her lip.

'Cheers, love. Here.' He fossicked in his pocket and brought out his hankie before gently wiping her mouth.

She smiled and looked around, and he followed her eyes. The sky was a vivid blue and occasionally a white corella flew into view. There was a very gentle breeze that made the leaves shift just enough to be audible, and the purple of the hills glowed under a brilliant sun.

'This is fun,' he said.

'This is fun,' she confirmed.

❧

'Mum, who's my uncle?' Aria asked as she was undressing for her bath.

Chelsea stilled. She wasn't sure how to answer; she had always promised herself she'd be truthful with Aria, no matter how painful or hard it was. 'How did you hear about Dale?' she asked, already knowing the answer. Her father must have said something.

'Papa said you and my uncle liked twirling grass in your fingers.'

Chelsea smiled at her use of words. She was obviously repeating exactly what Tom had said. 'We did. Windmill grass it was called. We'd pretend it was the propeller from a plane and see how fast we could whizz it around.'

Making a noise like a plane, Aria held out her arms like wings. 'I'm going to visit my uncle. *Zoom.*'

'I wish you could,' Chelsea said, feeling her voice catch in her throat. 'You can't see him, honey. My brother, or your Uncle Dale, isn't here anymore.' She could hear the low hum of her father's voice on the telephone.

Aria looked at her quizzically. 'Where is he?'

Chelsea squatted down and looked her daughter in the eye while smoothing back her hair from her forehead. 'He died. When he was very young.'

'Oh.'

Seeing that Aria was struggling with the concept, she explained, 'Do you remember how we looked after Tori's goldfish while she was away? And one morning we found it floating on top of the water? The fish died and we had to bury it, remember?'

Aria nodded, a frown forming on her forehead. 'And Tori was sad. She cried.'

'That's right. Well, that happened to Dale. Not floating on top of the water . . .' Chelsea stopped. Trying to explain this was hard. 'He died in an accident. Papa and Nan didn't cope with his death very well. It's hard for them . . . for Papa—' she corrected herself—'to talk about it. It's probably better not to bring it up with him again.'

She thought about Dale's large smile on the night he died. He'd been wearing shorts and a casual shirt, trying to convince her to go to the engagement party with him.

'Carn, sis. You know you want to,' he said.

'I can't. I have to practise. If I don't . . .'

'I know, I know, if you don't get it right, you'll lose your position. Okay, I get it. Well, so be it. I'll carry on without you.' His tone had been light and they'd been the last words he'd said to her as he rushed out the door.

She'd heard him call out his goodbyes to Tom and Pip, then the engine of his ute started.

He hadn't come home.

'Would you be sad if I died?' Aria asked, interrupting her thoughts.

'Oh my God, honey, I couldn't imagine my life without you in it *ever*!' She pulled her daughter close and hugged her tightly. 'Yes, I would be very sad if that happened, but it's not going to. Okay? Now . . .' Chelsea let her go and, turning her gently around, pushed her towards the bathroom. 'Come on, your bath is waiting for you. Then, at teatime, I have something very important to talk to you about.'

Chapter 8

In the coolness of the sitting room, Chelsea moved quietly so she wouldn't let her father know what she was doing.

After her conversation with Aria, she wasn't sure if she wanted to have another talk about Dale. For a long time, she'd stood in front of the fireplace and gazed at the photo of her brother on the mantelpiece. It was twelve years since he'd died.

She'd been eighteen and remembered it as if it had happened yesterday. Her mother's screaming, her father's dark despair, the heavy blanket of misery that sat over the house for months. In the end it had been her brother's death and her parents' inability to cope with life afterwards that had made her leave. Chelsea remembered how she'd chosen to stay home to be with her parents at such a tragic time. She'd ended up missing the musical she'd been practising for, knowing she needed to support them. But slowly, slowly they had dragged her down, and returning to work was the only option. Running away was her way of dealing with her own grief. She left in order to lose herself in music, to not have to think. Chelsea hadn't wanted to watch her parents disappear into a world of pain and sorrow, and she hadn't known how to help them either. Music had been the safest option.

Chelsea ran her hands over the arms of the couch. The dogs barking had been the first sign that something was wrong that night. She'd been seated at the piano, practising for the musical she was playing in, *Dusty*, which was to open in Sydney that February. It was the first musical she'd ever played in and she didn't want to muck it up. It was Christmas time, and her few precious days at home had been filled with eating too much and laughing with her family.

Pinto was long dead, so there was nothing to compete for the piano's attention, other than her family. And even they weren't taking up too much of her time. Her mum seemed to be disappointed in her, although why, Chelsea wasn't sure. She'd made it! Into *Dusty the Musical*. Wasn't that what her training had been about?

Apparently not, according to Pip. A solo career was all that mattered and Chelsea was wasting her time playing in a musical. Chelsea hadn't agreed. It was a stepping stone to help her get to the solo career she wanted. She remembered the argument she'd had with the conductor before they had broken up for Christmas.

'You need to watch me. I am your leader. You don't go making up your own riffs and rhythms. The performers are expecting to hear *exactly*—hear me—*exactly* what is written on the score. How can they be expected to perform at their best if you give them something they're not expecting?'

'Yes, sir,' she'd answered. But it was hard. Her fingers always seemed to have a life of their own. Adding in little extras or jazzing up the music in some way. If she wanted to keep her job, then she would have to make sure she played what was on the page. Not what was in her head. So she'd been practising. Slowly and painstakingly. Reading the music and following it perfectly.

Chelsea had heard the dogs bark and stopped, wondering if there was a fox outside. It had been a full moon, so any animal would have been visible. Then she'd noticed the flash of headlights heading towards the house. She remembered checking her watch and thinking Dale was home early, then continued to practise.

It had been the knocking that had made her think something was wrong. Dale would never have knocked. Especially if he'd had a couple of beers. He would've closed the front door with a bang and yelled that he was home— even if everyone else was asleep! Her brother had never known how to be quiet.

At the foreign sound, Chelsea had stopped playing, taken her fingers from the piano keys and sat still, her hands in her lap. She didn't know why. Twelve years later, she still didn't understand why she hadn't run to the door and yanked it open. It had been clear something was wrong.

The banging had echoed throughout the house and in the end it had been her mother who had got up, wrapped in a thick dressing gown, and opened the door. Her pitiful wail had brought her father running, but Chelsea had stayed sitting at the piano, her hands still folded in her lap.

'What are you doing?'

She jumped at the sound of her father's voice. He was standing in the doorway behind her, his arms crossed as if challenging her to tell him exactly what she was thinking.

'Remembering,' she answered.

She watched as his eyes flicked over Dale's photos and came back to rest on her. He stayed silent.

'Why did you tell Aria about Dale?' she finally asked.

'He came up in conversation.'

'I hadn't planned on telling her.'

Her father gave a grunt. 'What, hide away from his death like everything else?'

The words hit Chelsea's heart hard. She wanted to clutch at her chest and at the same time hit out at him. 'I didn't hide away,' she managed to choke out, ready to explain everything that had happened. 'Maybe I did from Dale's death, but not from Mum's!'

Before she could say anything further, Tom said, 'What are you doing here, Chelsea?' his voice low. 'Why did you bother to come back now? You've been gone for so long. Hardly seems worthwhile to turn up now when it's years after your mother's death.'

Chelsea didn't know how to answer; she'd asked herself the very same question. Instead she swallowed hard and lifted her chin. 'I wanted to . . .' She stopped. What did she want? All the secrets and lies out in the open? All the bitterness to disappear? To have a relationship with her dad? Her heart was screaming yes, but her mind wouldn't let her tongue work.

'It's dinnertime,' she answered. 'We should have this discussion when Aria is asleep.' She pushed past him and went into the kitchen. Quickly she washed the potatoes and started to slice them, before peeling the apple and carrot and slicing the cabbage to make a coleslaw.

'I'm hungry,' Aria said, coming into the kitchen. Her wet hair wasn't brushed but she held her brush out to Chelsea.

'That's lucky, there are chops and salad tonight.' She started brushing her daughter's tangled hair.

'Where's Papa?'

'Probably in his office. Here you go. Take that back to your bedroom, honey.'

Aria grabbed the brush and headed out of the kitchen, but she stopped and came back. 'Mummy, you're being funny.'

'About what?' she answered distractedly. The words suddenly hit Chelsea and she looked up. 'I'm not being funny. Well, I'm not laughing. What do you mean?'

'Like that time when Tori's goldfish died. You were funny.'

Chelsea had to think about that and she realised that she hadn't wanted to tell Aria about the death, so she'd probably acted 'funny' in the bathroom . . .

'Oh! Sometimes talking about my brother makes me sad, so I probably acted a bit strange, and being here reminds me of him and my mum.' The pot on the stove was boiling and she quickly scooped the pile of potatoes into it and threw in a heavy pinch of salt.

'Are you feeling sad, Mummy? Like when the goldfish died?'

Chelsea stopped and looked at her, her stomach constricting. 'I guess I am.'

The solemn little face looked up at her. 'Do you need a hug?'

Chelsea gave a little laugh. 'Yes, please.' She held out her arms and said, 'It is "funny" being back here. It's been a long time since I've been home.'

'When are *we* going home?'

'I'm not sure. Not until after Christmas at least.' Now wasn't the time to tell her there was nothing to go back to Sydney for, and the casual job playing in a bar in Adelaide had fizzled out. She hadn't even admitted to herself that she wasn't sure what she was going to do now.

'Okay.' Aria skipped out of the room.

'You can set the table when you've finished doing that!' Chelsea called after her. She stopped as the words came out of her mouth; she sounded just like her mum. She'd heard her friends say sometimes they just opened their mouths and their mothers came out, but it had never happened to her before.

Suddenly she was four again, running behind her mum with the knives and forks while Dale followed with the plates. 'The fork to the left and the knife to the right,' her mother would chant. Chelsea wanted to clap her hands in time to the memory. That's what she'd done when she was

a kid. 'The fork to the left and the knife to the right . . .'
One, two full beats then three short, sharp semiquavers,
before going back to the whole beat. She'd never sung it
to Aria and she wasn't sure if she should with her dad
within hearing.

It seemed as if they were tiptoeing around a great big
elephant in the room, not talking about Pip. The counsellor
she'd been to see after she'd got off the cruise ship had
told her it was good to talk about the person who'd died.
Mention their name and speak about them. But she was
treading on eggshells wondering how her dad would react.

As if she'd summoned him, her father walked in. 'I don't
like mashed potatoes,' he said as he saw the boiled potatoes
she was about to mash sitting on the bench.

'What?' Chelsea looked at him blankly. 'Yes, you do.'
She knew her mum had always made up extra helpings of
mash when she cooked it, so he could have it for lunch
the next day.

'No, I don't. I don't like the texture.'

'But . . . Mum used to . . . Is this a new thing?'

'New? No. Never liked them.'

Stifling the annoyance that rose within her, she asked,
'How would you like me to cook them for you?'

'In the oven.'

Chelsea found another potato and wiped oil over it in
preparation. 'What did the detective say when he phoned?'
she asked.

'Nothing much.' Her father turned to leave.

'Did he show you the brooch?'

'Couldn't show me over the phone. He described it.' Tom sounded noncommittal and it made Chelsea think he wasn't being truthful.

'Have you seen it before?'

'No.'

Chelsea's head snapped up. 'You don't sound sure.'

'Why would I have seen it? I don't know anything about a brooch.' His voice became loud and before Chelsea had a chance to respond, he turned and stormed out of the kitchen.

'What?' She stood staring after him incredulously, her hands half raised. There was something wrong with her dad. Sure, she'd expected him to be bitter towards her, and perhaps even angry. But not secretive and petulant.

The water pump outside came on, indicating Tom was in the shower. Quickly, Chelsea went into her father's office and looked for the book he always used for taking notes of phone calls. Since she was small it had been his habit to take notes so he could refer back to them later, especially if he was on a business phone call. 'You can never trust your memory,' he used to say. 'Even if you're one hundred percent positive you remember a conversation one way, you can be guaranteed someone else will remember it another way.'

Tom's desk was covered in papers, a far cry from the neat desk that Chelsea remembered. Maybe it was her mum who had always tidied it and this state was normal for him. Somehow she didn't think so.

Seeing the foolscap book next to the phone, she flipped it open to read what notes he'd written. The pages were blank save for a few doodles and a phone number. She cast around for another book, thinking the one on the desk must be new. There didn't seem to be any others.

The niggling feeling that something wasn't right with her dad hit her more strongly now. There were a lot of small incidents, but they added up to something troubling.

Frowning, she went back into the kitchen to check the dinner, wondering if she had time to go over to the overseer's house to talk to Cal. Maybe he'd know something. If he'd talk to her.

Cal had been stand-offish with her the whole time she'd been here. Probably with good reason. He would've known she hadn't returned for her mother's funeral and, in most people's estimation, that was unforgivable. Still, he didn't know the full story. No one in Barker did.

It was clear, however, he liked and respected her dad, so maybe that would help.

Closing the door quietly behind her, she ducked out into the heat and walked swiftly across the yard. It didn't take long for the heat to bring out sweat on her brow, even with the sun about to sink below the horizon. She stopped and looked to the west, where the sun was throwing its final rays onto the ranges. The tips were purple and pink, while the bases were a deep blue. The moon was above the hills; even with the sun still showing itself, she was casting an eerie glow. Chelsea's skin prickled at the sight and she wished she had a camera to capture the beauty of the landscape.

'Pretty, isn't it?'

Cal's voice came from behind her and she jumped.

'I didn't hear you there,' she said. 'Sorry.' Turning, she realised he must be coming back from a run; she'd never seen him dressed in anything but jeans and a blue work shirt. In fact, if her girlfriend Tori had been here, they would've joked that he must own at least seven blue work shirts or else he washed the same one every night.

Tonight he was wearing shorts and a singlet and she could see he had the physique of a runner.

'I didn't know you ran,' she said, then felt like a twit. Why would she? She'd had nothing to do with him!

'Yep, every night. Helps clear the mind.'

'Good habit.' She tried to remember the last time she'd done any form of exercise. Probably before Aria was born. Her pelvic floor wouldn't hold up to anything bouncy or strenuous, she was sure. A fly buzzed around her sweaty brow and she flicked it away.

'Are you going for a walk?' Cal asked. 'Better stick to the roads since it's almost dark. You might get lost otherwise.'

Chelsea frowned. Was that a dig that she hadn't been here for a long time? 'Actually,' she said, sticking her chin in the air, 'I was coming to talk to you.'

'Really?' Cal crossed his arms. 'What about?'

'Dad.'

Cal didn't answer, instead he lunged into a calf stretch and didn't look at her.

'I think there's something wrong with him.' Chelsea averted her eyes; she didn't want him thinking she was admiring his physique.

Still silence.

'He's acting strangely,' Chelsea pressed on. 'He told me tonight he didn't like mashed potatoes.'

Cal looked up at her and raised his eyebrows. She realised how stupid that comment sounded without the back story.

'I mean . . .' Trying again, she said, 'He's always loved mashed potatoes. Mum used to make them all the time for him.'

'Bloke can change his mind.'

'But—'

'Look Chelsea, I don't know what you expected when you turned up back here, but have a think about it from Tom's perspective. You haven't been back home for who knows how long. You didn't come to your mother's funeral. It was me who got your dad through that—sat and listened to him talk or cry. Me who made all the excuses under the sun for you, a woman I didn't even know, when you didn't bother to phone him and tell him you weren't coming or ask what happened. There was total silence from you until about a month afterwards. And even then it was just a phone call. Not a visit.' He stood up straight, a look of disgust on his face.

Chelsea wanted to take a step back; she felt as if she'd been slapped. Instead she stood her ground as he continued to admonish her.

Cal continued. 'I think you've got to expect some things have changed and if he doesn't like potatoes anymore, then who cares? Maybe you don't cook them like Pip did. Cook him something else.'

'Right.' Hearing her mum's name tumble so effortlessly out of his mouth made her remember Cal had known her.

He knew more about her parents than she did, and it left her feeling empty.

The sun had gone now and the beauty of the evening with it. Chelsea started to walk back to the house, but she could feel Cal watching her, so she stopped and turned to face him. 'Do you know why I didn't come back?' she asked.

'No. There isn't an excuse that would wash with me. There won't be an excuse that washes with your father. Not being at your mother's funeral is unforgivable.'

The anger that bubbled up inside her was almost at boiling point. How she managed to keep her tone calm, she wasn't sure. 'I didn't come back because I didn't find out about my mother's death until everything was all over and done with.'

Chelsea walked away to the sound of his stony silence.

Chapter 9

The dinner table was quiet. Chelsea was still smarting from her run-in with Cal, and Tom seemed to have nothing he wanted to talk about. Aria was watching both of them with wide eyes but seemed to know not to chatter.

Finally, Chelsea put down her knife and fork and looked at her daughter. 'You know how I said there was something I wanted to talk to you about, Aria? I hear there's a Christmas pageant in Barker on Sunday. Would you like to go?'

'What's a pageant?'

'A parade of all things Christmassy. Decorated cars, dancers, that sort of thing. And you know what the best bit is?'

Aria shook her head.

'Father Christmas always comes and you get to sit on his knee and tell him what you want for Christmas.' Aria gave a squeal of delight and Tom looked up from his meal.

'Is it that close to Christmas already?' Tom glanced around the kitchen as if seeing it for the first time. 'Would you like me to get a pine tree to decorate for Christmas?' he asked Aria.

'A real tree? In the house? Wow!' Aria's excitement was contagious.

'That's what we used to do all the time. I'll take a trip to Barker and see if we can get some decorations.'

'There'll be some in the cellar.' Tom looked over at the cellar door. 'That's where Pip always kept them.'

There was silence at the mention of her mum's name, then Chelsea said, 'Great, I'll look for them tomorrow.'

'And, Aria,' said Tom, 'I think you and I might have a little job to do. We have to go to the shed tonight and check something out, okay?'

'Okay, Papa. What is it?'

'A secret!' He touched his finger to his lips and smiled at her.

Aria's eyes couldn't get any wider, Chelsea was sure.

'Were there pageants when you were little, Mummy?'

'Uh-huh. One Christmas my friend Lily and I rode our horses in it.'

'Really?'

Chelsea laughed at her daughter's face. 'We did. Pinto, that was my horse, he had tinsel around his bridle and woven into his mane and tail. Lily's horse didn't like the shininess, so we just tied baubles on her tail so she couldn't see them and get frightened. Pinto was bombproof, so he just plodded down the main street like he was walking through a paddock. The yelling and cheering didn't bother him at all. Didn't bother either of the horses, actually. Then another year, I was on a float.'

'Were you dressed up like a fairy?' Aria got the question in before Chelsea could say anything more.

'No, not a fairy. A cowgirl. Think it was the float for school and we had to dress up as our favourite character out of a book. I can remember Kelly, another school friend, went as George from the Famous Five.'

'Who did you go as?'

'Norah, from the Billabong series. Oh! I should read them to you while we're here, Aria. They were my favourite books when I was just a bit older than you, but I still think you'd like them. The books should be here somewhere, shouldn't they, Dad?'

'Probably in the cellar too,' he muttered before taking another mouthful.

'I'll see if I can find them.' There was a pause before Chelsea continued her story. 'The pageant would finish at the old folks' home and Father Christmas would be there. We'd get to sit on his knee and tell him what we wanted for Christmas. Then the whole town would sing Christmas carols by candlelight. That's when you used to arrive, Dad. Just in time for the singing. Do they still do that?' she asked, looking over at him then quickly looking away as she saw a glistening in his eyes.

'Uh . . .' muttered Tom.

Chelsea didn't know which way to look. He wasn't crying but he was close to it. She felt the urge to apologise for upsetting him. For talking about the past.

She heard a movement and looked up to see Aria get off her chair and go to her grandfather. She put her hand on his arm and looked up at him. 'Are you sad?' she asked. 'Mummy's always told me it's okay to cry.'

Tom patted her hand and cleared his throat. 'Do you want to go to the shed and find the secret?'

Aria nodded and slipped her hand into his.

Opening her mouth, Chelsea tried to say something, but her voice wouldn't work. Her chest was so full, it felt like her heart was about to explode. Aria had said the exact words she had always said to her . . . The ones Chelsea's mum had said to her when she'd been little. 'It's okay to cry.'

Tom ran his spare hand roughly over his face and when he looked over at Chelsea he was smiling. 'Come on then,' he said gruffly, and he pushed his chair back, disappearing out the door before Aria could catch him.

Later that night, Chelsea opened the door into the cellar and cautiously took the first step down into the darkness. She held the torch in front of her, knowing that when she got to the bottom, the light switch would be on the left-hand side of the door frame. She was still grappling with the way that everything on Shandona was still so familiar, even after all these years.

The stone and wooden steps were uneven and she knew she had to be careful. Her Great-Grandfather Baxter, who used to live on Shandona, would say every time someone went down these stairs: 'You'll fall to your death going down there . . .'

Chelsea remembered Baxter quite well, even though she was six when he died. They'd both loved music. Baxter was her father's grandfather and outlived his wife, Adelia, by twelve months. In the time he'd lived in the family homestead, he'd shouted words of wisdom from the old faded armchair in the sitting room while Chelsea's grand-mother cared for him. When people complained about the lack of rain, his favourite response was always: 'A farmer has to be a gambler. There's no way he could do what he does otherwise.'

The steps down into the cellar reminded her of the treasure hunt her parents had organised for her birthday one year. There'd been a lively discussion over whether the girls from school should be allowed to search in the cellar, but her mum had won out and one of the clues had been: *Where the sunlight never reaches, and it is always cool.*

The girls had followed the clues down, down, with a few squeals of fear and excitement, only to find Dale waiting for them at the bottom, wearing a gremlin mask, making horrible noises! Dale had been a trickster, a practical joker. Like the time Pip had asked him to mow the lawn. Dale had mustered the closest mob of sheep and put them on the lawn. That joke had backfired badly after the ewes ate part of Pip's garden and trampled the rest. Chelsea remembered her mum's reaction: a few short choice words and a punishment of community service—her own as Dale had to work for free and restore the garden to its former glory.

Her thoughts drifted to her mum's death. She felt so guilty over not being here. Not knowing. Not supporting her dad. Her counsellor had told her that guilt was a wasted emotion—there was no point in beating herself up about it. Her work hadn't allowed her to return once she'd found out. Or maybe she'd thought that if she stayed away, then it wouldn't be real, and she'd used her work as an excuse.

Either way, as Cal had reminded her this evening, she'd failed as a daughter.

She'd failed at everything! Being a daughter, a musician, at relationships, at life in general. The only thing she was proud of was Aria, but that didn't make her a good mother. The ever-present lump in her throat expanded and stopped her breathing for a moment. A tear ran down her cheek and she brushed it away angrily. Reaching out for the light switch, she flicked it on and a dim glow lit up the small room.

It looked just the same—lino covering the cement floor and newspapers lining the wooden shelves—and it smelled damp. In the corner there was a steel trunk, which Chelsea hoped contained the books she was looking for.

When her mum and grandmother were alive, the cellar was stocked with jars of pickles, relishes and bottled fruit, harvested from the orchard at the side of the house. After trips to Adelaide, there would be bulk buys of oranges and lemons from roadside fruit and veg vendors. The fruit would be stored in the dark to keep it fresh longer. But now the shelves were bare, save for a few cardboard boxes that were covered in dust and cobwebs.

The trunk had her grandmother's name painted on the outside. Evelyn had gone to boarding school and this had been how she'd carried her belongings. Flicking the catch upwards, Chelsea tried to lift the lid, but it was stuck fast. Rusted closed.

Chelsea rubbed her fingers along the hinges and scratched at the rust, hoping to loosen them, then tried to wiggle the lid. It came up a little way, enough for her to move the lid up and down and get it to open more and more each time. Finally, with a loud screech, the lid opened fully. There weren't any books inside, only neatly stacked old documents and photo albums. Quickly she leafed through each one but didn't see anything that interested her.

She opened each of the cardboard boxes till she found the Christmas decorations, which she put at the base of the stairs to take back up with her. She also discovered a lot of archived cash books. She gave them a cursory glance; they dated back to the first years of her parents' marriage.

Pulling out the first cash book, she recognised her mother's writing. Seeing it made her think of all the birthday cards she'd kept in her apartment in Sydney. Everything her mum had sent to her, she still had. The letters, the cards, the angry demands to try harder. Everything. And she was glad she had, because Chelsea hadn't known that when she'd left Shandona last time, she'd never see her mum again.

When she'd heard about her mother's death and finally got back to Sydney, she'd pulled out the letters and cards and reread them all. They'd prompted tears, both happy and sad, and a lot of memories. They'd also unsettled her, so she'd sorted them into years and put them away again. She wouldn't admit to too many people that since Pip had died, every year on her birthday she went back and ran her fingers over her mother's writing, trying to feel her presence. Sometimes, when she held the envelopes to her cheek, she even thought she could smell the moisturiser her mother had used on her hands. Chelsea wished she'd handled the years since she'd finished at the Conservatorium differently; wished she'd handled her relationship with her mum with more care, because the truth was no one lived forever. Now her mum was dead and Chelsea was left with regret and guilt.

Now here were more memories, even though they were historical ones. Going back over to the trunk, she sat cross-legged on the floor and started to look through its contents. She remembered the detective saying something about looking through photo albums to find if she could see anyone wearing the brooch he'd shown her.

The pages were delicate, and in between each page there was a sheet of tracing paper to protect the photos from being damaged. Seeing faces of people she'd loved as a child made her smile, even though tears were hovering. The photo album seemed to start when Baxter and Adelia were building the main homestead. The black and white photos showed a half-built house. There was one with

Baxter standing on a wooden plank held up by drums. He was wearing baggy pants with suspenders and had what she thought was a handkerchief wrapped around his head. With a trowel in hand and a large smile on his face, he looked as if he were telling a funny story to the man standing next him. The next page showed her grandfather, Leo, in the sheep yards with a stock agent. She traced the outline of her grandfather's face in another photograph and laughed out loud when she came across a picture of her granny wearing a yellow golfing outfit! The knickerbockers looked as if they belonged back in the early 1900s.

'I hope you were going to a fancy-dress party, Gran,' she said quietly. 'That's a pretty shocking outfit!'

There were photos of the finished house and paddocks flush with green grass—not that Chelsea could tell it was green because the photos were black and white, but the land was covered with feed that came up to the ewes' bellies. Then there was a photo of a horse-drawn wagon filled with wool bales. Chelsea carefully removed the picture and turned it over to see if there was anything written on the back. *Wool clip from 1948. 50 bales. The most we've ever produced.*

'Wow,' she whispered, slipping it back into the holder. She hadn't seen these photos before.

Other photos showed local cricket matches and people Chelsea didn't know sitting on picnic rugs and watching the game and laughing. They depicted much more enjoyable times than the family was experiencing now and she loved the sense of history and happiness they exuded.

What had gone wrong? she wondered. Tori would say her family had run over a Chinaman. Tori was also the most un-politically correct person she knew! And her best friend.

She wondered why families were happy for generations, then the universe decided it was time to give that happiness to another family. Things took an unexpected turn and the next generation couldn't get along. It certainly felt like that for her family now.

Looking back, Chelsea knew it wasn't Dale's death that had started the downward slide for them. It was her going to the Conservatorium. Perhaps it was because her parents had put themselves back into debt to make her music dream happen—the scholarship had only covered the fees and her mother had been fond of telling her about all the other expenses involved in keeping her at the Conservatorium. Debt did funny things to people—nowadays there was a name for it: 'debt stress'. Back when she was growing up, it didn't have a name, but the stress came out in anger and blame. Towards her. And the bad seasons, which had come one after the other, only compounded the problem.

And after Dale's death, well, it had all been downhill from there.

Sighing, she put the photo album back into the trunk.

There had been no sign of the brooch.

Or the Billabong books.

Chapter 10

Dave switched off his car lights and let his head rest against the back of the seat for a couple of seconds. Running his hands over his face, he could feel he needed a shave. Kim would give him a good-natured chip about that later tonight, he was sure.

'I always get a pimple rash when you kiss me and haven't shaved,' she'd say. Then he imagined her lowering her voice and throwing him the sultry, sexy look that made him want to kiss her, and saying, 'And I *want* you to kiss me.' He realised he was smiling. Nice thought. Oh yeah, a really nice thought.

Yanking open the car door and grabbing his briefcase, he got out and walked up the path. He should have been home much earlier, in time to go for a walk, but the shire president had wanted to chew his ear about safety and road blocks for the pageant. Something Dave had undertaken for the many years he'd lived in Barker; he knew exactly what he was doing. For some reason, this year the president was worried about the road closures and the welfare of the public.

As if that wasn't my priority too, Dave thought, annoyed.

'Hey, sweetie, I'm home!' he called as he walked through his front door.

He was greeted by the thump of a tail and the smell of chicken curry.

'Hello there, old fella.' Dave reached down to pat Bob, an old kelpie he had adopted after his owner had died. Bob was stretched out on the lino in the kitchen, under the airconditioner—the coolest spot in the house. He raised his head and looked at Dave before trying to lick his hand.

'Hello, you,' Kim said from behind him.

Dave straightened and held out his arms. 'Hello, you, too.' He dropped a kiss on her head as she hugged him. 'Dinner smells good.'

'Unfortunately it's not for you.'

Dave sighed theatrically. 'Is it ever?'

'Haha, it's usually all about you! Anyway, this one is for a family whose son is in hospital. You know the Gallaways from up near Blinman?'

'Hmm, vaguely know the name,' Dave answered as he reached into the fridge and pulled out a beer.

'Their son, Michael, has just been diagnosed with a childhood form of cancer. Mum has moved to Adelaide while he has treatment. Not wanting to upset the rest of the family, education-wise, Dad has stayed home with the two girls to keep the station going and so on. You know the story.'

'I hate hearing about kids who get sick.'

'Me too. That's why I've got to help. So instead of chicken curry, we're having chops and salad. I've spent most of the day cooking for this family and the other clients I told you about. I'm a bit cooked out.'

'Understandable. How's the roadhouse?' He sat at the kitchen bench and watched as Kim lifted the large pot of curry from the stove and started to ladle it into plastic containers that had already been half filled with rice.

'All back on track. The girls are better now, so I don't need to go in tomorrow. I'll be able to finish off this order and then deliver it. I want to cook a Christmas lunch for them tomorrow, so they have something special on the day. There was talk about them going to Adelaide and spending the day at the hospital, but it turns out Michael will still be having chemo, so they're going to wait until after this round of treatment before heading down there. How awful, having treatment on Christmas Day.'

'There's never a good time for it.' Dave shook his head, imagining the pain the family would be feeling. 'God, what a horrible thing to have to go through—at any time, let alone Christmas. Families should be together at Christmas.'

Kim raised her eyebrows at him. When it came to families, they disagreed a bit. Kim's parents were dead, and her sister and her husband had moved away from the district after the death of their son in a farming accident. Her niece was now working on a farm in Canada and Kim missed everyone terribly.

No matter how many times she'd tried to get Dave to go back to the farm and visit his family, he still wouldn't budge. 'Hanging on to all that anger isn't healthy,' she'd told him more than once.

His standard response was: 'I'm not angry.'

'Then why won't you go?'

'There's no need to.'

Dave knew she hadn't given up on getting him to visit the farm. Kim would see his brother's accident as the perfect reason to.

He raised his eyebrows at her and asked, 'You're driving all the way to Blinman tomorrow?'

She sighed heavily, letting him know she was aware he was ignoring her. 'Not all the way. The father is going to meet me halfway.' Putting the pot down, she reached over and put her hand on Dave's arm. 'Have you heard anything more about your brother?'

Dave shook his head. 'I was going to ring Mandy tonight, but I got caught up at the station. I'll have to call tomorrow. I did try and ring Mum yesterday, but she didn't answer.'

'Any news on the skeleton front?'

'Yeah, actually. Have a look at this.' He pulled out his phone. 'Have you ever seen a brooch like this?'

She looked at the picture. 'That's really beautiful. Where'd you find it?'

'The forensic team found it in the dirt underneath the skeleton. I'd like to ID the owner, because if we do, I think we'll know who the body is. Do you know the Taylors?'

Kim continued to study the photo. 'What, out on Barker North Road? Yeah, they've got a sad family history there. The son was killed at an engagement party accident. Can't remember how long ago it was exactly, but it'd have to be at least ten years. And the mum died in the last couple of years too. That was a strange one—I don't think you'd started here by then, not full-time anyway, so you wouldn't have been called out. Don't really know what happened, but there was a rumour she died of a brain bleed or heart attack. Can't remember which. The daughter, she's an amazing musician. Plays the piano.' Kim paused and looked up. 'Did some concerts overseas. I remember hearing her play at one of the school concerts and at a few public functions and she made the piano sing. Don't know much about music but her playing transported people, you know. The weird thing is, though, she didn't come back for her mother's funeral, so I'm not sure whether there was a falling-out with the family or what.'

'Well, if it's the girl I met today, then she's staying with Tom for Christmas. Chelsea. And she's got a little girl of four. Her name's Aria.'

Kim straightened and nodded. 'That's her! How great she's come home.'

'There seems to be a bit of animosity between father and daughter.'

'Oh, dear. That's a shame. I really don't know what happened. I don't know who'd miss their own mother's funeral.' She looked pointedly at Dave, who had avoided his own father's funeral, despite Kim pressuring him.

He changed the subject.

'The only thing which is confusing me at the moment, is Finlay seems to think the remains are male. I'm sure a male wouldn't wear this brooch.'

'Maybe he was going to give it to someone.'

'There was a box with the body. I'm wondering if there might be more jewellery in it. Maybe he was a merchant or something similar.'

Kim handed the phone back and got two plates out, before going to the fridge and removing the salad ingredients.

There was movement near the airconditioner and Bob came into the kitchen and sat next to the oven with a sigh. He watched hopefully as the two worked side by side. Dave started to slice the tomato and cucumber while Kim seasoned the chops.

'I guess. But if he was, wouldn't whoever buried him have taken the jewellery? I mean, that brooch looks like it's worth a fortune.'

'People were a lot more honest back then.'

'Back when? Do you have a date? And being honest doesn't mean you bury it. They would've handed it into the police.'

Dave nodded, acknowledging that what she said was right. 'Not yet, and I'm not sure when I'll get one. Fact is, the bones are old, and if there isn't a strong chance of an arrest, I'm not sure they'll spend much time on it.'

'But what if it is a murder and they're still walking around out there?'

Dave shrugged. 'If the remains are fifty years old, the offender could be dead. We're wasting our time then.'

'That only makes the death in the late sixties. That's when it was like, "Peace, man".' She made her voice sound as if she were stoned and grinned at Dave.

He didn't grin back; he was too busy thinking. 'I wonder when the merchants stopped coming through. You know there were traders still operating when I first moved here.'

'Yeah, out of the backs of trucks rather than off camels, like they used to.'

'There were cameleers at Beltana Station and Blinman,' Dave reminded her.

'That was back in the late 1800s, you dag! No matter how old the bones are, I'm sure they won't date back that far.'

Looking down at the chopping board, Dave hid a smile. He loved the way Kim would disagree with him. She challenged his thinking and he liked that. 'You could be right, honey,' he answered.

'Could be? I know I am!'

'Don't go getting all self-righteous on me just because you've picked a small hole in my theory.' There was laughter in his voice. 'But if they were that old, we would've left them in the ground. It wouldn't have been in the public interest to bring them up. Finlay didn't stop excavating, so they have to be reasonably recent—as in this century!' He threw her a cheeky grin.

'What would happen to the grave if it was that old?' Kim asked seriously. 'You couldn't just leave it there unmarked— someone else might find the bones.'

'We'd document it, fence it off. Get in contact with the historical society, make it known someone was buried there, and that's it.'

Kim looked indignant. 'But what if they were murdered? Wouldn't you even try to investigate?'

'Who would we arrest from the 1800s? They'd all be dead!' Dave chortled. 'No point in taking on cases like that!'

Kim was silent for a moment and Dave knew she was working everything over. He wondered what she'd say next.

He didn't have to wait long.

'You know what you could do with that brooch?'

'What's that?'

'Why don't you ring some of the local jewellers and see if they've seen anything like it before?'

Dave grinned. 'We'll make a detective of you yet. That's on my list for tomorrow.'

Kim picked up the chops and headed out onto the patio to the barbecue. Bob got up and followed her out, hoping for a titbit.

Placing the salad on the plates, Dave followed her out. 'Seriously, you'd make a good detective, you know.'

'Nah, I'll leave that up to you. I like cooking. And speaking of cooking, Lily Jackson contacted me today and asked if I'd cook for the pageant on Sunday night.'

'She's left it a bit late. What does she want you to do?'

'Sounds like the school is going to have a fundraiser selling gourmet burgers and finger food. She wondered if I'd help.'

'And you said yes.' It wasn't a question.

'Of course!'

'Damn. That means I'll have to sit in the squad car by myself.'

Kim giggled. The previous year she'd gone with him and turned the siren on and off whenever she'd felt like it. The kids on the street had loved it—their parents not so much. The siren was loud and usually Dave would have had only the lights flashing. Whatever Kim did, she always spiced things up.

'Oh! I've just had an idea.'

Dave looked at her cautiously. 'This could be a worry.'

'Why don't you run a raffle on the night and whoever wins gets to sit in the squad car with you. You could donate the money to the school or library or something. The kids would *love* it!'

The chops were sizzling now so Dave reached out to take the tongs from Kim and started to turn them.

'That's a good idea,' he said. 'I always knew you weren't just a pretty face.'

From behind, she wrapped her arms around his waist. 'I love you.'

'And I love you.'

Dave felt her head rest against his shoulder blades for a moment and then move away.

The next morning Dave drafted an email to five local jewellery stores and attached the photo of the brooch. After hitting the send button, he picked up the phone and called the first shop on his list. The woman he spoke to didn't know anything about it and couldn't give him any information.

The next three shops were the same and he was beginning to feel frustrated as he dialled the fifth shop.

'Diamond Sea Jewellers, Roxy speaking.'

'Good morning. It's Detective Dave Burrows calling from the Barker police station. Could I speak to the owner or manager, please?'

'That's me, how can I help?'

'Thanks for taking my call, Roxy. I've just sent you an email with a photo of an antique brooch. I was wondering if you could take a look at it. I'm after any information you might have about it.'

'What type of information?'

'If you've seen anything like this before. What age it might be. Is it handmade? That type of thing. I can call back if you're busy.'

'No, it's fine. I'd rather do it now. One moment.'

Dave listened as a recorded message informed him that his call was important to Diamond Sea Jewellers and to please continue to hold.

'Hello?'

'Yes, I'm here.' Dave grabbed a pen and pulled a notepad towards him.

'It's a beautiful piece.'

'Do you have any thoughts on it?'

The jeweller paused. 'I think it's handmade. The rope twirling up the stems of the roses has been engraved by hand. See how each mark is different. Some are straight, some aren't. And the petals of the rose have been shaped by hand too. Again, they're not all the same as they would be if they'd been done by machine.'

'Have you seen a piece like this before?'

'No, I haven't, but I wish I had.'

'Do you have any idea how old it might be?'

'It's hard to say without examining it. Most jewellers would have left their signature on it somewhere. I can't see anything on the back to indicate who made it, and that in itself is unusual. It's certainly not recent. The craftsmanship is perhaps around the 1910s or 1920s.'

'That old?' Dave asked, his stomach sinking.

'Without having examined the piece it's hard to be accurate.'

'Have you been in the industry long, Roxy?'

'Are you needing my credentials, Detective?'

'Curiosity.'

She laughed. 'I thought that killed the cat. I am a third-generation jeweller. I did my apprenticeship under my father, who did his under *his* father. I'm a classically trained gold-smith and have been qualified for thirty years. I hope that's enough for you.'

'Sounds like you've got a long history.'

'I do. Mine is the only family-owned jewellers in the mid-north and I'm very proud of that.'

'Do you design your own pieces?'

'Usually, but with only me here, it is difficult to design and make as well as be on the floor, selling. I do a lot of my creating outside work hours.'

'Is your father still alive? Would he know anything about this piece?'

'No, I'm sorry. He died two years ago.' There was a pause. 'Now let me ask you a question, Detective. Where did you find it? I can see there is a lot of dirt on it, so it must have come from the ground.'

'I can't tell you much as it's part of an investigation but, yes, we found it buried with a few other things.'

'I see. Well, if I can be of any further assistance to you, please call again.'

'Thank you for your help.' Dave hung up the phone and tapped at his paper. From the 1910s or 1920s? Maybe it had been made then but given to the person who was buried there at a later time.

The bones couldn't be that old, could they? Otherwise Finlay would've stopped and told him to ring the historical society rather than wasting time and resources on a case that wouldn't get a conviction.

Chapter 11

Dave's phone dinged with a text message. He smiled as he saw Kim's name come up.

Have you rung your family?

His smile dropped. Instead of answering he put the phone down and went out the front of the station to see Joan.

She was sitting in front of the computer, typing up a report about a speeding driver Jack had pulled up on his way home from the forensic scene.

'Kim had an idea about raising money for the school,' he said without preamble.

'Oh yes?' Joan didn't look up and her fingers didn't slow as they flew across the keys, making Dave dizzy.

'She thought we might be able to run a raffle and the winner could ride in the squad car with Jack and me during the pageant. Is that easy to organise?'

'Should be. What do you want, like a gold coin donation?'

'Yeah, that'd be enough.'

Joan stopped typing and made some notes on the pad next to her. 'Okay, so I'll draw up a numbered board and people can buy the numbers. Then we'll draw a number out of the hat and whoever's number is picked can go for a ride.' She started to type again.

'Great, I'll leave it with you.'

'Is Jack going to be directing traffic?'

'Nah, the council are going to put up "road closed" signs and signpost the detours. That should be enough. We'll shut down the main street from 5 pm and reopen it at 8 pm once everyone moves up to the old folks' home. The president is having kittens this year. Seems to think we're not doing enough to protect everyone's safety. But we don't need to do anything more than we've done before.'

'Council elections are coming up early next year. Probably doesn't want anything to go wrong before he gets voted back in,' Joan said, still staring at the screen.

'Oh, that's the issue, is it? I thought he was being a bit pedantic.'

'Downright annoying, I'd say,' Joan answered cynically.

Dave heard his phone ding again. 'Thanks, Joan. I'm not sure this station would run without you.'

Joan looked up at him, the pleasure clear on her face. 'Don't be daft.'

Dave patted her on the shoulder and went back to his office. Kim had sent him another message. *????*

'All right, all right,' he told the text. 'I'll ring them now.' Mandy's phone rang four times before it diverted to the message bank.

'Yeah, Mandy, it's Dave.' He cleared his throat and felt stupid. He was quite capable of delivering bad news to victims' families, or asking the right questions to get people to talk to him, but he couldn't work out what to say in a message to his sister-in-law.

'Just, um, wondering how things are going over there. How Dean is and how you guys are all holding up.' He paused. 'Let me know.' He touched the disconnect button and wondered if he should ring his mum. Before he could talk himself out of it, he dialled the number he knew by heart and listened to it ring.

'Dave.' His mum's voice was deep and croaky from sleep. 'Hello, darling, how are you?'

'Probably better to ask how you all are,' he answered as he picked up a pen and doodled on the pad in front of him. 'You sound like you were asleep.'

'I haven't spoken to anyone this morning.' It sounded like she took a sip of something—tea maybe. Dave glanced at his watch and realised that, with daylight saving, it was only 7 am in the west.

'We're all holding up. Dean's out of danger. Amazingly they managed to save his arm, but they're not guaranteeing he's going to have a lot of use of it. And of course he's going to have a long road to recovery. Lots of physio and probably more operations. It's incredible what doctors can do these days. I really don't know how they saved it.'

'Well, that's fantastic news.'

'It is, and we're all very pleased and grateful.' She paused, and Dave waited. 'He's very depressed though.'

Dave tapped his pen up and down. 'I'm sure it's going to be a long and difficult road for him. It certainly won't be easy, knowing how much work there is at home. He's always been able to do everything himself and it'll take a massive amount of adjustment to realise he's going to be reliant on other people. That'll be what is the hardest for him, Mum.'

'The doctor said he might be angry for a while—just because he can't do things the way he used to. Adapting, they called it.' She sighed. 'He's always been so independent. Now he's going to have to rely on other people. It's a whole mindset change.'

'Unfortunately, that'll be part of the healing process. He's going to have to go through a whole heap of emotions before he comes to terms with this. And it's going to take time. A lot of time.' Dave had seen this many times in his line of work; didn't matter if it was due to a death, divorce or accident, the grief process took a person through denial, guilt, anger and depression before acceptance was possible. 'What about Mandy, how's she?'

'Oh, she's been a tower of strength. I don't know what we'd do without her and I don't know how she can be so strong. She's been there every step of the way, spoken to the doctors, everything. Now she's started to help with his physio . . .' Her voice trailed off and Dave suddenly realised she was frightened.

'Mum, why didn't you tell me they'd separated?'

He heard her blow out a breath and waited.

'Dave, things aren't always black and white. You should know that in your job. They didn't want anyone to know. Not until Christy had finished uni and both kids were settled. They weren't at home very often, and when they visited over the holidays, I think the act was kept up very well. Neither of them seemed to realise there were any problems between their parents. I didn't necessarily agree, Dave, but I had to respect their wishes.'

'But how did it happen? I thought they were solid?'

'I don't know. Sometimes people just grow apart. Fall out of love. There wasn't anyone else.' She paused. 'Well, not that I know of.'

'He didn't hit her, did he? He didn't have Dad's anger problems?' As he said it, he thought back to his conversation with Mandy: 'I don't hate him, Dave.'

Still he had to ask.

'Dave!'

He stayed silent. He knew his father had been volatile, and he'd heard the put-downs and emotional abuse his mum had been subjected to, but he'd never asked directly about physical violence before. He remembered an argument at the dinner table only days before his father kicked him off the family farm. His dad, at the end of the table, slammed his fist onto the wooden table-top. His eyes bulging, he yelled at Dave's mum: 'Stay out of it, woman! You don't know what you're talking about!' Dave remembered the fear in his mother's voice as she begged him to calm down.

'He never hit me,' she finally said. 'Never. Yes, he used to get angry. Yell a bit. Say things in the heat of the moment. But most of us are like that. I know you'll find it hard to understand, but he was a good, kind man. Respected.'

Not in my eyes, thought Dave. Instead he said, 'Mum, the way he treated you was abusive. He didn't have to hit you, he did it with his words and by manipulation. I'm glad you weren't subjected to physical abuse, but that doesn't make what you experienced any less traumatic. Dad could've been reported for what he did to you.' Dave knew he sounded harsh. He couldn't help it. His excuse for not going back to the farm was the way his father had treated him, but deep down it wasn't just that. It was the way his father had treated his mother. And her inability to fight back. 'Sorry, Mum,' he added, trying to soften his words.

He heard her sigh again and their silence stretched across the Nullarbor.

'Are you worried that Mandy will leave after Dean gets out of hospital?' Dave asked eventually. 'That everything will fall to you?'

Another silence. 'I don't know what I'm thinking.'

'Is there anything you want me to do?' he asked, fighting the hollow feeling in his stomach as he spoke. 'Do they need help with the harvest or anything? How long will Dean be in Perth for?' He paused before saying, 'I'll come if you need me.'

'There's still so many things that are unknown. The neighbours have been wonderful. They've organised a group to take their headers and trucks over after Christmas to harvest it all. With six or seven headers, it'll only take a couple of days. Some of the neighbours have their own trucks, and a freight company has donated the use of three of theirs. We're incredibly grateful.'

'I'd never want to live anywhere else but the country for that exact reason,' Dave said, feeling relief wash through him. It didn't sound like he'd be needed. 'People just love helping each other out. It's nice they're all doing that for you, Mum.'

'Do you remember Georgie and Jack Nixon? I think you used to play cricket with Jack.'

'Yeah, I remember.' His mum had obviously forgotten Dave had written letters to her when he'd left and he'd sent them via Georgie and Jack. He'd worried that his father wouldn't pass them on, whereas he knew Georgie would. And Jack? Well, he'd been the one who'd organised Dean's bucks' night. The night everything had gone wrong. The night he'd been kicked off the farm. Jack had also driven to Esperance to see Dave when he'd been working as a farmhand down there and tried to convince him to come home. To tell him his dad was sorry. Jack's talk hadn't changed Dave's mind.

'Georgie and Jack have been the driving force behind it all.'

'They're good people.' Jack's words echoed in Dave's ears: *'Look, I know your dad can be a bastard. Short-tempered and all that. But you need to come home. For your mum.'*

For your mum. That's what Kim would say too.

The phone rang at the front desk and he heard Joan answer it. Then she appeared in the doorway, making frantic motions with her hands.

'Look, I gotta go, Mum. But if there is anything Kim and I can do, make sure you give us a ring, okay?'

'You know what you could do, Dave?'

'What's that?'

'Stay in touch a little more. I'm old. I'd like to see you and meet Kim. Your father isn't here anymore.'

For your mum.

Dave paused. 'Sure, Mum. I'll do that. Talk to you soon. Bye.' He looked at Joan.

'It's Dr Fletcher from the morgue,' she said. 'He needs to talk to you urgently. Line one.'

Dave snatched up the phone and pressed the flashing red button. 'You've got news already?' He was surprised.

'You're lucky it's a slow week, Dave. Normally I would've put it right down the bottom of the to-do pile. However, you know there was a box that was buried with the remains?'

'Yes?'

'It contains the body of a baby.'

Dave opened his mouth to say something, but nothing came out.

Dr Fletcher continued. 'The body was wrapped in a hessian bag—like the ones that would have held flour and sugar back in the 1920s and 1930s.'

'He or she?'

'Can't tell. Too early for the gender to be evident in the bones.'

'How did it die?'

'Again, the bones don't tell me anything. Could've been sick or born prematurely and didn't survive, or could have been stillborn. Any other number of reasons.'

'What about the adult skeleton?'

'I haven't looked at him yet. I rang because I thought you'd want to know. It's not often you find a baby's remains in a rotted hessian bag tucked inside a box.'

Dave thought hard, wanting to ask more questions, but it didn't seem there were many he could ask if the bones hadn't given up any of their secrets.

'Not sure how much time I should put into this,' Dave said, thinking out loud. 'Until I have a reason to think there was a murder, these could be just two natural deaths.'

'They could be,' Dr Fletcher agreed. 'And that'll be your problem to work out. But I think the baby's remains change things, don't you? I'm starting on the other skeleton today, so there will be results on him soon enough.'

'Yeah. Was there anything else in the box? More jewellery or something to help with IDing them both?'

'No, and the hessian bag was almost non-existent. Back in the early 1900s, these types of bags had individual tags sewn on to indicate which company the flour came from. I haven't found anything like that—I'm sure it's just disintegrated along with the bag. I had a case a few years ago—the body in the bag. Do you remember it?'

'Vaguely,' Dave said. 'Something about a body found wrapped in bags, in a cave near Mount Gambier?'

'That's the one. The body was a freshy, so not like this, but it had been wrapped in the same type of hessian bag.'

'So . . .'

'We were able to identify the hessian bags through the tags. It turned out the great-grandfather of the murderer had worked for the company that produced the bags which had been stored at his great-granddaughter's house. See where I'm going?'

'Yeah, yeah. The bags linked the murderer to the body because his great-grandfather had worked at the factory and kept the bags. But you don't have the labels on this bag.'

'Unfortunately, no. I toyed with the idea the hessian bags might be from the same company, but I couldn't prove this without the label.'

'Right. What about year of death?'

There was a movement as if Dr Fletcher was changing the phone to his other ear. 'I really want to check it against the other skeletal remains, but I'm thinking maybe seventy or eighty years ago.'

Dave blew out his breath and leaned back in his chair, rubbing his face. There really didn't seem to be any point in pursuing this. 'It's too long ago.'

'Well, it is for any hope of arrest, but there's always the family to think about. Surely someone somewhere has been missing a family member? And there is the baby.' A silence came down the phone, although Dave thought he could hear Dr Fletcher clicking a pen in the background. 'Look, Dave, I know it seems like a long shot, so if you're not going to keep going with the case, you'll need to let me know. I'll release the body to be buried. I'm not going to tie up my resources.'

'No, no,' Dave answered quickly. There was something to this one, he just knew it. 'We'll keep going with it.'

After Dave had hung up the phone, he paced around the office, thinking. A seventy-year-old grave really didn't warrant much time spent on it at all, but that changed with the baby. The fact they were buried together, in the same grave, intrigued him. Were they father and child? Were they even related? If they weren't, how had they come to be in the ground together?

He rubbed his chin as he thought.

'You wearing out the carpet?' Jack's voice broke his concentration.

'Thinking,' he answered.

'Careful. You might overdo it.'

'Dr Fletcher just called from the morgue.'

'Oh yeah?' Jack pulled out a chair and sat down. 'Anything interesting?'

'Very.' He quickly brought Jack up to date on the developments.

'How the hell are we supposed to investigate deaths that are so old?'

'Look, we're not supposed to spend any time on something this old. There's no chance of an arrest because the perp will more than likely have passed away. But as Fletcher pointed out to me today, there's always the family to think about and the body of a baby . . .' He blew out a heavy sigh. 'Well, to me that changes things.'

'Why?' Jack asked.

'If they were murdered . . . Well, what sort of person kills a child? Someone who should be held accountable.'

Jack nodded his understanding and Dave continued, 'Surely, if we're able to identify the remains, we can trace their family and let them know what happened to their loved ones. I'm fascinated by this, so I'll work it just so long as it doesn't interfere with anything around here. You good with that?'

'If that's what you want to do, go for it. Not like there's anyone from HQ to check on you out here!'

Dave chuckled. 'I'll google a few things. See what Trove has on it. You never know, we might get lucky and find a newspaper story about a missing man and baby. Problem solved.'

'That's like expecting every body to be found with identification papers. Dream on, boss.'

Chapter 12

The morning of the pageant dawned clear, and it was hot before the sun had even risen.

Chelsea had been up early, making chocolate mint slice and rum balls for Christmas Day, and now, with Aria and Tom on their secret mission—still one she knew nothing about—she was alone in the house and her fingers were itchy.

She wanted to sit down at the piano and play. To escape the world of pressures and secrets. Every time she thought about playing, her heart ached. It was what she longed to do, but she wouldn't let herself. That life was behind her now. She had to put her mind to finding a career that would support her and Aria, and there wasn't time for frivolities. The piano was just that. It couldn't earn her a living anymore.

One of the reasons she'd come back to Shandona had been to see her father, to talk to him and find out about her mother's death. To understand what had happened and to grieve. But there were other reasons too, not least the need to work out what she was going to do now that conductors would no longer work with her.

When the paper had been delivered on the mail run yesterday, she'd taken it to bed with her and combed the employment pages. She'd also joined a Facebook page for people seeking work in Adelaide and found a professional resumé-writing service. Even with that, she knew it wouldn't be easy to find work. Since she was thirteen all she had done was play the piano.

She'd thought of teaching the instrument, but how could she do that? She had no idea how to teach! Hadn't done any training. And teaching kids who weren't talented? Ugh. No, thank you. The thought of clashing notes and children lacking hand-eye coordination sent shivers down her spine.

Panic had started to set in, although she was doing her best to stave it off by cooking and keeping busy. Walking early in the mornings had helped too, avoiding the evening time because that's when Cal went for a run. She certainly didn't have anything to say to him after his accusations.

An invisible force pulled her into the sitting room and drew her to the piano. The smooth, dark wood of the Beale was cool to her touch and the keys begged to be played.

The piano, made back in 1935, had been her Great-Grandfather Baxter's. With gold etching and a tone to die for, even eighty-three years on, it was in immaculate condition. He'd played it until he'd died. It had been his playing that had drawn her to the piano and, even though his fingers weren't as nimble as they'd been in his younger days, Great-Granda Baxter had still been able to make the instrument sing.

Her finger touched the F sharp key and she felt the electricity run though her. She *had* to play. The urge was stronger than her willpower.

Sitting down, she placed her fingers on the keys and left them there before pressing them down in a chord. The sound was a little off key—she assumed it hadn't been played since she'd left. But that could be fixed.

Quickly she swung into 'River Flows In You' by one of her favourite composers, Yiruma. It was sad and sweet and sounded just like a river flowing. Losing herself in the song, she shut her eyes and swayed as she played, the melodic tune easing her like a balm.

People were surprised she loved Yiruma's music, given she'd been classically trained, but to Chelsea it didn't matter whether a piece was classical or not; if the melody moved her, she would play it. This diversity had given her concert playing depth. Besides, she liked composing music herself, so she had a respect for pianists who were able to make a living out of it. Sometimes she wished she'd done the same thing; then she would've been free to play what and how she wanted.

Her fingers ran up and down the keyboard as if she'd never stopped playing. In reality she hadn't touched a piano for three months. The music was like air to her; she finally felt the stirring inside, as if she were alive again. The part of her soul she'd shut down had been opened a crack and now her emotions were pouring out onto the keyboard.

Once again, she was sending the music soaring to the ceiling and she had an audience of hundreds, as there'd been when she'd played at the Sydney Opera House. The applause she had received that night had carried her through the darkest times of her career—when she'd had to take jobs on cruise ships, not because she wanted to but because she had to.

Chelsea didn't want to think about the cruise ship, because then she'd have to think about Aria's father, and how he'd broken her heart.

As the song came to an end, Chelsea realised she had tears on her cheeks. She took her hands from the keyboard and laid them in her lap, just as she had when the police had come to tell them about Dale.

The first cruise she'd done, her gigs had been in the whiskey bar on the fourth deck. She'd play for an hour, four times a day, to people who didn't care about music; they were more interested in seeing how much they could drink, since most of them had bought the drinks package. She'd played Beethoven and Bach mixed up with Yiruma and piano versions of popular artists like Taylor Swift and Bruno Mars. The tunes had dipped and soared with the gentle rocking of the ship. She'd ignored the people who didn't care, playing only for herself and her own enjoyment. At least no one had told her she'd added too many embellishments to the pieces she played. At the end of the set, barely anyone even realised she'd left.

Her second job had been with a different cruise liner and had been a much better experience. There had been people who appreciated fine music and clapped enthusiastically when the piece was over.

The other two times had been much the same as the first and she'd had to keep reminding herself she had a child to look after and no choice but to perform for these unappreciative audiences. And each time she performed Aria was with Tori, waiting for her mum to come and get her. Normally taking a child onto a ship wouldn't have been allowed, but that had been part of Chelsea's negotiations—she wouldn't perform unless she could have Aria and Tori with her.

No! She pushed her body back from the piano and stood up with such force she tipped the stool over.

This time the word came from her: 'No!' She couldn't let herself get drawn back into the world of music. No one would take her on as a pianist anymore. Being headstrong and stubborn had put too many people offside. There wasn't a conductor in Australia who would work with her again. She had to put the music behind her, shut up the part that made her whole and learn to live without it. Slamming down the piano lid, she vowed never to touch it again, no matter how overwhelming the urge to play was.

'Mummy, you were playing!' Aria was standing in the doorway, a look of wonder on her face. 'I like it when you do.'

'What are you talking about, Aria?' Chelsea spoke over the top of her daughter. 'I play all the time.'

'No, you don't.'

'Don't you?' her father asked, looking at the piano. 'I thought you played every day. You need to keep up the practice or the Conservatorium won't have you back.'

Chelsea looked at her father. 'What?'

Her dad jerked his gaze back to her. 'Practise, Chelsea. It's something you need to do every day.'

They were the same words her mum used to say to her.

'But, Dad, I'm not at the Conservatorium anymore.' That weird flickering feeling of worry returned.

'You're not?' A look of confusion passed over his face. 'Oh no, of course you're not! That's right, I forgot,' he blustered.

Chelsea caught Aria gazing at the two of them. Perhaps she shouldn't say anything in front of her daughter, but if she didn't the moment would be lost. 'Dad . . .'

'Aria and I have something to show you,' he interrupted, smiling tightly. The bewilderment that had been in his eyes just moments before was now replaced with clarity, as if he hadn't said anything strange.

'That sounds exciting,' she said slowly. 'I wonder what it could be?'

Aria grabbed her hand and tugged at it. 'Come on! I'll show you, Mummy.'

She followed her daughter and dad outside and there, parked on the verandah, was Chelsea's old bike, complete with rusty trainer wheels. The handlebars had tinsel wound around them and there were shiny baubles hanging from each handle. The spokes had also been decorated with tinsel, and stretched over the basket on the back was a Father Christmas hat with a bell on the end.

Laughter bubbled out of Chelsea, despite only moments ago being in tears. 'That's utterly fabulous! What are you going to do with it? The pageant?'

'I've taught Aria to ride the bike and, yep, she's going to take part in the pageant this evening,' Tom said proudly.

Aria was jumping up and down with excitement. 'I'm going to be in the pageant! I'm going to be in the pageant!'

'Just like I used to,' Chelsea said. She turned to Aria. 'Show me how you ride it, honey. I can't wait to see.'

'Watch me, Mummy.' Aria mounted the bike and after a few little wobbles she rode down the pathway, the plumbago hitting her in the face as she went. An empty plastic water bottle zip-tied to the spokes made a clicking noise as she rode, and the decorations twinkled in the sunlight. The noise from the bottle would draw the judges' attention and hopefully they'd be so impressed by the creativity of the backyard decorations they'd give Aria the prize for the best decorated bike. Chelsea recognised her father's strategy from her own childhood.

Aria turned around and rode back, the smile on her face so wide Chelsea couldn't help but laugh.

'That's so exciting!' she said when Aria got off the bike. 'How did you get it organised, Dad?'

'I read in the community paper Lily Jackson was organising for the kindy kids to get together and decorate their bikes or scooters and ride them in the pageant behind the primary school float. I thought I'd give her a ring and see if it was okay to include Aria, and she thought it was a great idea. Took me a while to find your bike, but it was at the back of the machinery shed. Cleaned it up and this is the way it turned out.'

'Lily Jackson, she's still around?' Chelsea asked, remembering her childhood friend.

'Yeah. Married now, but I don't know who to. Not a farmer. She asked about you.'

'Did she?' Chelsea felt her breathing quicken.

'I said I thought you'd catch up with her when you went into town. Now, the next thing we have to do is decorate the Christmas—'

He broke off as Aria interrupted.

'Mummy, Papa cut down a big, big pine tree.' She spread her arms as wide as she could. 'Bigger than this. It's in the back of the ute.'

'Then you'd better help him carry it in and I'll get the decorations.' Chelsea grabbed a bucket from the outside laundry and filled it with stones and sand. Thank goodness for Aria. It seemed the little girl was the only thing keeping the tension between herself and Tom from bubbling over.

Tom carried in the tree with help from Aria, and between the three of them they got it standing up straight.

'Here, Aria,' Tom said, handing her a length of tinsel. 'Put it where you like.'

Digging in her pocket, Chelsea pulled out her mobile phone and snapped a couple of photos, while Aria hung the tinsel over the branches and struggled to get the baubles to stay on the needles.

Finally there was only the silver star to put on top. Tom was rolling it around in his hands as if uncertain what to do with it. When he handed it to Chelsea, his hands were shaking.

'Your mum made this,' he told her in a weak voice. 'I didn't think I ever wanted to see it again. Well,' he grimaced, 'I guess I did, but it brings back too many memories.'

Chelsea put her hand on her father's arm and looked him in the eye. 'Like the time Dale and I tried to climb to the top of the windmill to hang it from up there. We thought Father Christmas needed guidance to bring his sleigh into land the way the jets needed lights. We were sure the setting sun would make it twinkle and he'd be able to see the house!'

'God, Pip almost had a heart attack when she realised you'd scampered all the way to the top!'

'Well, Dale told me to.'

'And you always did everything your brother said!'

Chelsea's breath caught in her throat. He sounded like the father she remembered. 'I did!' She made herself indignant. 'That's why I always got into trouble—I did his dirty work for him.'

'That's not quite how I remember it,' Tom said with a slight laugh. 'Although pretty close. Right . . .' He glanced around and Chelsea knew the conversation was finished. 'We'd better get ready to . . .' He stopped and looked at Aria. 'I guess we'd better get that star to the top of the tree before anything else. Come here and climb up on my shoulders, you should be able to reach from there.' He picked Aria up and settled her on his shoulders, then she leaned out to place the star on top of the tree.

'I've done it,' Aria said, and Tom lowered her down again and looked at Chelsea.

'Remember . . .' they both asked at the same time.

'Group hug,' Chelsea finished.

'Group hug!' Aria called, and was squashed in between the two adults. 'Tori, Mum and I have group hugs too.'

'Who's Tori?' Tom asked as he let go.

'Mum's friend.'

'We always had a group hug once we'd finished decorating the tree,' Chelsea told Aria. 'My mum, your Nan, always used to say Christmas was about family and we should take every opportunity to celebrate our families. We had hugs with Tori when I got home from work, didn't we?'

'Yes,' Aria said, then she paused. 'I like Nan.'

Tom's lips were pressed tightly together, but somehow he managed to say, 'I did too.'

Chapter 13

The main street had been decorated, and Chelsea and Aria could hear the cheery conversations through the car window and smell the cooking from the barbecues. Lights hung from the wooden beams of the shop verandahs and Christmas ornaments decorated the trees that ran down the middle of the main street. There were Santa, sleigh and reindeer decorations in people's front yards, and a large Christmas tree had been erected next to the town hall.

Aria leaned out the window, her hair flapping around her face as she watched all the excitement, while Chelsea looked for somewhere to park.

'God! It's not like it should be hard to find a park in Barker,' she muttered to herself, turning down the street indicated by the detour sign.

Finally she pulled in under a shady tree and turned off the engine. The loud music and chatter swirling around the main street made Chelsea feel excited. The annual pageant had been one of her favourite events. Even more so when she'd been involved in it.

The floats were always bright and fun—the St John Cadets usually had one, as did the bowling club. Over the years there'd been a dance school one, with girls dressed as ballerinas. The footy club always hammed things up with the girls from the netball club, and a TV character like Fireman Sam or Bob the Builder usually made an appearance. The best was left for the last car of the parade. Father Christmas was driven around in a Model T Ford, waving royally to everyone who was watching. The children on the side of the road screamed with delight and lined up in front of the town hall, where the procession came to a stop, to put in their last-minute Christmas orders.

One year, the lady from the Uniting Church who always played the piano for carols by candlelight had called in sick. Chelsea had been asked to fill in and that night, even though she was so young—only fifteen—she'd been the town's darling. She wondered what type of reception she'd get tonight.

In true South Australian mid-north style, the heat was stifling and the flies gathered as soon as she opened the door. Even before she'd unloaded Aria's bike from the back, she was sweating.

Filled with nervous apprehension, she pushed Aria in the direction of the police station, where everyone was assembling. Would Lily recognise her? Would she recognise Lily? She hadn't spoken to her for years—not since Dale's funeral. And for no real reason save that she'd been busy focusing on her career. There had never been much time for friendships or relationships.

As she walked past a small group of people, she noticed they looked over and stared at her. Then they leaned forwards and whispered to each other, before glancing her way again. Chelsea held her head high and as she and Aria approached the crowds, she could see a woman with long blonde hair and sunglasses, dressed in a tank top and shorts. She was holding a clipboard and seemed to be directing people. She was familiar, but Chelsea wasn't convinced it was her friend.

'Come on, sweetie, come over this way. I'm sure this lady will be able to—'

'Chelsea?'

She turned at the man's voice and felt the blood drain from her face. 'Jason.'

Aria slipped her hand into Chelsea's. 'Mummy?'

'What—' Jason seemed to swallow hard before he could talk again. 'What are you doing here?'

'Home for Christmas,' she answered, squeezing Aria's hand for support. 'And you? Are you helping out somewhere?'

'Me? Um, yeah. I'm, ah, I help with the sound equipment.'

'Oh.' She racked her brains to remember what his job had been when she'd left. 'Are you not on the farm anymore?'

'Yeah, still there, but I like helping out with the tech stuff.'

'Sounds good. Well, I'd better find Lily. Um . . .'

'Is this your little girl?'

'Ah, yeah, this is Aria. Aria, sweetie, this is, um,' she groped for the right words. How do you introduce the man who killed your brother? 'This is Jason.'

'Hello, Aria. You have a pretty name. And that's a cool bike you've got decorated there.'

'Thank you.' Aria cuddled into Chelsea's side.

'We don't want to miss anything, so we'd better go.' Chelsea started to move away, but Jason took a step forwards and grabbed her arm.

'Can we catch up?' His tone was pleading. 'I'd like to talk to you.'

'I'm not sure how long I'm here for,' she hedged.

'Come on, Mummy.' Aria tugged at her arm impatiently.

'Look, I've really got to go. Sorry.' She turned away and started walking towards the woman with the clipboard.

After a few steps she had to stop, take her hand from Aria's and wipe both hands on her skirt. She was hot and sweaty, her heart thumping as if she'd just walked on stage at the Opera House. Without turning around, she gathered herself and together they kept walking, even though Chelsea knew Jason's eyes were on her back the whole time.

Half an hour later, with no Lily in sight, the parade started with the blast of a truck's horn. Chelsea had found her way to a spot in front of the supermarket where she'd arranged to meet her dad so they could watch Aria ride by on her bike.

Tom wasn't there yet, but Amal was standing outside the shop and nodded hello to her. How nice it was to see a friendly face.

'How are you enjoying being home, Chelsea?' he asked.

She wasn't overly surprised he remembered her. Still the gossip would've come thick and fast once people knew she was back in town, and she guessed he'd heard people talking in the shop.

'Really nice, thank you. Are you ready for Christmas?' As soon as she said the words she wanted to kick herself. Did he even celebrate Christmas?

'Is anyone ever really ready for Christmas?' he asked.

'Good point.' She changed the subject quickly in case it wasn't appropriate. 'Do you have children involved?'

'I do. Two. Boy and a girl. Probably of a similar age to yours. How old is Aria? Four? Five?'

People jostled past them and called hello to Amal. He greeted them with a large smile. Chelsea couldn't help but think that when she was growing up, Amal wouldn't have been greeted with the same amount of enthusiasm and warmth. In some instances, change was wonderful.

'Four.'

'Mmm. Nikko—we call her Nik—is six, and Rebaz is four.'

'Lovely ages. You've got a great memory,' she said. 'To remember our names.'

'There are always new people passing through at this time of the year. I do my best to make them feel welcome.'

'That's really lovely of you, Amal. How long have you lived here for?' She waved at the clown who was dancing down the street, blowing up balloons and passing them to the excited kids.

'Eight years. But we are from Adelaide. Not that far away. Most of our family are still there, but we wanted to get away from the city.'

'Couldn't get too much further away,' Chelsea joked.

'It is cheaper to live here. The children like it. My wife likes it, so we are content to stay. There is space and air to breathe.'

'I know what you mean.'

They paused as the footy club float went by. The guys were dressed as girls in long blonde wigs, and the netballers were dressed as blokes in footy shorts pulled up as far as they would go. As they passed, they threw out lollies and the kids raced out into the street to pick them up.

'Can't see people in the city getting away with doing that anymore,' Chelsea said with a smile.

'No, you are right. What about you, Chelsea? How long is it since you have visited?'

'Maybe too long, Amal. I wasn't sure I ever wanted to come back.'

He smiled sympathetically. 'Often there is no other place to go to heal than one's birthplace.'

To Chelsea it sounded like he understood.

'Do I need to heal?' she asked, her voice sounding like she was issuing a challenge.

'Everyone needs healing in one way or another.'

She glanced over at him and saw he was staring straight in front. Wondering if he spoke from experience, Chelsea felt her thumb start to run over her hand—an unconscious reaction she had when she was anxious.

A loud cheer went up from the crowd and the clapping started all over again. She leaned forwards to look down the road and saw a group of about ten children riding in pairs as fast as they could. Aria was in the front with a girl riding next to her. She was chatting away to her partner—so much so, Chelsea wasn't sure her daughter was looking at the road.

'Look at that,' Chelsea said softly. In how many other places would a child who'd only just arrived in town be riding in a pageant and making friends after only a few days. Maybe Barker had its benefits. 'We've never stayed in one place long enough for Aria to be able to make many friends. With my work . . .'

'What do you do?'

'I am . . . was a concert pianist.' Chelsea looked down at her hands. It hurt to say 'was'.

'But no more?'

'No,' she replied softly. 'No more.'

'If Aria likes it here, Barker might be the place for you to settle down. I'm sure your father would like to have you close by.'

'Ha! Maybe not.' She started to wave as the young cyclists drew parallel with her. 'Aria! Over here!' She waved and jumped up and down, waiting for her daughter to look over. After a couple of shouts, Aria glanced over and gave Chelsea a large smile, but then went straight back to talking to the girl next to her. 'I guess that's a good sign,' Chelsea said, turning to Amal. 'Too busy having fun to take notice of me.'

But Amal had gone and, in his place, stood Lily.

'Hello, Chelsea,' she said softly. 'It's good to see you. You haven't changed at all.'

'Lily? Oh my God, Lily.' Her voice broke as she leaned forwards to hug her childhood friend but pulled back when it wasn't returned. Clearing her throat, she asked, 'How are you? Look at you! Still as skinny as ever. And your hair—you've cut it!'

'I'm fine. What about you? You look exactly the same— glamorous without trying. Like your mum.'

Chelsea shook her head. 'I don't know about that. I guess we've all changed in some way. What are you doing now? I heard you got married.'

'I did. I'm Lily Gill these days. Do you remember Dylan Gill? His dad was the shire president when we were at school and his mum worked in the library.'

'Vaguely. He was a few years older than us?'

'Yeah, that's him. We married six years ago, and we run the local IT store now. Well, he does. I'm a stay-at-home mum.' She stared at her hard as if defying Chelsea to say anything.

'Wow, who would've thought we'd end up in Barker! We had such big plans. Remember the daydreaming we used to do?'

'Yeah, who would've thought,' Lily answered. 'But you need money to be able to live dreams. Anyway, I wouldn't change it. The kids are my world.'

'That's wonderful. How old?' Kids were a safe subject and Chelsea felt as if Lily was appraising her.

'The girl your little one is talking to is my eldest, then a two-year-old son.' Chelsea whipped around to get another look at Aria's partner, but all she could see now was her back and a long blonde ponytail swinging in time as she pushed the pedals around and around.

'What's her name?'

'Alecia. She's four.'

'Same as Aria.' She took a breath and said, 'Isn't that funny?' A smile spread across Chelsea's face. 'We always liked the same things and now we've named our daughters by the same letter!'

Lily didn't smile.

Taking a deep breath, Chelsea looked out across the street. 'I'm sorry—'

At the same time Lily said: 'Why didn't you—'

They both stopped and looked at each other, then Lily indicated for Chelsea to go first.

'I'm sorry I didn't write after Dale's funeral.' Chelsea said. 'I know I said I was going to and I started about a thousand times, but I never finished. I couldn't find the words to say anything meaningful. After Dale's death, nothing made any sense to me. Him dying . . . it seemed . . .' She frowned. 'Like a wasted life. Everything I did seemed

154

pointless. The only thing that kept me going was my music. I'm very sorry.'

'I waited for ages. I wanted to invite you to my wedding—I tried. I sent you an invitation. I wanted you to be my bridesmaid, but you never answered. I knew you struggled after Dale died, but not even a congratulations telegram on the day? Did we really come to this, Chelsea? All you were doing was running away and not dealing with his death.'

Chelsea's heart sank. 'You invited me? I didn't—'

'Yeah, I did.' She crossed her arms and looked away, as if she didn't want to look at Chelsea anymore. Listen to her lies.

'I wasn't running away.'

'That was how it seemed to all of us. To Kelly. And how about Jason? Dale's death was an accident. Your parents needed you too.'

Chelsea was looking down at the dirty pavement and kicking at the cement but, at Lily's words, her head snapped up. 'No, they didn't!' she said with such force that Lily took a step back.

Another cheer went up as the Model T Ford from Chelsea's childhood came into view carrying Santa. People started jostling to get to the front of the crowd and the two women were separated.

Chelsea looked at the people around her and saw a few faces she recognised, but they weren't looking at her, they were too engrossed in the parade and lifting smaller children on to their shoulders for a better view.

'Why didn't you answer the invitation?' Lily's voice came from behind her and was full of hurt.

Spinning around, she answered, 'I never got your invitation. I didn't even know you were married until Dad told me. I'm sorry, I would have answered if I'd got it. I would've loved to have been your bridesmaid. Where did you send it?'

'To your flat in Melbourne. Your mum gave me the address. It was after you'd finished your European tour. I read about you in the paper. We were all so proud of what you were doing. And I wanted you to be my bridesmaid.'

Then it all became clear. She hadn't been living in Melbourne, and she hadn't updated her address for her mum because she had been just about to go on her first cruise and hadn't wanted anyone to know what a failure she was. The European tour had been a disaster; even though the crowds had loved her, the conductors hadn't. There had been angry words and insults traded between her and them.

While Chelsea had been the feature, she'd still had an orchestra playing with her, and her relationship with the other musicians had also been tense.

It had been the world's most famous conductor, Gaspard Dubois, who had told her he would never work with her again.

'Difficult. Wilful. Arrogant. Defiant and disobedient!' he'd shouted at her in broken English. 'I will not work with you anymore.'

Gossip travels fast in the music industry and that was that.

Looking back, Chelsea knew she hadn't been a nice person. She'd been everything Gaspard Dubois had said, but she'd never thought it would cost her career. Her cheeks burned with embarrassment as she thought back to that final showdown outside her dressing room.

'Oh, Lily. I need to explain.' The silence between them stretched out because Chelsea wasn't sure how to explain. 'Can we . . .' she looked around. 'Can we have a glass of wine and talk? I've got a lot to tell you.'

'Mummy, Mummy!' Two voices called out in unison as they ran to their mothers, holding hands.

'This is my friend Aria, Mummy,' Alecia said, looking at Lily. 'She's staying on a farm.'

'That's my mum,' Aria said, pointing at Chelsea.

Chelsea collected herself and smiled at the excited girls. 'And your mummies know each other!' she said. 'Lily and I went to school here and we were best friends.' She could feel Lily looking at her but continued to smile.

'That's funny,' Alecia said. 'Our mums were best friends and now we are too!'

'Come on,' Lily said. 'Do you want to line up to see Father Christmas?'

'Yeah!' the girls shouted together.

'Well, off you go. We'll follow behind you.'

The girls ran across the road without fear of traffic, since the roads were closed, and joined the queue of kids waiting to see Santa.

'Maybe we need to have a talk,' Lily said to Chelsea as they followed their daughters.

Chelsea stopped and put a hand on Lily's arm. 'I'm truly sorry, Lily. I would've come if I'd known. I'd like to explain.'

'Coffee, then. After Christmas. I don't drink.'

'I'll ring and make a time,' Chelsea promised.

'When do you leave?'

'I don't know yet.' She shrugged. 'Do you have much to do with Dad?'

'What? Me? No. He doesn't talk to any of us now.' Lily said hello to a couple of people, and although Chelsea knew their faces, she couldn't remember their names, so she just nodded and ignored their curious glances.

'Any of the people involved that night or just anyone?'

'Any of us—Jason, me, Kelly. But now you mention it, probably not too many people at all.'

'I think there's something wrong with him,' she confided.

'Like what?'

They were interrupted by Aria running back to them, bubbling with excitement. She was waving a piece of paper and Alecia wasn't far behind her.

'Mum! Papa bought me a ride in the police car!'

'What?' Chelsea was puzzled. 'How do you buy a ride in a police car?'

'Ah, I know,' Lily said. 'Dave Burrows is raising money for the school, so he offered a ride in the car to the winning ticket. I think you're going for a ride with Santa. Detective Dave was going to take him to the reindeer and sleigh and while he did that he was going to give the lucky winner a ride. Look, there's your Papa.'

Aria's eyes were wide. 'No way,' she said making the 'way' long and drawn out.

Chelsea couldn't help giggling as she turned and saw her dad waving to Aria. 'Where on earth have you heard that saying?' she asked.

'Cal says it all the time.'

'Does he now?' Chelsea ignored the little jab of anxiety at the mention of his name. She needed to go back and talk to him, whether he liked her or not; Cal knew her father better than anyone and she was sure he'd have some thoughts on Tom.

'I'm going too!' Alecia cried. 'I can, can't I, Mummy?'

'Absolutely.'

The girls dragged their mothers over to the police car, pulling them so quickly that they bumped into people and had to apologise as they went.

'G'day, Lily,' Dave said as they approached. He was wearing his dress uniform, leaning against the patrol car. 'Kept Kim busy cooking gourmet burgers?'

'Thank God for her!' Lily answered with a smile. 'We were going to be very stuck without someone experienced in these things. She's been run off her feet.'

'Ah well, you know she needs to be kept out of mischief! How are you, Chelsea?' Dave turned his gaze to her and at once she was transported back to the house. To the piano. Where she'd sat silently while another policeman, many years ago, announced her brother's death.

She swallowed. 'Hi. Sounds like Aria is having a ride with you.'

'Me too!' Alecia cried.

'Oh, goodness me, yes, you too,' Chelsea said, patting the little girl on the shoulder.

'Yeah, both these girls are going to ride in the police car and hang out with Santa while I drive him to the edge of town. I hear he has another car waiting to take him to the airport where his sleigh and reindeers are waiting.'

'Can we go to the airport too?'

Dave shook his head solemnly. 'No can do, sorry, girls. The airport is full of security because Santa is so important. You don't have the required clearances.'

The girls' eyes were so wide as they stared up at the detective that Chelsea had to look down so Aria and Alecia didn't see her laugh. They turned and looked at each other, then grabbed each other's hands before giving a little squeal of excitement.

As she watched them, Chelsea's mouth fell open and she looked at Lily to see if she'd noticed, to see if she remembered. These two girls could have been the two of them when they were four.

'I have room for one more. Would one of you ladies like to accompany us?'

Chelsea and Lily looked at each other.

'You go,' said Chelsea. 'I'll see if I can find Dad.'

Chapter 14

Chelsea leaned down and brushed Aria's hair away from her face as she slept. Her long dark lashes touched her cheeks and she breathed evenly. When Aria was asleep like this, she reminded Chelsea so much of her father. When they had shared a bunk on the ship together, Chelsea had loved to watch him sleep. She had often propped herself up on one elbow and gazed at him. Aria's deep brown eyes and long dark lashes were the same as her father's, as was the colour of her hair. Seeing the similarities made Chelsea's heart ache; she tried not to think about him too often.

At the end of Aria's bed, Chelsea had placed a pillowcase full of little Santa presents: a book, a new set of crayons, colouring books and a tube of touch bubbles. The main present she'd put underneath the Christmas tree shortly. It wasn't much; she didn't have a lot of money left, but the cute backpack and lunchbox set would be great for when Aria started kindy next year.

The thought sent shivers through her. Where was she going to put her into school? As Aria gave a deep sigh and settled into a deeper sleep Chelsea backed quietly out of the room, determined not to think about the future yet.

Back in her room, she pulled out the wrapping paper she'd bought in Barker and looked for the sticky tape. She knew she'd bought some. It wasn't there. Bugger. Must've slipped out of the bag.

Creeping out into the kitchen, she pulled open a couple of knick-knack drawers and had a rifle through them but didn't find any. There wasn't any in her dad's office. Surely there'd at least be some masking tape somewhere! Or electrical tape—what farmhouse didn't have that?

Would there be anything in her mother's office, she wondered. She went to the small room next to the sitting room and looked at the door, which was tightly shut.

It'd been like that since she'd arrived, and not once had she seen her father go in or come out. And Chelsea hadn't felt free to go in. In some ways she felt like a visitor in her old home.

Slowly she reached out and opened the door. The hinges, in need of oiling, let out a long screech. She froze for a moment before looking over her shoulder in case Tom or Aria had woken.

A strange thought popped into her mind. The loud screeching might be symbolic of emotions and feelings long since locked away and needing to come out. To be talked about and dealt with. That's what Baxter would've said.

Great-Granda Baxter had always been one to look out for signs—'From the universe, girl,' he'd say.

Granny, Great-Granda Baxter's daughter-in-law, would shake her head and shush him. 'Don't frighten the child. If the Lord heard you talk like that, he'd strike you down.'

Chelsea wished she could recall her gran as clearly as Baxter. Trouble was, she was always busy looking after him and everyone else. Chelsea remembered her beautiful sponges and bread rolls rather than her personality—but she knew she'd loved her gran with all her heart and she knew her gran had loved her.

Maybe it would be better not to remember too much tonight. Not to remember the feeling of her mum's hand on her forehead when she came to kiss her goodnight. Or her reaction when Chelsea managed to stop a goal during the netball grand final. Or just the feeling she had when her mum came in after a long day in the sheep yards and sat quietly in the sitting room, listening as Chelsea practised. No, the memories were too painful and she felt too much regret.

Feeling around, she found the long light cord and yanked it. The dim illumination showed her mother's study: a desk stuffed with papers and old invoices, and on the wall a corkboard covered in photos of Dale. There he was at school—running on sports day, face smeared with red zinc, the colour of his sports house. Baring his teeth—or lack thereof, as he was missing his two front ones. Shearing sheep in the yards with their father, their arms around each other's shoulders.

And this one. Chelsea pulled the pin out and sat down at her mother's desk, never taking her eyes from the picture. In it Dale's hair was cut into a mullet and he was wearing a pink tank top. He could've been a double for Jason Donovan in *Neighbours*. He was sitting on the back of his ute, the tailgate down, his arm around a black and tan kelpie, and it seemed as if the two were grinning at each other.

It was the photo that had been used on the order of service for his funeral and Chelsea was sure it was the last photo that had ever been taken of him.

'Dale and Dixie,' she muttered. 'Inseparable.'

Her mum had obviously made this board after Dale died. She didn't remember it being in the office when she was growing up. When she'd been younger her mum would be sitting at her desk, her glasses perched on the end of her nose and strands of hair escaping from her ponytail. She'd have the phone tucked in between her shoulder and her ear, talking to someone about a netball training regimen or laughing with a friend. Her feet would be up on her desk and she'd be leaning back in her chair, laughing raucously. And then there was Dixie . . .

Damn, she really didn't want to think about this now. But Dixie forced her way into her mind.

For the first five weeks after Dale's death, Dixie had sat at the front door barely moving. Every time a vehicle pulled up, she'd race to the end of the path and look hopeful. When the dog realised it wasn't her master coming home, she'd slink back up the path and slump at the door again, her chin on her paws. If she'd been a human, Chelsea was sure there would have been tears slipping down her furry cheeks.

'Stop it,' she whispered as she tore her eyes away from the photos. 'Not now. We've got to get through tomorrow first.'

She hurried over to the desk and pulled open the drawers, looking for some sticky tape. After all, she had presents to wrap and cooking to do. It was still hours before she could go to bed.

Nothing in the first drawer other than pens, paperclips and rubber bands. The second drawer was full of used envelopes. The third drawer held a box.

It took a moment for Chelsea to work out what it was. There was the outline of a blue flower on the lid, along with her mum's name and the date that would be burned in Chelsea's memory forever—the date of her mum's death.

Pursing her lips, she continued to look at the container. She wasn't sure what it held, but it must be something to do with her mum's funeral.

Dale's funeral was the only one Chelsea remembered clearly. In one way she was glad about that: it meant most of the people she loved hadn't died. But oh, how she wished she'd been able to go to her mother's funeral. No one knew the guilt she experienced every single day because she hadn't been there.

Dale's funeral she relived often, still seeing it as if she were there. There was a lot of noise—people crying, but also laughing at some of the stories that were told. There'd been music—'Angels' by Robbie Williams and 'Chasing Cars' by Snow Patrol. Then Chelsea had played 'Wind Beneath

My Wings' as a piano solo. She remembered pressing the keys automatically, as if in a trance. She could remember the sobbing as the pallbearers, from Dale's cricket club, carried out the coffin.

Pulling her eyes away from the box, she looked around the rest of the room. Nothing else seemed to have changed since she'd been in here last, all those years ago. The blue curtains still hung over the window to block out the midday sun, and the office chair was placed by the window, where her mum loved to sit and drink her morning coffee while she looked over the creek and listened to the birds' cacophony of song.

Not wanting to disturb anything, she picked up the container and sat down on her mother's chair with it in her lap. Chelsea spent a long time tracing around the edges, trying not to think about her mum being buried on the cold grey day she imagined it had been. Maybe the wind would've whipped around the mourners standing at the graveside so they scurried out of the cold after the coffin had been lowered into the ground. After all, there was no way it would've been sunny the day her mother was buried.

Before she could stop herself, she took the lid off the box and stared inside. It was full of cards.

Dear Tom, We're sorry to hear about the loss of Pip. At peace now.

To Tom, In your darkest times, remember how Pip always made you feel. She can never be lost if you do.

Tom, Let us know if we can do anything, mate.

As Chelsea flicked through them all, she realised her name wasn't on any of them. They were all addressed to Tom. Not even Tom and family.

She guessed the community remembered he'd already lost a son, and his daughter hadn't been seen in years. Maybe she'd been forgotten until she'd arrived home this week.

Towards the bottom she found an order of service. Written on the front page below a photo Chelsea didn't recognise was: *Philippa Teresa Taylor born on the 6th of March 1955 and left her earthly body on the 19th of August 2015.*

She studied the photograph. Her mother was sitting on a fallen log in the creek just below the house. She was laughing at someone who was out of the picture, but it was the paper-thin skin and overly large smile that took Chelsea's breath away. She looked ill. Had she been? No one had told her if she had. Or was it the after-effects of grief?

Opening the order of service, she saw the funeral had been conducted by Pastor Bill Higgins—not a name she knew—and the pallbearers had been four of the neighbouring farmers.

Chelsea looked up, tears threatening—except this time she didn't see the walls of the office, she saw a cold church with a walnut-coloured coffin at the altar. A man she didn't know dressed in robes, telling everyone how Pip would be reunited with Dale in heaven. She heard the electric piano start to play and the pallbearers walk to the front to escort the coffin on the final journey from the church. Her father walking behind, grief-stricken, and Cal alongside him, his face solemn and grave. The hush of the church as the procession made its way to the hearse and then on to ...

Chelsea blinked. The tears rolled down her cheeks and fell onto her T-shirt. She'd still not asked her dad where her mum had been buried. For some reason she hoped it wasn't in the cemetery. It was so cold there. So structured. Her mum would've needed to be free—her ashes scattered on Shandona.

'What are you doing in here?'

Chelsea startled at the sound of her father's voice. She looked up and saw him standing in the doorway. He was dressed in boxers and a singlet and looked pained.

'I need to know about Mum,' she said.

Tom looked at her steadily. 'Why? You didn't come. I didn't think you cared.'

Chelsea jumped up from her chair and went over to him. Standing ramrod straight, staring him in the eyes, her voice was strong as she said, 'I've told you why. I didn't get the messages. I didn't know. I didn't know until after we got back into port. I hadn't taken my phone with me when I went on that cruise ship. I didn't want you and Mum to know that I'd failed. I didn't want any communication. Dad, I didn't get your messages.'

'Why didn't you come home afterwards?'

Chelsea looked down at the box. 'I don't know.'

Chapter 15

Chelsea sat at the piano; it was where she went when she needed to feel safe.

Tom sat on the chair with a glass of water and looked down at his hands. She noticed they were shaking slightly. His fingers were permanently stained with purple dirt and grease; no matter how long he scrubbed them, they were never absolutely clean. They were strong hands. Hands that would take care of her and Aria. Hands that had wiped her tears as a child and clapped when she'd finished a performance.

'I didn't know she was going to die.' Tom's voice broke a little. 'If I had I wouldn't have gone into town that night.'

Chelsea looked down at the floor and rubbed at the stain on the carpet just in front of the stool. She thought she remembered spilling Milo there when she was little, but she couldn't be sure.

'Jacko and Terry had asked me to play corporate bowls and normally she would've come too, but that night she didn't. Said she was tired. So I went by myself. There wasn't too much happening here; we had to start thinking about shearing, but that was a week or two away.

'We had a couple of beers afterwards and I came home. Pip was already in bed, so I didn't turn the light on, just got undressed and into bed. Usually she would've said something to me, or asked how it had all gone, but she didn't say a word. I thought she must've been asleep.' Tom swallowed hard and breathed in deeply through his nose before continuing.

'I lay there for a bit, thinking about what we had to do the next day, and then I realised something. I couldn't hear her breathing. So, I . . .' He paused and started to mash his teeth together. 'I put my hand on her. There was nothing.'

Chelsea gulped a little as a few tears trickled down her cheeks. She wanted to comfort her dad, but his posture didn't invite that.

They both sat in the low light, looking at the floor. Chelsea's mind was exploding with questions, but she wasn't sure if she should ask them. How awful to be lying alongside your wife and realising she'd taken her final breath.

Of course, she must ask, she told herself. She might never get another opportunity.

'Was she sick?' she finally managed to choke out. 'The photo on the Order of Service . . . She didn't look, um, healthy. Mum looked—' pausing, Chelsea finally said—'frail.'

Her dad shook his head. 'No. She'd lost so much weight since Dale had died. That was the pain and misery you could see in that photo, even though she was smiling. The autopsy—'

'Autopsy?' The word shot from her mouth before she could stop it.

'They had to do one.' Tom shrugged as he spoke. 'The doctor didn't know why she'd died. It was a heart attack. Massive. But you know what I think? I think her heart got weak from all the sadness. Then it couldn't keep going.'

'Heart attack? But she was fit—she didn't look like she was a candidate for a heart attack.' Chelsea couldn't believe it. Her strong, active mother had a blockage in her arteries and her heart had stopped at sixty.

'Yes.' Tom sounded angry now.

Chelsea saw him get up and start to pace the room.

'It's not fair,' he said, angrily, as he walked. 'There's a book on the bedside table. One of those biographies she liked to read. I never liked them, but I wanted to hold and read the pages she had.' Dragging in a breath, he kept talking, faster and faster. 'But I can't read past where the bookmark is. Why should I know more about the book than she did?

'I look at the clothes in her wardrobe and imagine what she looked like in them. I can't clean it out—I don't want to. If I do, I might lose her again. I dunno, to move on seems like some kind of . . .' He cast around the room helplessly. 'Some kind of unfaithfulness.' He stopped and looked at Chelsea. 'Sounds ridiculous. But every step I take, I'm leaving her further and further behind, and while I'm losing her, I'm losing myself.' He looked at Chelsea, a pleading expression in his eyes. 'Why, why the hell do I feel like this?'

She had no idea what to say, because it was just like hearing her father talk after Dale had died.

'I'm sorry, Dad.'

'Sorry?' An explosion of grim laughter escaped from him. 'Sorry?' He dragged his eyes away from her now and walked to the window. 'Not only was I dealing with your mother's death, the whole town kept asking about you: "Chelsea will come home to help you now, I'm sure." And "Where's Chelsea? Be home soon, will she? I would've thought she'd come back for her mother's funeral." Then they'd tut-tut and I'd be left trying to explain where you were when even *I* didn't know.'

The bitterness in his voice was undeniable and she shifted uncomfortably on the piano stool. There was anger inside her too but she'd trained herself not to let her feelings interfere with her performance, and somehow she'd become adept at not letting them interfere in her personal life either. Tori had summed it up one day: 'What you feel is what you feel—neither right nor wrong, because they're your emotions, your feelings.' They'd been sitting on the balcony in Sydney, drinking wine. 'But if you react to other people's emotions, then they're controlling you. There's a difference between reacting and responding.'

It had taken her a long time to work out the difference, but finally she had. And here, in the sitting room, with her dad, she had a choice—to react or to respond. React to his anger with all the hurt and resentment she was feeling, or respond by using that hurt and anger in a positive way.

Taking a few deep breaths, she said in a low voice, 'I'm sorry I wasn't here, Dad. I would've been if I could. And I'm sorry it's taken me so long to come back home. I didn't want to come home,' she finally admitted. 'I was scared.' She wasn't sure if it was worth explaining again that the messages hadn't got through.

'Scared? What on earth for?'

'About this,' she held open her hands and indicated their surroundings. 'To see how you were feeling, to face that Mum wasn't here anymore. It was easier to stay away when I'd been away for so long, to pretend things hadn't changed out here.' She stopped and lifted her fingers to the piano then pressed three keys in a minor chord. 'To have to come back and be in the shadow of Dale again. I didn't matter after he died. You and Mum forgot about me. I understood that you were hurting, so I left. Went back and concentrated on the piano.'

There was silence.

'Is that how you feel?' Tom finally asked.

'Yes.' Chelsea dropped her head as she sat there. 'And don't forget,' she continued softly, 'neither of you came to me when Aria was born. Why was that?'

'We couldn't. It would've hurt too much.' He took a breath. 'You'll understand one day.'

❧

Chelsea woke to the sound of Aria laughing and jumping on her bed.

'He came, he came!' she cried, and tipped up the pillowcase on the bed so the presents tumbled out.

'Merry Christmas, my gorgeous girl,' Chelsea said, sitting up to give her a hug. 'What did you get?'

'Crayons and colouring-in books and . . .' Aria started and then showed her the rest.

Chelsea rubbed her eyes, which were tired from all the crying she'd done after she'd finally gone to bed last night.

The final thing her dad had said to her was: 'You'll understand one day.' He hadn't spoken another word. The confused look in his eyes had returned and he'd shut down.

His reaction had made her wonder if highly emotional situations triggered the confusion. She'd wanted to google it but had decided she was too tired, and she'd still needed to find some sticky tape. It had been nearly midnight by the time she'd wrapped the rest of the presents and put them under the tree, and finished the last of the cooking. Then she'd gone outside to sit and look at the moon, which cast an eerie glow across the landscape. The lights in Cal's house were still on and she'd wondered what he was doing for Christmas Day.

'Did Father Christmas drink the milk you put out?' Chelsea asked, dragging her thoughts back to her daughter.

'Yes! And he ate half of the biscuit!'

Chelsea, despite not having had a coffee yet, laughed out loud at her daughter's excitement. What a beautiful start to the day. She only hoped her dad would be okay when he appeared.

'Can I open my presents?' Aria asked, collecting every-thing from the bed and skipping towards the kitchen.

'Not until Papa is up and we've had breakfast,' she answered. 'Now I'm going to make some coffee. Do you want a Milo?'

'Yes, please. Can I let Scout off?' she said, referring to Tom's old border collie.

'All right. I'll bring the drinks out and we can sit on the chairs and watch the galahs in the creek until Papa comes out.' But Chelsea was talking to herself because the door slammed before she could finish the sentence.

Throwing the covers off, she shrugged into her dressing gown and went into the kitchen to turn on the kettle and get out the coffee plunger. While she waited, she leaned on the sink and watched Aria through the window.

Even though it'd been a hard decision to come back, she was sure it was a good one for her daughter. The rela-tionship between Aria and her grandfather was wonderful, and her daughter had gone from a shy, withdrawn little girl who didn't speak to many people to an open, smiling, happy child. And it had only taken a few days.

Outside, Aria bounced with Scout for a few steps, then picked up the tennis ball lying on the dry lawn and threw it towards the creek. Scout dashed off after it then brought the ball back to her, and they repeated the action until the hot drinks were ready.

'Hello, Scout,' Chelsea said as she settled on the edge of the creek on a chair and bent down to pat the dog who had flopped at her feet. The few minutes of play were more than enough for a dog who had fifteen years on the dial and a lot of grey around his muzzle.

'Merry Christmas.'

Chelsea turned to see Cal standing behind her, his hands in the pockets of his blue jeans, the now-familiar blue shirt tucked into the waistband.

'Merry Christmas,' she answered, looking back towards the dry river bed. She took a sip of her coffee.

'Cal! Guess what Father Christmas brought me!' Aria tugged at his sleeve.

'Tell me?' he said, squatting down and looking her in the eye. 'Did you get lots of nice presents?'

'Can I show you?'

'Of course.'

'I'll get them,' Aria said and ran off.

Chelsea stared out over the creek. The ewes in the paddock closest to the house were wending their way in to get a drink at the trough and feed from the trail of grain Cal had fed to them this morning. It was still damp enough underfoot for there not to be any dust, and the pinpricks of green, even though not high, were growing around the base of each tree and in the hollows where water had lain a little longer.

'Do you want a coffee?' she finally asked, thinking Christmas Day was a good day for manners.

'That'd be good.' He pulled up a camp chair and sat down.

'How do you have it?'

'White and one, thanks.'

Chelsea passed Aria on her way out of the house, her arms full of presents and excitement on her face. It gave Chelsea pause; her little girl was so happy here. How could she think of leaving once Christmas was over?

In the kitchen she fixed the coffee and went down to her dad's room. 'Dad?' she whispered.

'I'm awake.'

She heard a thud and then a door click. 'I'll be out soon.'

'Merry Christmas, Dad,' she said quietly.

Outside, as she handed Cal his coffee, he smiled, a full, genuine smile—one she hadn't seen before. 'Aria did well on the Father Christmas front,' he said.

Raising her eyebrows in a conspiratorial way, she said, 'She did. Lucky girl.'

'I hope you don't mind, but I bought her a gift.'

With the cup halfway to her mouth, she stopped and looked over at him. 'Did you?' She hoped her surprise wasn't too obvious.

He nodded. 'Is it okay if I give it to her when she comes back out? She's just putting her presents away.'

'Sure. That's really kind of you.'

He shrugged. 'I owe you an apology too.'

Chelsea put down her coffee cup and crossed her arms. She had to wait until a flock of white corellas had flown over, calling noisily, before she could answer. 'Oh?'

'You're right, I have seen a change in Tom in the four years I've been here.' He picked at the sleeve of his shirt and adjusted the collar before looking over at her. 'I don't know what it is, but he's changed.'

'In what way?'

Cal considered the question. 'In a forgetful way.'

Chelsea nodded. 'Dementia?'

Shaking his head, he said, 'I'm no doctor, but he's pretty young to have that.'

'I don't know much about it either, except—'

'Can I have a ride on your motorbike, Cal?' Aria came hopping out of the house and ran across to them, throwing herself on Cal's lap.

'Steady there, you'll knock an old man off his chair!'

'It's Christmas Day, Aria. Cal has to go and visit his family.'

'Actually,' said Cal, 'would you come over to the ute with me, Aria? I have something I think you'll like.'

Aria's eyes. 'Another present?'

'I need some help with the ute, that's all,' Cal answered as he put his coffee down. 'And you're just the girl for it.'

Torn between wanting to see what the present was and not wanting to seem too interested, Chelsea stayed put. Perhaps Cal wasn't as awful as she'd originally thought. It was clear he had a high opinion of Tom, and the way he treated Aria—well, that just made her want to melt . . . which of course Chelsea refused to do because he had been arrogant and dismissive of her. 'So? He doesn't like me.' Chelsea gave a disgruntled groan. She was going to have to reconsider her opinion of him, but still keep her distance at the same time.

Chelsea could hear the pump running, so she knew her dad was in the shower. She thought about the information Cal had just given her. Her heart ached, but it helped to know she wasn't the only one noticing her dad had a problem. When had these lapses first started? And why? Could emotional stress cause forgetfulness? Chelsea didn't know.

Startled by a sudden squeal, Chelsea jumped up and ran towards the noise. It was Aria! What was wrong?

'I love it!' Chelsea heard her say and she immediately relaxed. 'Thanks, Cal. *Mummy!*'

Chelsea started to laugh as Aria rounded the corner wearing a child-size Akubra hat. 'Oh, wow, you look just like a cowgirl! It's so gorgeous on you.' Her startled gaze went to Cal's kind face. 'That's very generous of you, Cal. And not necessary. Her stomach betrayed her resolve to keep her distance by doing a flip-flop as he smiled at her.

Putting her hands on her hips, Aria strutted down the path towards Chelsea as if modelling the hat. 'It's all mine! I'm going to find Papa to show him. I can work in the sheep yards now!'

'Thank you, Cal. Where did you find one so small?'

'The Giftory in Barker. Saw the hat in the window and thought I knew someone who would fit right into it.'

Chelsea shook her head, not sure what to say. 'It's an incredible present. Thank you. She'll never want to leave.'

Turning to look at her, Cal considered her carefully. 'Do you think you will?'

She fidgeted. 'I never thought about staying for good.'

'I imagine you've got concerts to perform at and stuff. This place isn't the most central, I guess.'

Chelsea didn't know what came over her. 'I don't play anymore.' She wanted to take the words back the minute she'd said them out loud. It was only true if she said them.

But she had. And that made her never returning to the concert halls again a reality. Emotion welled in her chest and she had to walk away quickly, not wanting Cal to see her cry.

'What do you mean? Why not? That's what you do.'

'Not anymore. And please don't mention it to Dad. I haven't told him yet. I didn't even mean to tell you.' She walked up the path to the house, Cal following her. 'I don't want to talk about it.'

'Okay. If you don't want to talk, you don't want to talk. No skin off my nose. But as my mum would say, a problem shared is a problem halved.' He stopped but Chelsea kept walking. 'Look, I reckon we got off on the wrong foot. I'm protective of Tom and I was worried when you came back that he'd get hurt again. I can see you're not here to do that.'

Chelsea stopped and turned around.

Cal continued: 'I love him like he was my dad and, yeah, I was pissed off with you for not caring enough to come home when he needed you. You're telling me there's more to that story than meets the eye.' He stopped and cocked his head to the side. 'When you're ready, I hope you'll confide in me, because I'd like to take back all the bad thoughts I've had about you!' He grinned and winked at her.

Maybe he thought he'd softened those words with his cute smile, but Chelsea felt defensive and she crossed her arms and stared at him.

'Look,' Cal said, switching back to the original topic, 'you've asked if I've noticed a difference in Tom, because you've obviously seen a change yourself.' He sighed. 'I came to talk to you about that and it's clear you need to get some things off your chest too.' He looked at her steadily, causing butterflies in her stomach again. 'You think we should have a chat? Because we've got the same goals in mind, whether you want to admit it or not.'

'And what might they be?' She was still pretending that she didn't want to be on the same page after his cutting remark, but somehow she knew they were going to be.

'Making sure Tom and Aria are okay.'

Chapter 16

Aria didn't want to take her hat off all day, or the leather RM Williams boots Tom had given her. The boots were so cute on her little feet but they couldn't be worn inside, and the hat couldn't be worn at the table. Chelsea had had to negotiate to have it sitting beside her plate rather than on her head.

'It's all about manners, Aria,' she'd told her, trying to sound stern. 'You should be able to eat with the shearers and dine with the Queen.' She'd caught Tom looking over at her and realised it was something Pip used to say.

By mid-afternoon the hot lunch combined with the heat of the day had resulted in a food coma and Aria was stretched out on the floor, sound asleep, her hat over her face. Scout had been curled up beside her until Tom had chased him out with a growl. 'Dogs don't belong inside!'

Chelsea stopped cleaning up and looked at her daughter, her dark hair falling to one side from under the hat brim as she slept. The love she felt for her was so intense it hurt physically. Her heart wanted to burst when the feeling was that strong. And these feelings made her wonder why her mother hadn't come to see her after she'd written and told them about Aria. Maybe she'd ask her dad again about this when the time was right. Perhaps it had been because she wasn't married. Or perhaps there was something else. It sounded like it when he'd said, 'It would've hurt too much.' She couldn't imagine letting her own daughter give birth to a brand new human life by herself. She would've wanted to be there, holding Aria's hand, helping afterwards, taking the baby so she could sleep. Giving her advice and letting her know everything would be okay. Having a newborn was a steep learning curve and a mother's love and advice would make such a difference.

'I don't understand,' she whispered as she continued to stare at her sleeping daughter.

She snapped a couple of pictures on her mobile for Tori, but because there was no mobile reception out here she'd have to wait until she was next in Barker to send them.

Seeking some cooler air, Chelsea went into the sitting room and flopped on the couch, her legs over the side and her head resting on the arm. Even though there had only been three of them for Christmas lunch, it felt like she'd cooked for twenty! Maybe the late night and emotion had something to do with the tiredness she was feeling.

Closing her eyes, she reflected on the time she'd been here. Other than the concern about her dad, she'd enjoyed the space, the openness. Not the heat. Definitely not the heat. But it cooled down some evenings and the mornings were, while not cold, at least fresh. She remembered how her mother used to get up before dawn and get as many outside jobs done as she could. 'No point being out there in the heat of the day,' she'd always said.

She remembered her dad getting up early too. Heading off in the ute to shift or feed sheep before it was too hot. He'd told her it was easier to muster the ewes while they were out feeding and getting a drink than when they were camped under the trees at midday.

Often he'd come in smelling of sweat and covered in dust, and Pip would hand him a cold drink of homemade lemon cordial and a cold wet flannel to help cool him down. As Dale had begun to do more work on the farm, she'd started the same routine with him too.

Looking back, it was clear how much Pip had cared for them. Chelsea sighed, wondering what had made her change. Dale's death had had such an impact on both her parents. They'd withdrawn into themselves for sure, but it was before then. The arguments they'd had when she'd come home from the Conservatorium were furious. Pip had accused her of not making the most of the opportunities she'd been given. Told her how disappointed she was with Chelsea's attitude.

The Conservatorium had been challenging for Chelsea and she probably hadn't handled it the way her mum would've liked. Being thrust into routine and strictness, when she'd been used to the freedom of the farm, had made life unbearable in the first few years. There had been so many times she'd picked up the phone and rung her mum and dad, begging to be allowed to come back, only to be met with: 'Come on, Chelsea, this is what you wanted. We've sacrificed a lot for you to have this opportunity. You must keep at it.'

Then the bullying had started. 'You won't make it in this world, Chelsea,' one of the girls had said to her. 'You're too unsophisticated. You've been raised with dust and sheep shit under your fingernails. No matter how good you are, you'll never be able to make it on stage. You just don't have the finesse.' After that, she'd been ostracised, and the taunts had become increasingly vicious.

Chelsea had withdrawn deeper into herself. She'd wanted to write to Lily and tell her everything, but she couldn't bring herself to do it. She wouldn't let anyone know that this whole music game was harder than she'd ever imagined. But she couldn't give up; her mum wouldn't let her. So she did the only thing she could: ignored the hurt every time the bullies said anything; ignored the disapproval that radiated from her mother; and ignored the tutors who were pushing her towards becoming a classical performer rather than the free-spirited musician she wanted to be.

She'd started to rebel against the confines of the Conservatorium. The complaints to her parents arrived thick and fast. When she was fifteen had been crunch time. Her mother was called to Adelaide at the end of first term and the principal had issued them both with an ultimatum: 'Chelsea, you have to shape up or ship out.'

Pip hadn't said anything to her on the way home. Chelsea remembered arriving home to bare ground, heat beyond hell-hot and skinny sheep. It had been the worst drought Tom and Pip had ever seen, and Chelsea was reminded almost every day of how they had gone back into debt for her and now there was no way of making money because they'd had to sell all their sheep, save the core breeding ewes. And now they were nearly broke. It was not said aloud but Chelsea heard the 'because of you' at the end of every sentence.

Chelsea had been glad to get back to the Conservatorium after those holidays. To play and forget everything else. This time she worked hard, harder than any of the other students, and because of this she often wasn't available when phone calls from her parents came. She rarely returned them. Chelsea protected her heart and feelings by becoming abrupt and rude, demanding the best of herself and of other performers around her.

She became a person she'd never wanted to be nor thought she ever would be. Her strained relationship with her parents had never got back on track, then Dale had died and it couldn't be salvaged.

Aria let out a little groan in her sleep and the thought of his kind present brought Cal and his comments about her dad to mind again. What could she do to help? Realistically, she was the only family he had left, so she couldn't not help. Her dad had sacrificed a lot for her and it was time for her to return the favour.

Cal's question earlier had got her thinking in a different way—was there some chance she'd like to stay at Shandona?

A note from the piano sounded, then another and another. Opening an eye, she stayed exactly where she was when she saw her dad sitting on the stool, his hands on the keys. He couldn't know she was there.

The tune he was trying to play was 'Red River Valley'—it had been one of her mum's favourites, but it was clear her dad couldn't quite remember the notes.

She coughed slightly, to make him aware she was on the couch; the music didn't stop but the keys were pushed down with more force and the notes jarred as he hit the wrong ones. Chelsea closed her eyes and tried to imagine the score in her head. Not that she needed to; more it was for an overview of the notes. Holding her hands up in the air, she pressed her fingers down onto imaginary keys and heard the whole tune playing in her mind. It was an easy piece.

For a little while she watched her dad try to find the right notes. He was becoming increasingly frustrated. Chelsea had an inkling of how her mum might have felt on the side of a netball court, calling out instructions to her. Maybe she'd experienced the frustration Chelsea was feeling with her dad now. It wasn't a difficult piece, so why couldn't he get the notes right?

Getting up quietly, she went and sat beside him. He jumped, then started to get up.

'Don't,' he said. 'I—'

'Stay,' Chelsea said quietly. 'Let's see if we can figure this out together.'

Carefully she touched the right keys. 'Here,' placing his fingers where hers had just been. Then she began to hum the tune as she pushed his fingers down in time to what she was humming.

'*From this valley they say you are leaving* . . .' Tom started to sing quietly. As he did so, it was as if all the notes fell into place. Then he made a mistake, touching two notes side by side. They made a harsh clashing noise, and Tom frowned, testing another key for a different note.

'Try the beginning again,' Chelsea suggested. 'Here and here.' Again, she placed his fingers on the keys and started to hum.

'*From this valley they say you are leaving* . . .'

His fingers moved of their own accord to each different note and chord. This time there were no mistakes and he started on the second line.

'*We will miss your bright eyes and sweet smile* . . .'

Chelsea broke into a smile as this time he didn't falter once through the whole verse. She nodded in time and sung with him softly until he'd played the whole song.

When he finished, he started the piece again.

'I don't want to forget,' he said quietly, looking at his fingers as they moved across the keyboard.

Chelsea got up from the stool and went to stand against the wall. Even though Tom was remembering all the notes, he was jittery, and the way he pushed the keys down was edgy rather than gliding, the way her old teacher Mrs Maher had shown her. But that was okay; she guessed it was a while since her dad had sat down at the piano. She'd been a bit edgy when she'd first laid her fingers on the keys a few days ago, after three months' break.

Her dad started from the beginning for the third time.

Not wanting to interrupt, she walked over to the bookshelves that lined one wall of the room, and looked through the titles, hoping there was something she could read. The Billabong series she wanted to read to Aria was still missing; maybe the books had ended up in here.

The first shelf was filled with the biographies her mum had liked to read: John Howard, Frank McCourt, Maya Angelou. Her dad liked westerns and they filled the next shelf. Then there were novels: mysteries and crime.

The piano still played; she'd lost count of how many times Tom had played 'Red River Valley' now.

She wasn't sure she could read something dark at the moment. She needed something light and happy. A laugh-out-loud book. Something like *Bridget Jones's Diary*.

A cover depicting the back of a naked man lying in bed caught her attention. At first glance she thought it was Cal, then she mentally slapped herself. As if he'd be on the cover of a novel. And why was she even thinking like that anyway?

She was intrigued as to why this book was sitting on her mum's bookshelf when she'd never usually read that sort of thing.

When she looked at the title she raised her eyebrows in astonishment. *The Man Who Made Husbands Jealous*. When she saw the word 'bonking' in the blurb, she had to stifle a giggle. *Oh my God!* she thought. *Mum, really?*

Shooting a quick glance at her dad, she wondered if he knew there was a raunchy novel in the bookshelf of his very conservative home. It looked like the perfect book for her right now, so she tucked it under her arm.

She realised the piano playing had stopped. Turning around, she saw Tom watching her.

'Do you remember it now?' she asked.

He nodded. 'I used to play it all the time,' he said. 'For Granda Baxter. All those American folk songs, he loved them. Never understood why when we have great folk songs over here but, still, that was him.'

'"Clementine" and "Oh! Susanna". We used to sing them to him.'

'And "Home On The Range"!'

Chelsea smiled at the memories—they were good ones.

'Wait here. I've got something for you.' Tom got up from the piano and left the room.

Wondering what it was, Chelsea lay back down on the couch and flicked through the novel. The naughtiness of it grabbed her attention and she was giggling to herself when Tom came back in the room again, holding a box. It was larger than the one which contained her mother's funeral cards, and she could see from the way her dad was carrying it that the box was heavy.

'You asked why,' was all he said as he handed it to her. 'Maybe you'll understand now.'

Chapter 17

'Here you are, Mr Oakes,' Kim said, handing the elderly man a tray. 'You've got prawns in a mango salad for entrée, roast chicken and pork, veggies and gravy for main, and a piece of pav for dessert. Dave is bringing it in now.'

'Thank you, lassie. Sounds just like the Christmas dinners me ma used to make, 'cept we never got prawns. If we were lucky there might be a few yabbies around, but not real often.'

'I know! But prawns are just so nice they're hard to leave off the menu these days—especially now they're easier to get. We're lucky that Ashley Binder from over in Port Pirie donated them to us this year. It's really great when stores do that.'

'That country spirit.' With shaking hands, Mr Oakes took the serviette Kim offered him and tucked it into his collar, before lifting the plastic lid from the entrée.

Dave came in with another tray and opened the fridge. 'G'day, Mr Oakes. Got a pretty big piece of pav waiting for you right after you finish what's on your tray there.'

'It's a wonder you're not the size of a house the way your wife cooks, young man!'

'Yeah, she's pretty good at it.' Dave looked around at the pictures on the wall. They showed a group of young men dressed in jeans and bright shirts, wearing large hats and sunglasses. 'Your grandsons?' he asked.

Mr Oakes looked up with a reflective expression on his face. 'Sure are. Different to my generation, let me tell you.'

Dave laughed. 'I hear that all the time. You farmed?'

'Oh yeah. Broke me heart when I had to leave and come into town. Especially when my head was still all right. Just me body which was giving up. The family got a bit concerned about me all the way out there on me own. Legs are no good,' he said, patting his wasted thighs. 'Me dear old girl passed away in her sleep five years ago, so it was time for me to go. Miss the paddocks and me dog,' he told them.

'Where was your place?' Dave asked, still examining the photos. The country looked similar to Tom Taylor's.

'About twenty miles east of Barker. Where the deep gorges run with water when it rains and the hills are high. I tell you, we had some interesting times mustering that country. Rocks and steep hills. We'd muster on horses. We were hard on them though.'

'Pretty country out through there,' Dave said as Kim washed the few dishes sitting in the sink and listened to them chat. He saw her glance at her watch and he guessed she was thinking about the next delivery, but risked another question anyway.

'Hard on the horses how?'

'Rabbit holes and ankles don't go well together.'

'Oh, I see what you mean. Yeah, real *Man from Snowy River* stuff, except in the Flinders Ranges. Do you know if there used to be cameleer trains throughout that area sixty or so years ago?' He heard Kim sigh quietly. She knew he wouldn't be able to help but ask, just in case this elderly man had some information that would assist him in identifying the remains.

'Oh, that's a long time ago. But, yeah, there was them and other men who had horses and drays and would sell things off the back. They'd turn up at the house and offer me mum socks and boots. Maybe a pair of overalls. But there wasn't any money back then, so sometimes we'd get something but more often than not we didn't.

'Sometimes,' Mr Oakes pushed himself up in his chair, his face animated. 'Sometimes, people would steal things off the back. Usually most people were honest back then, but sometimes life was tough and women'd try and grab a few extra spuds or a bag of sugar without them seeing. Specially during the Depression years.'

'That would've caused a few upsets.'

'It did, that's for sure.'

'Anyone ever get murdered because of that?'

The old man's eyebrows shot up. 'Murder? You betcha! No rules back then. Anything and everything happened.'

He picked up the fork and speared a prawn. 'Anyways, you two had better be off and finish the rest of the deliveries, hadn't you?' He leaned forwards and sniffed the food. 'I tell you, Kim, this is going to be the best Christmas dinner I've had in years, even if me girl didn't cook it.'

'I hope so,' Kim answered cheekily as she bent down to kiss his cheek. 'I'll be back tomorrow with leftovers for Boxing Day. Do you need anything else?'

'No, no. I'm fine. Thank you.'

Dave clapped him on the shoulder. 'Happy Christmas,' he said. 'Can I ask one more thing?'

Mr Oakes stopped with a prawn halfway to his mouth. 'I feel like I'm being interviewed.'

'More like a curiosity question.'

'Fire away then.' He waved the fork around as an indication for Dave to continue.

'Do you remember there ever being a death of any kind up around the reserve on Taylor's property?'

The faded blue eyes focused on Dave. 'Now why would you be asking about such a specific area?'

Dave dug into his pocket and brought out his phone. 'We found this in the ground up there. Have you ever seen anything like it before?'

Mr Oakes put down his fork and reached for the phone. 'Are you ever off duty?'

Kim muttered a good-natured 'humph' and put her arm around Dave's waist. 'Not likely,' she answered for him.

'And you found this up on the reserve area, you say?'

'Yeah, it was buried up there.' Dave held his breath, hoping the old man would say it belonged to his grandmother or something else that would make his job easy! But he knew that was unlikely.

Mr Oakes shook his head. 'How the hell did you find that then? There are millions of acres out there and you just happened to stumble across this piece of jewellery?' His watery eyes regarded Dave curiously.

'We were called out there for another reason. This just happened to come to the surface—excuse the pun!—while we were looking at something else.'

Mr Oakes handed the phone back. 'Can't say I've ever seen anything like that before. Wish I'd been able to give it to my girl. She liked pretty things, but I couldn't afford many of them.'

'We're all like that, Mr Oakes,' Kim said with a laugh. 'Anyway, we'd better get on. Have a few other deliveries to make yet.'

'Yes, yes, be away with you. Hurry home to enjoy your own Christmas lunch. Happy Christmas!'

Out in the car, Kim leaned across and gave Dave's thigh a gentle slap. 'Are you going to interrogate every one of my clients?' she asked. 'If you are, then I don't think I'll take you with me again.'

Dave held up his hands in protest. 'Hey, just making the most of a useful situation. Never know what you might get out of an oldie. Look at how I solved the one last year with the help from the minister's diaries.'

'And you were hoping you were going to solve the mystery right then and there, weren't you?'

Winking at her, he asked where they were going next.

❧

After the deliveries were all finished, they headed home to enjoy the spread that Kim had prepared before they'd left that morning.

Their lunch was different—cold crayfish and salad and a couple of glasses of wine.

'What did Mandy and Dean and the rest of the family do today?' Kim asked as she pushed a small mouthful of cray onto her fork.

'They were at the hospital. Dean hasn't been allowed out yet.'

'Yuck, hospital food for Christmas lunch.'

'I'm sure Mum would've taken something nice in though. Christmas lunch when I was growing up was all about roast turkey, veggies and Christmas pudding. I bet she still made a pudding.' Dave winked at Kim and reached for his glass of wine. 'Sometimes I reckon all you think about is food.'

Kim gave him a smouldering look. 'Not all the time.'

'Hmm, crayfish or you?' Dave said, getting up from the table. 'I don't think there's a choice.' He held his hand out to her, and she stood up and they headed to the bedroom.

❧

Later, as they were doing the dishes together, Kim's mobile rang.

'Hello, Mr Oakes, is everything okay?' she asked, putting the phone on loudspeaker while she dried her hands on a tea towel. Dave had rinsed out the sink and was moving on to wipe down the bench.

'Fine, fine. Lovely dinner. Thank you,' Mr Oakes responded. 'You're a very good cook, Kim.'

'Thank you.' She paused, wondering what he wanted.

'Is your policeman friend there?'

Her eyes flicked across to Dave. 'He sure is. I'll just pass you over.' Holding out the phone, she cocked her head at him with a half-smile. 'Looks like you're back on duty,' she said, and took the sponge out of his hand.

'Dave Burrows here, Mr Oakes,' Dave said, taking the phone and walking into their home office.

'You asked about a death up on the reserve.'

Grabbing a notebook and pen, he said, 'Yeah, I did. Do you know something?'

'Well, my mum told me an old story once. Not sure if it's true, but I thought I'd better pass it on. Goes back to the early 1900s, when the travelling hawkers used to go through. There was a family living on the reserve; lived in a semi-permanent shanty village. They had canvas tents and a fire pit that was always going. Mum said she could smell the smoke most afternoons when the wind blew from the north. There was a freshwater well there, so they had a constant supply, which made it easy for them to stay put. There were a few chooks and goats for meat and eggs. Almost like a farmyard.'

Dave made a few notes and turned to the computer to bring up the Trove website. 'How long did they live there?' he asked.

'Oh, mate, I dunno. Like I said, this was just me mum's story. But the thing about it was, everyone was a bit wary of them. The fella that lived there, rumour had it that he was being chased by police for a murder in New South Wales.'

'A murder?' Dave's fingers hovered above the keyboard.

'Yes, sir. According to my mother, he was a nasty piece of work, beating dogs and women alike. Anyway, one day they just weren't there. Up and left, just like that. No word about where they were going or why.

'Two days later the police rode into our farm. I was real little, but I remember the mounted troopers coming.

'When I was older and Mum told me this story, she said they wanted the man for questioning in relation to two shootings. One in Broken Hill where the man fired a gun at a young lad. He was left on the main street picking shotgun pellets out of his leg.'

Dave blew out a breath.

'And the other one. A girl. Her throat had been slit.'

'Slit? Was she related to him, or his wife?' To Dave that sounded like a crime of passion.

'Mother said it was his daughter. That'd she'd seen him do something real bad and threatened to dob him in to the coppers, so he got rid of her.'

Nothing surprised Dave anymore, but the thought of a father murdering his own daughter horrified him. 'Can you remember the name of this family, or would there be records anywhere?'

'Nah, I just remember the story. It's a long time ago now and most of the people would be dead.'

'Any letters or diaries from your parents still around?'

'Me parents couldn't write.'

Damn. Actually, that didn't surprise Dave. When he'd met Mr Oakes this morning, he'd assessed him as the sort of bloke who'd sign a cheque then turn it around for the shopkeeper to fill in the amount. His formal education would have been sparse but his life experiences rich.

'Well, I've got to say, that's all really interesting.'

'Does it help with your piece of jewellery?' Mr Oakes asked hopefully.

'I'll have to do a bit of research, but any information about the reserve is going to be useful.' Not sure how useful, Dave thought, but any information was good at the moment, when he had nothing.

'What about other neighbours, can you remember if they're the same families that are around now?'

'That's testing me memory a bit. Back then, people were transient. Not people who owned land as such—although there are farms in the area which are fifth generation owned. But life's no different to today. If they didn't pay their bills, they got kicked off. Or not even that. Some of them just walked away when they couldn't afford to stay. Workers would drift in and out and, like we talked about before, there were the merchants. And the swaggies and the shearers. Transient, as I said.'

Dave nodded, then he realised Mr Oakes couldn't see him. 'I've heard of that happening.' He paused. 'What about the Taylor family? Were they on Shandona back then?'

'Now that was owned by Evelyn and Leo, wasn't it?'

'If their son was Tom, then yes.'

'Yeah, I know of Tom. Evelyn was older'n me. But my she was pretty. Not as pretty as my girl, but pretty. And Leo seemed like a good solid farmer. We used to play tennis together on Sunday afternoons. Had a pretty good social crowd, but we never caught up anymore'n that.'

Dave waited until he'd heard the whole of the farming biography before he asked again, 'So the family owned and lived on Shandona back in the early 1900s? When these other people were living on the reserve?'

A low hissing came down the line as Mr Oakes was silent for a moment, before saying, 'You know what, there was a fight about that reserve. I remember it now. Me dad and ma, they got all worried about it. Gawd, I'd forgotten all about it.

'The Taylor family got some kind of long-term lease from the government. Dunno how it worked, but it was ninety-nine years and a peppercorn lease.

'I reckon there was a fight between the Taylors and this family who was camping on the reserve, with old man Taylor trying to get 'em off it.'

'What type of a fight?'

'Fight as in he asked them to leave and they wouldn't. P'haps incident is a better word. I don't remember hearing anything about it getting physical or anything but I mightn't've heard about that. Remember, I was just a whippersnapper back then. But,' he lowered his voice conspiratorially, 'what I did used to do is, when there was something different going on and Ma and Dad were talking about it, after us kids had gone to bed, I'd sneak out and listen. They never saw me. That's how I heard so much. But I don't remember there being anything said about him hurting them, but he certainly threatened them. He wanted them off his land.

'Funny, though,' he continued. 'They never seemed like the type of people to back down from a fight.'

'And then one day the squatters just weren't there?' Dave asked.

'Yeah, just like that.'

Chapter 18

Chelsea had spent the last hour looking at the box her father had given her, wondering what secrets were inside. What answers did it hold? And did she want to find out?

Tori said that when it came to someone's secrets it was sometimes kinder not to know about them. The trouble was that Chelsea knew there was at least one secret her mum had kept, because her dad had said she'd understand one day. Now was that day if she chose to open the lid on the box. Would it make any difference now? Would it bring any peace?

With shaking hands, she opened the lid and looked inside. On the top there was a journal, which she took out and laid on the bed. Then there was a photo album and another journal. One by one, she laid them next to each other. Three small jewellery boxes and four large scrapbooks, a plastic folder full of documents. The cover was clear and the paper on top was her parents' marriage certificate.

Thomas Leo Taylor married Philippa Teresa Kent on the 21st of May 1980 at the Barker Church, South Australia.

She looked underneath it and saw a death certificate.

Name: Philippa Teresa Taylor
Place of Birth: Jamestown Hospital
Date of Birth: 6th March 1955
Date of Death: 19th August 2015
Place of Death: Shandona Farm, Hunter Road, Barker,
   South Australia
Cause of Death: Heart failure
Married: Yes
Date of Marriage: 21st May 1980
Spouse: Thomas Leo Taylor
Children (Living): Chelsea Philippa Taylor (Born: 15th
   September 1988)
Children (Deceased): Dale Baxter Taylor (Born: 9th June
   1982 – Death: Dec. 5th January 2006)
Crystal Grace Taylor (Born: 29th June 1984 – Death:
   Dec. 29th June 1984)
Andrew John Taylor (Born: 4th June 1986 – Death: Dec.
   4th June 1986)

Carefully, Chelsea put the page down on the bed and reread it to make sure she hadn't made a mistake.

There were two other children on the death certificate Chelsea had never heard of. How did they die?

Getting up, she went to find her dad. She was going to ask. It was time they sat down and discussed everything; from her decision to go to the Conservatorium to these babies, Dale's death, the reason she didn't get home for the funeral. She'd already explained that, but she was almost sure he hadn't taken it in or remembered.

'Dad?'

Aria was still asleep on the floor and her hat had fallen to one side. Picking it up, she placed it gently on the sleeping girl's face and went in search of her father. There was no answer when she called out at the door of his bedroom and she'd already looked in the office.

Outside, the sun was beginning to sink below the hills surrounding the house, casting long dark shadows across the gumtree-lined creeks. The range glowed a dark purple, getting deeper with the sun's movement towards the horizon. Out near the hills, there was a haze of dust, rising skywards, as the sheep came into the troughs for their nightly drink. Today's heat must have finally dried the land out enough for the dust to be raised.

Other than the occasional sheep baaing and galah calls, Chelsea couldn't hear anything. With Scout alongside her, she walked towards Cal's house, wondering if he was home yet. Then she saw the motorbike was missing from the garage. Her dad had obviously gone to check a trough. He'd mentioned earlier that he'd have to and, without Aria, the bike would have been quicker and easier.

Tonight it would be nice to have someone to talk to. A friend. Just to ask whether, if it were them, would they read the journals in the box. Tori's words had echoed in her ears since she'd opened it. 'Sometimes you're better off not knowing.'

And these children who were her brother and sister . . . She shook her head, unable to believe she didn't know about them. Why wouldn't her mum have told her she'd had other children who hadn't survived?

The spot where Cal usually parked his vehicle was empty, so she assumed he was still with his family. Did he have to work tomorrow? She wasn't sure but she assumed not.

Her dad used to settle in and watch the Boxing Day cricket Test, so maybe he'd do that again and Cal wouldn't come home tonight.

She continued to walk down towards the house dam, past the poly-tank and machinery sheds. The ground was stony and the thongs she was wearing were proving unsuitable. As she bent down to pull a stick out from under her toe, she realised her whole foot was purple from the dust on the road.

The corners of her mouth lifted upwards because, for once, it felt like home.

❧

It was dark by the time she returned to the house to find Aria curled up watching a Christmas movie on TV, her hat on her head.

'I lost you!' Aria said. 'I couldn't find you or Scout. Or Papa.'

'I was outside, going for a walk. I didn't plan to be gone this long. You okay?'

Aria nodded.

'Thought you would be. Are you hungry? It's almost teatime.'

'My tummy is still full!'

Chelsea laughed. 'Well, how about a bit of cold meat and bread? Or should we just wait until Papa comes home?'

'Wait.'

'Okay. We'll wait.'

The items on her bed were pulling her back towards her room and she wondered if she could look at a couple more things before she had to get tea, but the phone rang then, the outside bell announcing the call. She wondered if she should let the answering machine pick up but decided against it and went into her father's office.

'Hello?'

'Chelsea?'

Chelsea frowned, no one would be calling her here. None of her Sydney friends had the number for Shandona. She hadn't been and still wasn't keen to talk to anyone.

'Yes,' she answered cautiously.

'It's Lily.'

Relief flooded through her. 'Lily, hi. Merry Christmas.'

'Same to you. Had a nice day?'

'Hmm, it's been very quiet, but in a nice way. What about you?'

'It's been a great day! Busy, with the kids, but really enjoyable. Kids make Christmas, don't they?'

Chelsea stopped and thought about that. She remembered Christmas lunches with ten or fifteen people around the table. Aunties and uncles. Cousins and orphans. Orphans were people who didn't have anywhere else to go on the day. There were always two or three of them. There'd been laughter and high spirits around the table back then. Not the stilted silences of today.

'Yes, they do.'

'How's your dad?'

'He wasn't too bad today,' Chelsea answered, realising that apart from his piano playing, he had been pretty good. He'd laughed with Aria and pulled the crackers with her, helping with her paper crown. He'd read out the terrible jokes in a playful voice, laughing loudly at the punchlines. There hadn't been any memory lapses that she'd noticed.

And the piano—well, it was easy enough to forget the notes to a song if you hadn't played it in years. 'He played the piano. I had to remind him of the right notes, but that was okay. In fact, he was happy I helped him, I think. Do you remember how we always used to sing when you came out here and stayed overnight?'

'Yeah. And how we used to watch *Rage* on Saturday mornings and we'd try and copy the dances from the video clips?'

Chelsea could hear the smile in her voice.

'Yeah, I do! What about that song . . .' she hummed a few bars. 'What was it?'

'"All I Wanna Do Is Make Love To You" by Heart,' Lily said quickly.

'That's it! I remember singing that at the tops of our voices. God knows what Mum thought about the lyrics! They've got a whole new meaning now we've grown up.'

Lily giggled. 'I know. But we had fun around the piano too. If it wasn't you belting it out on the piano, it was your dad. And you'd get annoyed when he hogged it for too long!'

'Then Mum would turn up with netball exercises and try to get us to go outside and practise.' A thought struck her. 'Tell me you don't make your kids play netball?'

Lily laughed. 'None of my kids are old enough yet, but no, I'll never force them to play. Every time I go to a sports day and I hear a mum yelling "Run faster!" or "Come on, you're better than that!", I see your mum.'

'I know, right? Alongside that netball court, running up and down. "Come on, Chels, Lily's there. Share the ball around, girls! Oh, come on! You can do better than that!"' She took a breath. 'I hated it.'

'All the other girls loved her enthusiasm. And her.'

'As you and I know, I'm not all the other girls. Never have been.'

'No,' Lily answered quietly. 'Nope, you're certainly not.'

'Lily, did you go to my mum's funeral?' Chelsea stood looking out the window into the darkness. The birds had stopped talking with the sun's setting and now the crickets had taken over, their loud chirps echoing around the river. The leaves of the gums lifted and fell in time with the gentle breeze.

'Yeah, I did.' Lily's voice grew quieter. 'You didn't.' It was a statement rather than a question. Of course Lily knew she hadn't gone.

'No.' Chelsea looked down at the floor.

'Do you want to tell me why?'

'Would it make any difference? I'm sure you've already got an opinion, like the rest of town.'

'That's not true. All I know is you weren't there. Your dad was distraught, but Cal was there to help him. I'm sure you had your reasons.'

'I feel like everyone judges me; they do, don't they? I saw their looks at the pageant. I'd been hoping . . .' Her voice broke unexpectedly, but she charged on. 'I'd been hoping it would be different. That I could come home and feel like Barker really was my home. But I can't. Everything is so familiar but so strange. Dad is different, the town is different, so are you. Shandona is the only place I feel at home. Even here, sometimes I do and sometimes I don't. I don't really know why I thought I could just slot back in.'

'Of course we're different. We've all had things happen to us that have altered who we are. And we've grown up.' Lily took a breath. 'You sound so lost, Chels. I've missed you.'

Swallowing the lump in her throat, Chelsea said, 'I've missed you too,' and she was surprised when she realised she meant it.

'The funeral was lovely as funerals go,' Lily told her after they'd both got their emotions under control. 'There was a wreath of roses, I think they were yellow, and a photo of her on the coffin. It was of her sitting in one of the creeks.'

'The same as the one on the order of service?'

'Yeah. That's it. I think most of the community came— probably at least four hundred people. I know it was one of the larger ones the town has had.'

'What building houses that many people?' Chelsea wondered aloud as she sat down on the couch to listen.

'It was held in the town hall. You've got to remember, it wasn't just the netball club Pip was involved in. There was the tennis club and more recently she'd started up a squash club from scratch. She'd raised the money to build the court and organised everything almost singlehandedly. And don't forget the bowls club.'

'Bowls?' Then she remembered what her dad had told her about that night—he'd been at bowls.

'Bowls,' Lily confirmed. 'Every Tuesday night when pennants were on, she'd be down there competing or working behind the bar. So, all of those people went, along with the farming community. It was packed.'

Chelsea glanced over at Aria, who was still sitting on the couch watching TV, so she started to walk out of the room. 'Um, where . . . where is she buried?' Her voice was low.

There was a shocked silence. 'Haven't you talked to your dad about any of this?'

'No.' From her tone, Chelsea could tell Lily was incredulous. She didn't bother to defend her actions. This was her oldest friend. She hoped there'd be no judgement. 'No, not at all. He hasn't been at all open towards me and we haven't got to this particular conversation yet. Oh, there're times when I see a glimpse of who he was before Dale died, but he's a closed book mostly. Doesn't let anyone in or talk about anything emotional. In fact, he's still angry with me, which is probably why he's not talking much.

'But, on the upside, he's given me a cardboard box full of journals and other memorabilia and told me I should have a look at them. I think the problems go back to when I was being ratty at the Conservatorium. I've never told you, Lily, but I think Mum blamed me for nearly sending them broke. They had to borrow more money to send me there and then I didn't work as hard as I should've and we never got back on track from there. I was distant, so was she. Dale died and that was it.' She paused. 'But what if there's more in the box? Another reason?'

'God, Chels. Have you looked at it?'

Chelsea shook her head, then rolled her eyes at herself. 'No. Not yet.'

She jumped as there was a loud banging on the door. 'Shit!' Her hand flew to her chest and she ran towards the sound.

'What?'

'There's someone here.' Holding the phone, she reached the door and pulled it open. It was Cal.

'Hi,' he said with a smile, which disappeared when he saw her face. 'Are you okay?'

'Yeah, yeah, fine. Just got a fright. I wasn't expecting anyone at the door!'

'Hello, Cal.' Aria appeared at her mother's side, smiling up at him.

'Well, hello there, little lady. How was your Christmas?'

As Aria excitedly told Cal all about her day, Chelsea promised to ring Lily back and ended the phone call. She put the phone back in the cradle and waited until Aria had stopped chattering, then asked how Cal's day had been.

'Nice,' he replied. 'All my family were there for lunch. Mum cooked up the usual feast. Sounds like you guys had a good one too.' He indicated to Aria. 'So I was just looking for your dad.'

Chelsea glanced at her watch; it was nearly nine o'clock. 'The motorbike's gone, so I assumed he was out checking sheep.'

Cal's forehead creased into a deep frown. 'In the dark?'

'Uh, well,' Chelsea stumbled as she realised there was a problem. 'He left in the light.'

'If he's not back now, something's wrong. Come on.'

Chapter 19

The spotlights from the ute picked up the green glow of the sheep's eyes and encouraged every moth and midge within a kilometre radius to bomb the globes. Cal swung the ute from side to side, creating an arc of light, hoping to catch a reflection of Tom's bike, but there were so many places to look. Thirty-five square kilometres of land and not just flat country. It was rugged and hilly and covered with acacia trees, which hid everything from kangaroos and emus to cars that had run off the road, much less a motorbike. There were so many little dips and gullies, Tom could have been anywhere.

'What time did he leave?' Cal asked, keeping his tone casual so as not to alarm Aria any more than she already was.

'I don't really know,' Chelsea answered, her voice tight. 'It might've been four o'clock or a bit later.'

'And it's after nine now.'

Chelsea felt a soft little hand slip into hers. 'Mummy, I'm scared,' she said.

'I'm a little bit scared too, honey, but I'm sure there's nothing too much to be worried about. Papa knows this country like the back of his hand so it's probably something simple. Maybe he's got a flat tyre on the motorbike and he's walking home.' She saw Cal glance at her and knew instantly that wasn't what he was thinking.

'Has he, uh, shown any tendencies to, um . . .' She let the sentence fade in the hope Cal would pick up on her meaning. Aria didn't need to hear the question. When he didn't answer, she added, 'Especially since Mum died?' Maybe he'd given her the box and, with that done, it was time to end all of his sadness and pain.

Cal cleared his throat. 'Not that I know of.'

Chelsea picked up the two-way mic and put another call out: 'Tom Taylor, are you on channel?'

The static hissed back at her.

Reaching down, Cal flicked the channels over. 'Call the McKenzies. See if they'll come out and help us look.'

'Names?'

'Colleen and Hec.'

Chelsea did as she was asked and waited for a reply.

'Hec here, who'm I talking to?'

'It's Chelsea Taylor, Hec. My father is missing, and Cal and I are out trying to find him. We were hoping for a few extra vehicles.'

There was a pause. 'No worries. I'll head out now. Colleen will ring around for some more neighbours. Have you got a child with you, Chelsea? Is she out with you?'

Chelsea's head snapped back. How did . . . ?

'It's a small area,' Cal said, seeing her reaction.

'Ah, yes,' she answered, looking at Aria, who was peering through the windscreen.

'Tell Cal to meet Colleen at the ramp going over the main road and she'll take her home.' His tone brooked no argument, and all Chelsea felt was relief. There was no way she wanted Aria with them when they found her dad. Even if he only had a broken ankle or had got lost again.

Cal directed the ute back onto the road.

'I want to stay with you, Mummy,' Aria said as she registered what was happening.

'I think you'd be better with Colleen, honey. It might take us all night to find Papa and it's past your bedtime by a long way.'

Aria looked close to tears.

'Colleen is a beaut lady, Aria,' said Cal. 'She's heard all about you from your Papa and she makes yummy scones and custards. Plus she's got heaps of grandkids, so she knows what kids like. You'll have a lot of fun with her.'

'Has she got colouring-in books?'

'I bet she has. Probably with the coolest colouring pencils.'

'You'll come back and get me, Mummy?' Aria said with panic in her voice.

'Of course I will! As soon as we find Papa. But, honey, if it's really late when we find him, it might be better if I let you sleep there and pick you up tomorrow. Okay?'

'Okay.' But Aria didn't sound happy about it.

By the time they arrived at the ramp, there were five utes there. In the spotlight glow, she could see they were all old grey Toyota traybacks—some had spotlights on the roof and others on the bullbar. There was one with a mattress in the back and instantly Chelsea knew that would be a bed for her dad if he was injured and they had to take him to hospital.

The four men were in a circle around the bonnet of one of the utes, a map opened out in front of them. It was obvious they were discussing how to stage the search. Just out of the light, a grey-haired woman was leaning against a fence-post, listening to the men talk. As the lights of the ute flashed onto her, Chelsea saw she was holding a black kitten.

'That's Colleen,' Cal said, inclining his head towards her.

'Come on, Aria,' Chelsea said, getting out of the ute and taking her daughter's hand. 'Looks like she's got a special friend for you.'

After some quick introductions, Colleen handed the kitten to Aria, whose face lit up with wonder. Chelsea gave her a kiss goodbye, then Aria happily got into the car, settled the kitten on her lap and headed off to their homestead.

Chelsea just looked at the group of men, not sure if she should go over and join them, but the decision was taken out of her hands when Cal called her over.

'You all remember Chelsea,' Cal introduced her.

'Good to see you again. I'm Hec.' The tall sandy-haired man held his hand out to her, while the others nodded and smiled at her.

Somehow she felt accepted, even if she didn't know everyone's names.

'Right, Chelsea, can you tell us the last time you saw Tom and what sort of mood he was in?'

Chelsea ran her hands over her face as she thought about his state of mind. 'We'd had a nice Christmas Day and I thought he was okay. Peaceful, even. I'd been helping him remember a song on the piano and then he'd given me a box with a heap of Mum's things in it.' She paused. 'He didn't seem upset or angry. Just matter of fact. I know he said he had some troughs to check but he didn't say where.'

The men nodded.

'Okay, well . . .' Hec directed two of the men to start at the reserve and work their way back to the homestead.

'Cal, you and Chelsea, I think go from the shearing shed, out to the hills and back down Blind Corner Road, okay? I brought a spotlight—do you want it?'

'Yep, Chelsea can get on the back and use it while I drive,' Cal answered, going back to the ute and popping the bonnet so he could connect the spotlight.

'Right, and Blake and I'll do the main road leading back to the house. Everyone got their two-ways on?'

'Sure have.'

'Yeah.'

'Make sure you stay in contact. If we haven't found Tom in the next couple of hours, we'd better ring the police. They can organise the SES then.'

For the first time, a trickle of fear ran through Chelsea. Despite her original question about Tom's state of mind, she'd just assumed they'd find him with a broken ankle or a flat tyre. Now she realised it could be a lot more serious. Again, the box jumped into her thoughts. Surely he wouldn't have given her the box with the thought that it contained all the answers and now he didn't need to be around anymore? Or even if he hadn't meant to hurt himself, he could've hit a roo, and doing that on a motor-bike meant serious injury, if not death.

'Please let him be okay,' she whispered to herself.

Cal showed her how to use the spotlight and what to look for. 'Anything reflective,' he said. 'So, look for a light or numberplate. Hopefully he was wearing a high-vis jacket. And make sure you keep an eye on the road too—there might be skid marks off to the side if he's tried to miss a roo. Anything that you think is weird. You can't be wrong in these circumstances.'

Chelsea nodded and climbed up on the back of the ute.

'Make sure you hang on, and if you see something, bang on the roof or yell through the window.' Cal's face was as serious as she'd ever seen it, so she nodded her understanding and flicked on the light, turning it from left to right and staring into the distance, desperate to see something.

❧

'Is this the time I bargain with you, God?' Chelsea asked two hours later, when no one had found any sign of him. 'If I promise never to leave him again, will you bring him back safely to me, to us?'

God didn't answer, and Chelsea clenched her jaw and let her tired arm drop onto the roof of the cab, giving it a small break from holding the light, which had, after two hours of searching, become surprisingly heavy.

The dust had been flicking up behind the wheels of the ute and swirling around, and she'd learned very quickly to keep her mouth shut lest bugs and dust ended up in there.

'Do you want to drive for a little while and have a break?' Cal called from the open window as he slowed down a little. 'I'm only driving because I know the country better.'

'No, it's okay,' she said, frustrated and a little teary. All they'd seen were countless kangaroos and emus, a stray horse and a couple of cars on the road, people who'd been driving home after Christmas Day. Both cars had stopped when Cal had flashed his lights at them and he'd explained the situation. Neither driver had seen anything untoward but had promised to keep an eye out.

'Cal, you on channel?'

Chelsea recognised the voice as Hec's and leaned in towards the window to listen.

'Yeah.'

'Can you head towards the old pump house over in Nine Mile Bore's river?'

Cal slammed his foot on the brake and Chelsea held on tight until they came to a complete stop. He tumbled out of the vehicle and ran to the front, popping the bonnet and disconnecting the spotlight. He told Chelsea to get in; they'd found Tom.

Chelsea jumped down and got into the passenger's seat, her heart pounding. 'They found him?' she asked.

'Yeah, at the old pump house.'

The drive was fast, and Chelsea was sure they hit every bump in the road. Old Toyotas didn't ride so smoothly and there was a spring that pressed into her behind with every pot-hole.

Please let him be okay, she said again, this time silently. *I won't leave him again. I'll find something to do here. I understand he needs family now.* Pause. *Please, God.*

She couldn't remember the last time she'd prayed. Maybe it was when she was in labour and the drugs hadn't taken the pain away. Or maybe it was when she finally received the message on her mobile phone, the sobbing message from her father saying her mother had died. Then the next one, yelling, 'Why haven't I heard from you? Where are you? How can you not answer?' And the last one with no emotion: 'We buried your mum today.' There had been a long pause before the message disconnected. It was if he'd wanted to say more but couldn't find the words.

From then on, she'd left messages, explaining what had happened: 'Dad, oh God, Dad, I'm sorry. Pick up the phone. Talk to me! I've been out of range for three months. On the cruise ship I've been working on. I didn't tell you I was going because I didn't want you to be disappointed in me. I've only just got your messages. Dad!'

As Cal continued to drive, the voices got louder in her head. She wanted to cover her ears and shake them away.

'Dad, it's me. Please pick up the phone.'

'Dad, um, I know you don't want to speak to me, but I'd like to talk to you. Could you please ring me back?'

'It's Chelsea. In case you've forgotten.'

Finally she'd stopped leaving messages, until Tori had convinced her to go home for Christmas. She had told Chelsea she'd never be content until she'd seen her dad. 'You've both got too many things to sort out, so go and do it. I bet you find your future will fall into place from there.'

'Dad, it's me, Chelsea. Aria and I are coming for Christmas. I hope that'll be okay . . .'

He'd picked up the phone then. There'd been a silence and heavy breathing as Chelsea's heart had smashed through her chest with nerves and anxiety. 'Dad?'

'Yes,' he'd said. 'That'll be okay.'

Chapter 20

Lights from five utes shone onto the pump house and Chelsea could see that one of the men was bending over a figure stretched out on the ground. She caught a glimpse of the motorbike nearby and let out a sigh of relief. From where she stood, it looked like an accident rather than anything more sinister.

'We don't know yet,' Cal said as if he'd read her mind.

'What?'

'We don't know what state he's in yet.' Negotiating the ute closer and directing the lights towards Tom, he left the engine running and got out. From behind the seat he pulled out a first-aid kit and jogged over with the same urgency that Chelsea felt.

She wanted to go running in and throw herself over her father, to talk to him and make sure he was okay, but the men had surrounded him and blocked out her view.

Muttered words filtered through the quiet night. 'Call the ambulance?'

'Probably quicker to take him in ourselves.'

'. . . neck or back injuries?'

'Conscious. Tom? Tom, can you hear us? It's Hec McKenzie.'

Chelsea couldn't stop herself now; she ran towards the group and pushed her way through. 'Dad?' She drew in a sharp gasp as she saw his injuries.

His face was bloodied and seemed to have gravel rash down the side, and his foot was at an unnatural angle. His right arm was bleeding as well. Cal grabbed hold of her arm and pulled her back.

'Let Hec deal with him first,' he instructed. 'He's a volunteer ambulance officer so he knows what he's doing.'

'But—'

'Leave him to do his job.' Cal pulled her into a strong hug. 'He's going to be fine,' he said against her hair, 'but let them be for the moment.'

Chelsea hadn't been hugged in so long, she leaned against Cal for a moment, taking strength from his lean body. It felt good to let someone share the weight of responsibility. Then she remembered Cal was her father's workman and somebody she hardly knew. Backing away from him slowly, she put up her hand as if to ward him off.

'I'll let them be,' she said softly and went to stand near the ute, even though she desperately wanted to stay in his arms.

Within half an hour, Hec had strapped Tom's ankle and cleaned up his head wounds, and the five men lifted him carefully into one of the ute trays. Putting him on a mattress, which was there for this exact purpose, one man covered him with a blanket. Hec climbed up and sat next to him, holding his wrist to check Tom's pulse. Chelsea went over and put her hand on her dad's shoulder.

'Dad? You'll be okay. We're taking you to hospital. I don't know if you can hear me, but hang in there, okay?'

'Righto, let's go,' Hec said. 'Follow us, Cal. We'll be quicker going like this than calling the ambulance out on Christmas night, which might not even be around. See you at the hospital. I wish I had a green whistle to give to him.'

'Green whistle?' Chelsea asked.

'It's a painkiller that ambos are allowed to hand out,' Cal told her.

'Oh. What about Aria?'

'I'll call Colleen and let her know what's going on when we get into mobile range,' Hec answered. 'She's better off staying where she is for the night. I'm sure you won't be back out here before daylight.'

Cal took her arm and led her back to the ute.

As they took off towards town Chelsea looked in the rear-vision mirror and saw the other men loading the motorbike onto the back of another ute.

'Shit! I didn't thank them,' she said.

'You can do it another time. They're not going anywhere.'

'I don't even know all their names.'

'Don't worry about it. I do.'

They drove in silence, Chelsea keeping her eyes to the front, never straying from the vehicle ahead of them.

'What do you think happened?' she asked after a while.

Cal sighed. 'Bit hard to tell, but I reckon he probably hit a rock and got thrown sideways. Reckon it's safe to say it wasn't deliberate though.'

'Do you think he's broken his ankle?'

'Yeah, and maybe his arm. He was conscious for a very short time, but I think the pain probably knocked him out again. But it's a good thing he recognised Hec. That shows no brain damage.'

'And you know this how?'

'He said Hec's name.'

Her heart had slowed, but the anxiety in her tummy was still there. 'Are you sure?'

Cal gave her a sideways glance. 'Ah, no. Nope, not sure. I'm trying to make you feel better.'

An hysterical giggle escaped from Chelsea despite her fear. Folding her hands in her lap, she kept running her right thumb over her left hand, something she used to do before a concert.

'Hey, I know you're worried about it, but in my limited medical experience, I think he's going to be okay. Just a bit bashed and bruised and maybe a bit slow for a while.'

'I need to sort everything out with him,' Chelsea said softly, turning towards Cal. 'I'm taking a punt here and assuming you've heard lots about me that hasn't been good?'

Cal shrugged. 'I try to take people as I find them.'

'Were you a politician in a past life?'

He laughed, a rich, gravelly sound that reverberated around the cabin. 'Not that I know of. What do you want me to say? Yeah, I've heard about you. Not all of it good. I held Tom's hand while he cried, answered his "Why hasn't she come home?" questions. Anyway, what's the point in rehashing all of this?'

Pressing her lips together, Chelsea touched his arm. 'Do you want to know what happened? Why I wasn't here for her funeral?'

'Only if you want to tell me.'

Chelsea pinched her nose as tears threatened again. 'God, I think I've cried more since I've been home than I have in the last ten years.' She shook her head. 'So, I'll lay everything out bare.

'Five years ago, I was told there weren't any conductors in Australia who would work with me anymore. I was too hard, too high maintenance, too whatever. I was devastated. Very angry. I spoke to my agent and demanded she get them to change her mind.' She laughed mirthlessly. 'Stupid really. If every conductor had the same thought, no one was going to be able to change anyone's mind.

'Anyway, it was my own fault. I've been difficult to get along with ever since I started playing professionally. I put up barriers to people and treated them with no respect. See, I'd always wanted to play what I loved, which *wasn't* classical music. I'd been classically trained because that's what everyone thought I'd be best at, but it wasn't where my heart was. So I'd get frustrated and annoyed and snap at conductors or other orchestra members.

'Then I was lucky enough to get a tour in Europe. A soloist tour, but I still needed backing music so I had a small orchestra with me, and the best conductor in the world!'

The sign on the side of the road said there were fifty kilometres to Barker and she wondered how her dad was coping on the back of the ute. With the heat from the day still strong, even though the sun had long gone, he wouldn't be cold.

She went on to tell Cal how she'd fallen out with the conductor. How the music industry was small and now no one would work with her. 'I was horrible back then,' she finished. 'And I found out that touring wasn't as much fun as I thought it would be. Every day a new city, a new hotel, a new concert hall. It was exhausting.

'So, once the tour fell apart, I still had to make a living. I was never going to tell Mum and Dad what had happened. Well, if I could avoid it. After all the effort they put into my schooling. But I didn't know what to do because playing the piano was the only thing I knew.

'My friend, Tori, suggested I apply for a job as a soloist on a cruise ship. It wouldn't matter that much there. I was told hardly anyone listened to what was being played anyway; most people went to the bars to drink and talk, not listen to music.' Again, her right thumb was running over her left hand. 'So that's what I did.'

'Did you tell anyone?'

'No. Not a soul. Oh, Tori knew, but no one else. And it wasn't like I was in constant contact with Mum and Dad anyway. Six months could go by before we got in touch.' She shrugged. 'I thought I could hide what was going on from them. I didn't take my mobile on any of the ships with me, and they had no idea where I was or how to contact me.'

'But why did you want to hide it from them? I don't understand that.'

'God, Cal, don't you see? It's embarrassing. Degrading. I'm a . . . Well, I was a concert pianist. To be downgraded to playing on a cruise ship . . . They would have been horrified.'

'I don't think you gave them enough credit.'

'Mum would've been livid. They had sacrificed so much for me to have a career at the highest level of music. So when I got on the ships, I didn't take my phone. I deliberately wanted to cut off contact with the world.'

'You didn't get your dad's message,' Cal said.

In the darkness she looked over at him and saw the understanding on his face. Chelsea shook her head. 'No. Not until it was too late. When we docked back in Sydney and I was finally able to get messages, a month or so afterwards.'

'But why didn't you come straight here?'

'I couldn't! I tried to call and let Dad know what I was doing, but I had to get on a different ship. And I was scared. I didn't want to come home. If I stayed away I could pretend she hadn't gone. I did that for five years. After Aria was born I took her with me—in special circumstances you're able to take a child on board. And, as part of my contract, my friend Tori was allowed to come too and look after Aria.' She smiled sadly. 'See, I still had a bit of pull because my name is well known and my bio is reasonably impressive—if you discount the tour, that is. Anyway every time I came back, I rang, but he didn't pick up the phone. Until we got back in November and I couldn't face doing another cruise. That's when I tried again. It was going to be the last time.'

'I still don't understand why you didn't write or try to visit, but I guess all of that's in the past now.' He paused for a moment as if turning over all the information in his mind, then asked, 'Why can't you do another cruise?'

'Aria will be starting preschool this coming year. She needs to live somewhere stable. I haven't set down roots before and now I have to. The problem with that is, I don't have any other qualifications, so I've got no idea how I'm going to support us.'

Cal was quiet while Chelsea watched the red glow of the tail-lights in front of her as the white lines slipped by.

'You know, Tom didn't avoid answering the phone only with you,' Cal said, rubbing his hand along his thighs as if trying to wipe sweat away. 'He didn't answer the phone to anyone. He didn't go anywhere. If there was ever a man sleepwalking through life, it was Tom. For him, the world lost its meaning when Pip died.'

Chelsea opened her mouth but found she couldn't speak. She thought about her parents together. The way they'd clung to each other at Dale's funeral, the way they'd laughed together in the sheep yards and how they'd always talked to each other.

How could she have not seen it before? They were best friends. They didn't need anyone. Everyone else was a bonus. They just needed each other.

A sign told them it was another ten kilometres into Barker and Chelsea wanted to change the subject—there was too much emotion to face once they reached the hospital.

'Tell me about you,' she said. 'How did you come to work for Dad? I know I've asked before but . . .' Her voice trailed off, not sure what else to say.

'I answered an ad in the paper. He and Pip were keen to get someone in to do a bit more of the physical work. Not that they couldn't do it, but it was harder on them as they got older, and Pip was beginning to struggle with the heat. They just needed an extra pair of hands.

'I turned up, they liked the way I rode a motorbike and so they gave me the job!'

Chelsea could imagine her dad saying, '*Get on the bike and bring that mob in from eight. Once you've done that I'll tell you if you've got the job or not.*' He'd say things like that to Dale all the time.

'And your family? You said this morning they were in Port Pirie?'

'Yeah, Mum and Dad live there. Both retired school teachers. Two sisters and one brother, all working in Adelaide, and me. I'm the baby of the family.'

'How did you get involved in farming if your family aren't?'

Cal didn't answer straightaway but, when he did, Chelsea wasn't sure what his answer meant.

'Farming saved me.'

Chapter 21

Chelsea and the doctor stood in the hospital hallway, looking through the doorway at Tom.

She'd been shocked at how small and fragile he looked with his head wrapped in a bandage. It had taken a moment or two for Chelsea to even see a resemblance between the man in the bed and her father.

'The head injury has caused mild concussion. We've kept him awake for the amount of time needed, so it's fine that he's asleep now.

'The ankle, well, that's a nasty break and probably going to require surgery. Couple of pins to hold everything together, but we're going to have to wait until the swelling goes down so we can see exactly what we need to do.'

'Can you do the op here?' she asked.

'No, that'll be an Adelaide job. Has he got private health insurance?'

'I'll find out, but I'd imagine so. He always used to.'

'Do that and I can work out a plan from there. Look, the rest of it is reasonably superficial. His wrist has taken a bit of a battering where he's put his hand out to break his fall. Normally I would've expected a break there, but it seems as if it's mostly muscular. It'll take a bit of time, but he'll be back on his feet eventually.'

Chelsea nodded and chewed on her bottom lip. 'Doctor, there's something else I'd like to talk to you about.'

When he didn't say anything, she continued with a rush. 'I've been away for a few years and haven't seen my dad in that time. Since I've been back, I've noticed some strange things. Sometimes he seems to forget where he is or what words to use. I made mashed potatoes, knowing that's one of his favourite veggies, and he told me he didn't like them. My daughter told me that they got lost one time when they were out in the paddock. My father knows Shandona like the back of his hand. I can't believe he could've got lost out there.'

'Is there a family history of mental health problems or dementia?'

'Not that I'm aware of.'

The doctor pressed her for more details and Chelsea answered as best she could but, as she did so, she realised there was much more about her father that she didn't know.

No, she wasn't sure whether he was on any medications. No, as far as she was aware he hadn't had any bumps or falls lately. No, she wasn't sure if he was depressed.

'What about stress? Has he been under pressure lately?'

'My mother died nearly three years ago. I know that's caused him a huge amount of grief. I don't know if you categorise that as stress though.'

'The death of a spouse *is* classed as stress,' the doctor confirmed. 'Come and sit down and tell me about your father.' He indicated for her to follow him down the corridor and within minutes they were settled in his office.

The doctor tapped on his computer and quickly read through her father's medical records. 'From what I can see here, he hasn't been admitted into hospital before. I don't have access to his day-to-day medical records because I only come in to look after the emergency department on public holidays. The resident doctor will have more info if Tom's been to see him recently.'

'I couldn't tell you,' Chelsea said. 'Like I said, I've been away for a while.'

'Let's go back to your mother's death. Was it sudden?'

'Yes, very much so. She died in their bed and Dad didn't realise until after he'd been in bed with her for a little while.'

The doctor blew out a breath. 'Not nice.'

Chelsea shook her head.

'Any other deaths?'

'My brother died back in 2006. I don't think either of my parents ever got over his death. It was like they couldn't carry on. Everything was too much of an effort and no one else mattered except Dale.'

'That's not abnormal after the death of a child.' He leaned forwards and put his elbows on the desk. 'Grief is a strange beast. It manifests itself in so many different ways. And I'm sure you know that people often take their emotions out on the people they love.'

Chelsea thought he may have been talking from experience.

'So, do you think that could be the cause of his memory lapses? Because most of the time he seems sad but fine.'

'Sure could.' The doctor paused. 'Look, I think we certainly need to do some investigation into this. There are a few possibilities. It could be stress or medication related, or it could be the start of early onset dementia. He is young for a disease like that, but in my experience it can happen to anyone at any time. When we get him to Adelaide I'll order some tests, okay? But I'll have to talk to him about what we're going to do.'

Chelsea nodded. 'Okay.' She swallowed and looked down at the floor, trying to process everything.

'I've given him some drugs for the pain, so he's going to be out of it for a while. Why don't you head home and get some rest? We'll call you when he wakes up and you can come back in then. Is there someone you want us to phone to come and collect you or have you got a mobile?'

Thinking about Cal, she shook her head. 'No, it's okay. My friend caught a lift home and left me his ute.'

'Right. I guess I'll see you later then.' He gave her a smile and Chelsea realised he was about her age.

'I'm sorry, I don't remember your name.'

'Ryan. Ryan Miller.'

'Thank you, Ryan.'

∿

By the time she'd left the hospital it had been too late to collect Aria from Hec and Colleen's place. It was three in the morning when she'd finally walked back into the empty house.

She had been beyond tired but sleep kept eluding her, so she'd poured herself a glass of wine and laid down on the bed and closed her eyes. The next time she'd opened them, the sun had been high in the sky.

Seeing it was close to eleven am, she rang Hec and Colleen and told them she was heading back into the hospital as soon as she could. When Colleen said the hospital wasn't an ideal place for a little girl and offered to look after Aria for longer, Chelsea was grateful. It would give her the opportunity to get things sorted with her dad and Dr Miller.

Colleen put Hec on the phone. 'Thank you so much,' Chelsea said. 'We wouldn't have found him as quickly without your help.'

Hec played down her gratitude. 'He would've done it for us and it's the way we work out here. We don't let our friends and neighbours down.'

Chelsea felt like the words were aimed at her but decided to let them slide. She didn't need to answer to the whole town. The important people knew why she hadn't been here and that was all that mattered.

After Hec, Aria spoke to her.

'Mummy, I love Sooty. Can he come home with us?'

'Who's Sooty?'

'Colleen's kitten. He slept on my bed last night so I didn't get scared.'

'I don't think Colleen would like us to take her kitten, honey. But maybe we can get one later.'

'Mummy?'

'Yeah?'

'When are you coming to pick me up?'

'Probably after I get back from seeing Papa tomorrow. A hospital is such a boring place and I think you'll have much more fun with Colleen.'

'We're going to make biscuits soon. Ones with chocolate in them.' Aria sounded excited as she said 'chocolate'.

'Yum! My fav. Will you save me some?'

'Yes.'

'Thank you. Okay, I'm going to go and see Papa now. I love you.'

'Love you, Mummy.'

Chelsea hung up the phone, gathered her purse and phone and drove to Barker.

She spent a few hours at the hospital but Tom was still so drugged up, he slept the whole time. This time it was a nurse who suggested she go home and get some sleep. Tomorrow would be a different day, she told her.

When Chelsea got back to the house she called Lily. 'Dad had an accident,' she started without preamble.

'I heard,' Lily answered. 'I tried to call but there was no answer. Is he okay?'

'Yeah, he will be.'

'What about you?'

'I'm really tired—I didn't get a lot of sleep last night—but other than that, I'm fine,' Chelsea answered, ignoring the anxiety churning in her stomach.

'You know I'm here if you need anything.'

'Thank you.' She looked out the window and saw a mob of sheep on the move. Behind them was a motorbike and Cal in his familiar blue shirt. She needed to go and talk to him too.

'Lily,' Chelsea started. 'Lily, I need to tell you why I didn't get your wedding invitation, but I don't want to do it over the phone. Do you want to come out here for dinner tomorrow? Would your husband look after the kids?'

'I can come out. That'd be nice. But instead of you cooking, why don't I bring a barbecue chicken and some salad. Quick and easy and more time for catching up.'

'That would be really great,' Chelsea answered.

Hanging up the phone, she went out to see where Cal was. The dust from the sheep hung in the air; without a breath of breeze it would continue to hang like a shroud until it finally fell back to the ground. The sun was beginning its downward slide behind the hills and Chelsea realised he was shifting the mob now because it was cooler.

She pulled on her sandshoes and went outside, wondering if she could walk quickly enough to catch him.

As she walked, the flies buzzed around her face and crawled into her eyes, looking for moisture. She brushed them away and continued on, listening to the call of the birds as they settled in the trees for the night. It made her remember things she'd long forgotten.

Her father had taught her and Dale to drive along this road in the old Corolla he'd kept in the shed for the short runs to the mailbox, or to check a tank.

'Push your left foot in and put it into first,' Tom had instructed, his hand on hers to guide her through the gear changes. 'Now, when you let your foot off the clutch, you have to do it gently. Pretend there's a glass of water on your knee and you're not allowed to spill it. Once you feel the car begin to move, then you can push the accelerator down and you'll start to go forwards.'

Chelsea smiled to herself as she remembered the bunny hops and her father's annoyance every time she stalled the car. Which was often. Dale used to laugh at her and Pip had shushed him every time. 'You weren't perfect when you started,' she'd remind him.

Once she'd learned to drive, Tom had entrusted her to get sheep in or check bores, but she hadn't been very keen on that; that'd been Dale's forte. What she had loved was shearing time. Every shearing, she'd head up to the shed and sit in the corner, watching the shearers. She loved the feel of the wool on her skin and the banter in the shed. Most of the shearers were men she knew; cocky shearers they were called, other farmers who made a bit of extra money by shearing when they weren't busy on their own farms. They were always nice to her, and one of them, Daniel Mundy, had even let her hold a handpiece. He'd shown her how to hold the ewe in between her legs and slide the comb down her side. She'd ended up with a lot of prickles in her fingers—so many that the tips of her fingers had hurt and she hadn't been able to play the piano for a couple of days.

And while shearing was on, Pinto was put to good use too. Tom would set the shorn ewes out into the laneway, and Chelsea and Pinto would walk behind them until they were back in the paddock. When the sheep were safely behind the gates, Pinto would turn his head eagerly for home. He always went home more quickly.

How cool would it be to teach Aria to ride and drive, she thought. *I wonder if I could find a sedate pony I could teach her on.* Pinto would have been perfect, but he had died during her second year at the Conservatorium.

What about you? a little voice said. *Would you like to ride again?*

Chelsea stopped and looked around. The hills dwarfed her and suddenly, under a vast purple sunset sky, she felt small and insignificant. The pull that had drawn her home was stronger than ever, and she was standing right on the ground she was raised on. This was home, she realised. No matter where she'd travelled and what she'd seen, this was home. Shandona was where she belonged. There was nowhere else.

'Don't be stupid,' she muttered. 'How are you going to earn money here? You can't stay.'

Hearing a dog bark, Chelsea saw the motorbike was only a few hundred metres in front of her and she broke into a trot to catch Cal.

Scout saw her before Cal did and he ran over, his long pink tongue dangling out the side of his mouth.

'Hey, Scout,' she said, bending down to pat him.

Cal raised his hand in acknowledgement and turned the motorbike towards her, driving over slowly, his feet skimming along the ground to keep him upright.

'How is he?' he asked once he'd switched off the engine.

'Looks like surgery for his ankle, but everything else is reasonably superficial,' she said.

Wiping the sweat away from his brow, Cal smiled. His teeth were pure white compared to the red of his face, which was covered in dust. His forehead was wet with sweat and his blue eyes stood out, set off by his shirt. He had the sleeves rolled up and Chelsea could see the definition of the muscles in his arms. It made her want them around her, holding her. She remembered how safe she'd felt when he'd given her a hug last night, after they'd found her dad. His body had been hard against hers, yet his touch soft. And suddenly she ached to feel him again. Her heartbeat kicked up a notch.

'Poor bugger. God, I'm glad we found him when we did,' Cal said.

Chelsea looked down at the ground, her cheeks warm with a blush. She hoped he couldn't tell what she was thinking. 'I still don't know what he was doing out there. I didn't get to talk to him today because he was knocked out by the medication.'

'I don't think it was anything sinister,' Cal answered, his face serious. 'We'd been making plans the day before

Christmas, talking about moving these sheep here,' he nodded to the mob in front of him, 'all the way out to the pines where there was a little feed from the rain. I reckon that's what he'd started to do.'

Chelsea nodded. 'Well, that's good to know.' She paused. 'I told the doctor about his memory lapses.'

'Go back, Scout,' Cal instructed. The sheep had come to a standstill under the trees in the creek. 'Push 'em up!'

Scout ran off like a greyhound and pushed the sheep, running from side to side, to get them moving again. The ewes took off with a startled *baa* along the creek line. One by one they followed each other as they tried to move away from the working dog. Scout kept an eye on the stragglers and hung back, making sure they didn't stop. If they did, he gave a short, sharp bark and they bolted to catch up with the mob.

Chelsea loved watching Scout work but soon he'd had enough and, without encouragement from Cal, he stopped under a large gumtree, scratching at the dirt to find a cooler spot, and flopped down. He looked over at Cal to make sure that was all right, then dropped his head and shut his eyes.

'Oh, to be able to sleep like that,' Chelsea said with a laugh.

'What did the doc say about his memory?' Cal was staring off into the distance and Chelsea realised he was dreading the answer.

'You really do love my dad, don't you?' she asked suddenly.

Cal frowned. 'Yeah, I do. You know how I told you on the way into Barker that farming saved me? Well, it was more your dad, because he gave me the job.'

He fell silent but Chelsea didn't fill the gap. She sensed he was going to tell her something important.

'I was living over in Victoria, working at an abattoir. But I wasn't making enough money to pay off my loan for a second house. See, I'd been living with a woman and when she left me she was entitled to half of what I had, which was two houses—one debt-free. I had to pay her out.' His mouth twisted and Chelsea could see it hurt him to talk about it. 'I didn't have the money, so I got another loan, but the interest was more than I could afford on the wage I was on. One of the blokes I worked with told me he had a way to make some extra money on my days off if I wanted. Don't know if you know what it's like to be desperate, but it's not a lot of fun. So I asked what it was.' He paused. 'It was running drugs up to the border of New South Wales. It all went okay for a while, then one afternoon I had a police car follow me. I was on the way back from a delivery, so I knew I didn't have any of the drugs in the car, but it scared me enough never to want to do it again.' He stopped and ran his hands through his hair, before looking Chelsea in the eye. 'I handed in my resignation at the abattoir as soon as I got back. Packed up my gear, not that I had much, and hightailed it home to Mum and Dad. The near run-in made me realise what an idiot I was being.' He shrugged. 'So I got home, looked in the paper, saw this job, applied and here I am. Tom worked out I had a problem and, about a week after he hired me, he sat me down to ask about it. I told him about the debt and he helped me work out a payment plan for the bank.' He smiled. 'I've paid it all off now and I've done it through hard work. Your dad saved me.'

Chelsea didn't know what to say, so instead she put her hand on his arm and smiled. 'I'm glad he did that.'

Cal covered her hand with his and held her eyes. For a second, Chelsea thought he was going to kiss her. She leaned in slightly, still holding his eyes. Cal's slid away and the moment was gone.

'What about his memory?' he asked again.

Clearing her throat and slightly embarrassed that she had misread the situation, Chelsea moved away. Kicking at the dirt, she said, 'The doctor's going to order tests when he gets to Adelaide. Ryan has to talk to Dad first, but—'

'Who's Ryan?'

'The doctor. Once he's talked to Dad, he'll get everything rolling. He did say it could be stress related, but it may also be the early onset of dementia.'

Checking the sheep were still moving, Cal said, 'That's what I was afraid of.'

Chelsea said, 'Me too.'

Chapter 22

Dave and Kim sat next to each other in front of the computer in their home office. Boxing Day had started off quietly for them before they made another round of visits to Kim's customers. Today there hadn't been any old stories or information Dave could draw on to investigate the remains, so they'd taken to searching Google and Trove.

'Try "murders in South Australia in the early 1920s",' Dave said. Then he mused out loud, 'Still, we don't know if they were murdered or just died. What about "missing persons in the early 1920s"?'

'Hold on, hold on! I've just done the first one.'

They waited for the page to come up while in the background the Boxing Day Test commentators talked about run averages and a cracked pitch.

'Okay, here we go.' Dave ran his finger down the list. 'Nope, nope, nope. All interstate. Geez, they were a murderous lot back then. Oh, here we are, this is South

Australia. Have a read of this! *"Woman found with her throat slashed in Hammond."* That's not very far from here. 1902. *"On Monday evening of the 25th of May 1902, Mary Anna Roberts was found in the pig pen on a property just outside Hammond in the mid-north of South Australia. It was just on dark when Mrs Roberts' husband returned home to find her face-down in the pen. It was originally thought the pigs had mauled her after she fell into their enclosure; however, on further investigation it was found her throat had been cut with a ragged-edged knife. Investigations are ongoing."*

'Sweet Mother of God,' Kim said as she continued to scroll.

'And this! *"A child was reported missing from the town site of Wild Horse Flat after a team of Travelling Hawkers went through. Samuel George Daw, eight, had been playing in the small creek which runs at the back of the hamlet. He was reported missing when he didn't return home for lunch. The Travelling Hawkers had left Wild Horse Flat early that morning, after Samuel had left home to do his morning chores. Investigations are still continuing."'*

'How awful,' Kim said with her hand on her chest. 'What that mother must have gone through.' She scrolled to the end of the page but nothing else caught their attention. 'Shall we try a different search, Dave? "Missing child"? "Missing man"?'

He groaned. 'That'd be like looking for a needle in a haystack. How do we narrow it down?'

Kim turned to him. 'So, what are we actually googling for? You've got the remains of a baby and a male skeleton that was possibly buried on the reserve seventy to eighty years ago.'

'That's about it.'

'Right.' Kim typed in 'missing man and baby early 1900s'.

'"*Police arrested Arthur Clarence Dally in Toowoomba last night, in relation to Thursday night's shooting. There is still no sight of his partner, Lillian Alice Dally, and police believe she is being harboured by friends. Anyone with any information is asked to contact the Toowoomba police station.*" Not South Australia,' Dave said. He frowned. 'How does this Trove work? You type in something which is really clear and yet it comes back with all this other unrelated stuff.'

'That's why it's called Trove. It's a store of valuable things but you have to look through to find what you want. Don't be so impatient. You might miss the best bit.'

Dave glanced over at her and patted her knee. 'Thanks.'

'You're welcome.' Kim kept her eyes on the screen and rolled the mouse with her finger. 'More shootings, gambling . . .' Her voice trailed off. 'Engagements. Ha! I wonder if we could find our engagement notice.' Quickly she typed in their names and hit send.

'We'll be too recent, won't we?'

'Probably, but it's fun looking. Look at this.' She pointed to the screen as a page of scanned newspaper came up.

'There are all sorts of announcements on Trove going back to the 1950s. And further.'

Dave stopped and thought. 'Let's do a bit of research on the Taylor family. Mr Oakes said that Tom's parents were named Evelyn and Leo. Can we search them?'

Kim's fingers flew across the keyboard.

'"*Leo and Evelyn Taylor are pleased to announce the safe arrival of Thomas Leo Taylor at Calvary Hospital, Adelaide.*" There we go, got them!' Dave said, pleased. 'Okay, can we go back further? To when they were married, or even the generation before?'

'South Australia differs from most states in the amount of information they put on birth, deaths and marriage certificates,' Kim said as she searched for more information. 'They're not as detailed. And I know this from when I was researching my family tree. Oh wait! I've had an idea—what about Ancestory.com? I've still got a subscription. If we can get the birth dates of some of the people you want to find, then I should be able to do a search for them.'

Dave felt the familiar excitement flood through him. 'You know,' he said, 'those cop shows on TV really do a disservice to us real cops. They're always out fighting crime on the streets and talking to potential witnesses. No one really understands that ninety percent of police work is done behind a desk, and, my precious one, you'd make a great detective. But I'm sure I've told you that before!'

Kim laughed softly, keeping her eyes on the screen. 'Only because you've taught me well.' She closed down Trove and opened another window. 'Right, we need to start a new tree.' Dave knew she was talking more to herself than to him, so he stayed quiet while she worked.

'Name?'

Glancing at his notebook he read out Tom's full name and date of birth. He was glad he'd got all the usual inform-ation from Tom when he'd done the initial interview. Kim typed it in and then asked for Tom's father's name.

'All I've got is Leo Taylor. Don't know a middle name.'

'Let's just put in everything we've got. Hopefully we'll get a little green leaf, which will give us a hint.'

Ten minutes later they'd created a family tree which had very few details and nothing to indicate there was any extra help in the way of clues.

'Damn.' Dave scratched his head, feeling the excitement ebb out of him.

'Hang on, we're not done just yet.' Kim flicked to another screen and typed the name into Google. Three pages in she found it: '"*The funeral for Leo Graham Taylor will be held at the Barker Uniting Church on the 28th June 2003. The procession will then progress to the cemetery for internment.*"'

Dave pushed back his chair. 'Want to go for a look at the cemetery?' he asked.

❧

'Tell me why we're out here looking for another needle in a haystack in the middle of the afternoon when it's as hot as hell?' Kim asked. She held down her wide-brimmed hat as a gust of wind from the north lifted dust and leaves into a small willy-willy.

Dave read the directory at the front gate. It seemed there was a whole family of Taylors buried here.

'We've got Adelia Taylor dying back in 1993, then Leo and Evelyn and Philippa. Then there are younger ones: Crystal, Andrew and Dale. Shit. Those first two, they must have been stillborns or died straight after birth. Look here: Crystal was born on 29 June and died on the same day, whereas Andrew was born on 4 June and died the same day.' He stared at the names on the board, sadness spreading through him.

Kim stood next to him, linking her arm through his, and looked silently at the words in front of her.

'These must be Chelsea's brothers and sister. I'd forgotten you said Dale had died recently. Remind me again how he died and what the circumstances were.'

Kim took a deep breath. 'It was awful. I don't know all the details but there were three or four kids involved. Kelly and Shane Hunt, you know the people who own the Giftory?'

Dave turned to look at her. 'Yeah.'

'Them and Jason Putter. Then there was Dale, Chelsea's brother. They'd been drinking at the caravan park kitchen, celebrating Kelly and Shane's engagement. It'd been the talk of the town because it was a bit of a Romeo and Juliet scenario. Their parents had been at loggerheads over the placement of a boundary fence. Kelly's parents owned a caravan park on the outskirts of town and Shane's owned the pub next door. It had originally all been owned by one person, but when the previous owner sold, he made more money by splitting it in two. The settlement agents didn't pick up that the fence wasn't in the right spot. It cut off about ten metres from the park and they needed it to be able to add more cabins. They tried to buy some of the land from the pub, but the owners refused. Then they discovered the land *was* actually the caravan park's but, because the pub was using the land, they didn't want to give it back. Then all hell broke loose. Anyway, none of that really matters, but you can understand the problem.'

'Small-town rifts can be the start of dreadful wars,' Dave said, nodding.

'So, when those two announced their engagement, the town held its breath. Both sets of parents said they were happy about it—through gritted teeth.'

'So how did this affect Dale?'

'They were all mucking around, play fighting and carrying on—Shane, Jason and Dale. Then apparently Jason launched himself at Dale and got him in a headlock. They accidentally ran into a wall and Dale's neck was broken. He died before the ambulance arrived.'

'Shit.' He kept looking at Dale's name and thinking about having to be the police officer who did the inform on that. No parent ever expected their child would go out to a party and never return.

After another gust of wind and a shower of dirt granules Kim pulled at his arm. 'Come on, let's get the info you need and head home. We've got work ahead of us if you want to put all of these people into the family tree.'

They opened the gate and wandered among the graves, taking notes of the family names, dates of death and, if they were available, birth dates.

Down at the older end of the cemetery, Kim found a grave that had caved in, leaving a gaping hole around the edge.

She frowned as she stared at the hole. 'Hey Dave!' she called. 'Come and look at this!'

Dave finished what he was doing then walked over.

Kim pointed to the hole and said, 'Do you think they've escaped?'

He burst out laughing. 'Well, if they have, I reckon it might have been a while ago!'

❧

Back in their office, Kim entered the information they'd gathered while Dave seasoned some steaks and heated up the barbecue. He poured a glass of wine, placed it on the desk in front of her and started to massage her shoulders.

'Found anything?'

'I'm not sure. This is certainly a little odd.' She pointed to Adelia's name. 'It says here that Adelia was married to Oscar and he's named as the father on the birth certificates for Leo and three other siblings, whom we didn't find in the cemetery. See here, I was able to access the birth certificates. But she was married to Baxter.'

'People often go by their middle names. Or nickname.' Dave said. 'Maybe his real name was Oscar . . .'

Kim nodded. 'Hmm, maybe. He's not got a date of death that I can find, or a place of burial. He'd have to be dead now, because he was born in 1905.'

'You'd think so, wouldn't you? He'd be one hundred and thirteen and, as much as he might've had a good consti-tution, I don't reckon it would've been that good!'

'Exactly. I need to do a bit more research on Oscar and see if I can find him. He's probably been buried in a different cemetery with the other kids.' Kim picked up her glass of wine and took a sip.

'Where else can you look?'

'I'll go through Trove again and see if I can find a death notice. If not, I'll go to the Births, Deaths and Marriages office and see what they've got. There has to be a record of him somewhere.'

Dave thought for a moment. 'Or not.'

Chapter 23

'Come on, we need to get going,' Cal said as the sun dropped below the hills and a chill came into the air.

'I'll walk.'

'Nah, get on here. You'll be right. I won't let you fall off.'

'Huh, how can I be sure?' Chelsea asked, looking at the bike. 'Dale used to do his best to scare the crap out of me when he was dinking me. He'd line up a tree and drive straight at it, or drive really fast and stop really suddenly.'

'I'm not Dale,' was all Cal replied. 'Hop on.' He called to Scout, who jumped up in front of him, and Chelsea tried to get on the back and still look elegant.

Chelsea wrapped her arms around Cal's waist and held on tight. It was exhilarating feeling the cool wind against her face. Her hair whipped around the nape of her neck and she wanted to reach up and tie it back, but she also didn't want to stop holding on. She told herself it was for safety, but really it was because Cal felt so good. She hoped he hadn't realised that she'd wanted to kiss him earlier. Her emotions were all out of whack at the moment!

'How much do you know about sheep?' Cal had turned his face to the side so she could hear what he said.

'Sheep? Not much. I used to help in the yards and shearing shed when I was a kid, but that's a long time ago. My fingers and hands were pretty important, so I had to stop doing anything that could have caused them injury.'

'Fair call. Well, I'm shifting these because we're running out of feed in this paddock.'

'I realise that,' she said in a huffy tone. 'You asked about sheep not feed!'

Cal gave half a smile. 'I haven't finished yet.'

'Oh.'

He slowed the motorbike and came to a stop in front of a gate. 'Hop off.'

Chelsea put her left foot down and brought her other leg up to try and hop away from the bike without clobbering Cal in the back of the head.

Flicking the stand down, Cal got off and opened the gate. 'Can you stand there for me?' He pointed to the far side of the gate but back from the fence slightly. 'I'm going to run them along the fence and you need to stop them and get them to turn into the gateway, okay?'

'Sure.' She was nowhere near as confident as she sounded. Looking around, she wondered if Cal would get them close enough before the light faded. The sun had been gone for nearly ten minutes now, and although it was still light, the darkness was encroaching quickly.

Scout had held the sheep so they couldn't turn around and run back the way they'd come, and now, with a rev of the engine, Cal roared back around them and rode from side to side, encouraging the ewes down the fence line towards the gate.

Chelsea watched carefully as the sheep ran in her direction. She knew enough not to move in case she baulked them, but at the same time she wasn't sure when to make a noise to stop them running. She could hear Cal revving the engine, hurrying them along, and by the time they appeared from the cloud of dust, they were almost on top of her.

'Hey!' she yelled. 'Hey, hey, hey! Get in the gate, get in the gate! Ha!' She stamped her feet and waved her arms around as she remembered her mum doing and then, for good measure, blew a raspberry.

The sheep came to an abrupt standstill and looked at her before the leader took a step towards her.

'Nope! No, you don't!' she yelled again. 'Go in the gate! Shhh, shhh!' She felt like an idiot. What were you supposed to say to sheep to get them to go through a gateway? 'Come on, turn, you buggers!' With a few more movements a professional dancer would've been proud of, Chelsea took a couple of steps towards them and they turned. Seeing the gate and freedom, the leader ran through, with the rest of the mob following.

'Hey, good job!' Cal said as he parked the bike in front of the gate and turned off the engine. He got off and dragged the cocky gate across the ground, shutting it tightly. 'You look like you've done that more than once.'

With relief, Chelsea laughed. 'Maybe about twenty years ago, in another life.'

'They went through the gate, what more could you ask for?'

'Well, the head one went through and the rest followed. They're a bit like the Pied Piper. They follow the leader.'

'That's why all you've got to do is get that one to go in the right direction and you're home and hosed.' He looked up at the sky. 'Ah, the first few stars are out,' he said. 'Better head home, otherwise it'll be pitch black by the time we get there. I don't like being out on the bike after dark. Too many roos or emus to hit.'

Chelsea didn't argue. She was keen to get close to Cal again. 'Yeah, and I have to go and pick Aria up.'

He mounted the bike and whistled to Scout. Settling himself halfway down the seat, there was room for the dog on the front. 'Now you hop on where you were before.'

Gingerly, she lifted one leg over and tried to wiggle on without getting too close to him. She giggled uncomfortably. 'Sorry. I'm not very graceful.'

'Look fine to me,' he said gruffly, then turned the key before she could say anything more.

❧

Cal parked the bike in the shed and asked Chelsea if she wanted a beer.

'Thanks, but I'd better go and get organised. Once I've picked up Aria, I've got to find some things for the doctor. Private health insurance papers and so on.'

Nodding, Cal stretched out his back and said, 'You know where I am if you need me. Will you feed and tie up Scout?'

'I can do that, no worries.'

'Guess it's goodnight then,' he said and sauntered off towards his house.

Chelsea watched him go for a moment then called Scout to her side. She fed and watered the dog and made sure he was tied up securely. The last thing she wanted was to lose the work dog that everyone seemed to love.

'Night, old boy,' she said, giving him a final pat. 'I'm off for a shower. Bark if you want me.'

Scout wagged his tail, his head still in his food bowl.

❧

'Thanks again for looking after Aria so well,' Chelsea said to Colleen and Hec.

'No problem. She hasn't been any trouble at all, have you, Aria?' Colleen leaned in through the window and stroked Aria's hair.

'Can I *pleeeassse* take Sooty?' Aria implored.

'No, honey. She's not yours,' Chelsea answered. Mouthing 'sorry' to Colleen as Aria started to cry.

'I want to take Sooty!' she wailed.

'You can come back and play with her anytime,' Hec told Aria.

Chelsea thanked them and got into the car, waving goodbye as she drove away, while Aria continued to sob.

By the time they arrived home, Aria was asleep, so Chelsea carried her inside without waking her. Pulling the blankets up, she stared at her daughter before kissing her goodnight and tiptoeing out of the room.

After showering, Chelsea poured herself a glass of wine and took all the contents of the box out into the sitting room so she could look at them more easily. Opening the first scrapbook, she saw newspaper clippings of her mum and dad dressed in their wedding outfits. The caption read: *Congratulations to Mr and Mrs Thomas Taylor of Barker, who married last week in the Uniting Church. The reception was held at the Barker Football Club rooms.*

She examined her parents. Their smiles were large and carefree and they were looking at each other. Pip's veil had caught around Tom's neck and he was reaching up to pull it away. Running her fingers over their faces, she saw the love between them and her heart ached at how familiar her mum was even though she hadn't seen her for years. She looked at them a moment longer before moving on to the next page.

Birth notices for Dale, then birth and death notices for Andrew and Crystal. The scrapbook page looked wrinkled near the notices and some of the writing was illegible, as if her mother had sat there crying after gluing in the notices and her tears had dropped onto the page.

There was her own birth notice and a picture of her in the hospital crib.

It was clear her mum had been proud of her children. Every award Dale or Chelsea had ever won had been kept.

In the second scrapbook, on the first page, was the letter from the Adelaide Conservatorium of Music offering

Chelsea a place in their Talented Youngsters Program. In Pip's handwriting there was a big *yes* with a ring around it. After that, the newspaper clippings were of Chelsea's first performances. There were concerts at the Adelaide Festival Theatre and even one at Government House, when she'd played as an eighteen-year-old for the visit of British royal, Prince Edward.

For Chelsea it was bittersweet. She'd had the kind of success she'd dreamed of, but now it was all over.

Her mum had also glued in her reports from the Conservatorium: *Chelsea is a talented student but needs to learn to follow the score.*

Her talent far outweighs her ability to play exactly what is on the page.

Then came the clincher: *Headstrong. Strong-willed.*

The embarrassment and shame she'd felt back then, when the principal had first pulled her up and spoken to her, flooded her again.

She wished there had been some good reports her mum could have glued into the scrapbook.

From then on there was nothing more about Chelsea.

'Why did she keep these?' Chelsea said to the silence of the old house. 'To remind herself she was disappointed in me?'

A heaviness settled in her chest and once again she wished she could take back all those years. Redo them, not make the same mistakes.

Hindsight was a wonderful thing.

Hurriedly she reached for the last scrapbook and flipped through the pages. Cuttings of friends and family, Dale's death notices and newspaper articles on the enquiry into his death.

Stopping, she read those, seeing the word 'accidental' a few times. She was glad Jason had been cleared of any wrongdoing. He'd always been a nice boy in school, and it'd been clear straightaway that the boys had just been mucking around. Dale's death hadn't only ruined her parents' lives and changed hers, it had also set Jason, Shane and Kelly on a completely different path. Everyone was only one phone call or police visit away from having their lives changed forever.

Again, she was struck by the need for everything to be out in the open with her father. For so long she'd been frightened to say Dale's name in front of her parents because she didn't know what their reaction would be. Photos had been removed from the walls and only one remained on display. Why should they be afraid to say the name of a person who'd died—especially someone they had all loved so much?

She was to blame too. Aria hadn't been told about her uncle. That was Chelsea's fault. She'd fallen into the same trap. Don't mention Dale's name. He's dead. Let's pretend he didn't exist.

'No more,' she muttered quietly, a stern resolve in her heart to talk to her dad about it.

Chapter 24

Jack turned up at the station earlier than Dave had expected.

'Good Christmas?' Dave asked when his junior flopped down into the chair in front of him. It wouldn't have been great, Dave knew, because Jack had worked over the two public holidays, which was why he hadn't been expecting to see him until later in the afternoon.

'Busy,' he answered. 'I've handed out ten infringement notices—three of them for drug driving.'

'*Drug* driving?' Dave's voice rose in surprise. 'That's a first here in Barker. Were they locals?'

'One was. Jason Putter.'

'Oh.' Dave felt his heart sink. When he'd arrived this morning, he'd done a couple of searches on Dale Taylor's death. Then he'd investigated the men involved and found a long list of drink-driving and disorderly-conduct charges against Jason's name.

It was clear the man was still hurting greatly, consumed with guilt, and Dave surmised he was self-medicating. From the little he knew of Jason, he wasn't married and didn't seem to have a steady girlfriend. He was working for his father and helping out with sound systems on the occasional gig.

'That bloke needs some help,' Dave said and quickly told Jack about Jason's involvement in Dale's death.

'That's your speciality, community policing,' Jack said, rubbing his eyes.

'I might go and see him later on today. Anything else happen?'

'The ambos called to let me know that Tom Taylor had been involved in an accident out on the farm. I went to the hospital and spoke to the ER doctor, who had taken bloods to see if there was any drinking involved, but there wasn't, so I didn't need to do anything. He's still in hospital. Broken ankle and some serious gravel rash.'

'What happened there? Stock work?' Dave tapped his pen against the pad.

'Yeah, only one motorbike involved. Must have been shifting sheep or something and taken a tumble.

'Well, that was a busy enough couple of days. Was glad to be busy.' He continued to sit but didn't say anything more. 'And tomorrow I've got off and nothing to do!'

Dave cocked his head and stopped tapping. 'What's up?'

'Nothing, why?'

'Your face is longer than a grey cloud dropping rain from Perth to Adelaide. I'm listening.'

Jack sighed and again ran his hand over his eyes 'What's the point in having time off?' he asked. 'I haven't got a girlfriend to spend time with, and there's nothing to do at home during the week. I might as well be here helping you.'

Frowning, Dave thought about his answer. 'Well, mate, I'm more than happy for you to come in and work for the next couple of days, but that's not a long-term solution.'

'I know! And I don't know why I'm feeling like this. I love living here, I love my job. I've never been lonely before and don't freaking understand why I've suddenly started feeling like this. It's got knobs on it.'

'Right, well, I tell you what, can you go across and help Kim this morning? She's doing some research on the Taylor family, trying to find out whether or not our body could have anything to do with them. It's an off-the-record investigation, because we've really got nothing to go on, but your help would be appreciated.'

Jack brightened. 'That'd be good.'

'You're just wanting to eat me out of house and home. Anyway, get going over there and I'll ring Kim to let her know you're coming.'

Jack stood up and looked at his boss for a moment. 'Cheers, Dave. Appreciate it.'

Dave nodded and waited for him to go before picking up the phone. 'I'm sending Jack over to you,' he said when Kim answered. 'Can you find him some research work to do? He's really flat.'

'What's up?'

'Lonely mostly, I think.'

'I'll see what I can cook up for him,' Kim said, and Dave heard the smile in her voice. Suddenly he wondered what he'd orchestrated. Kim was the master of fix-its and set-ups.

Putting Jack out of his mind, he called his mother for an update. She didn't answer, but a few minutes later he received a text from her saying they were in physio with Dean and she'd call him back.

Satisfied he'd done what was required of him, he opened his emails and scrolled through, hoping there would be something from Dr Fletcher. There wasn't anything yet. Dave mucked around in the office for an hour or so, achieving nothing, then locked the door and put the notice on the window saying the station was closed and to contact his mobile if necessary.

He got into his car and drove to the hospital to see Tom Taylor.

❧

'Mr Taylor has only just woken up,' the nurse told him. 'I was about to ring his daughter and ask her to come in.'

'Could I have a couple of minutes with him?' Dave asked.

'I guess that'd be all right. You're not going to question him too much, are you?'

Dave flashed his most charming smile. 'I really only want to see how he is.'

'Oh, well then, go right on through. Room eight on the left.'

Thanking her, he started to walk down the corridor. He stuck his head into the room and said, 'G'day Tom. Up for a visitor?'

The man in the bed looked confused, then frightened, and he twisted the bedsheets in his hands.

'I'm Dave, the copper from the Barker station.'

'Oh, g'day. Sure, come on in.' His facial expression didn't change but his shoulders relaxed slightly.

Dave pulled up a chair next to the bed and smiled at him. 'You had a bit of an accident?' he said, hoping Tom had genuinely remembered who he was.

'Yeah. Bloody sheep. Went to shift them. Don't really remember what happened. Must've hit a rock or something. Went for a short flight. Over the handle bars. I thought my days of doing that were over when I stopped riding horses!'

With a quiet laugh, Dave said, 'Never been too partial to horses for that very reason. Didn't know motorbikes had similar tendencies.'

'Just as bad,' Tom said.

'Doc reckons you'll be up and about soon?'

'Haven't seen him yet, but my ankle's broken.' He stared at Dave with a puzzled expression on his face. 'Did I do something wrong?' he asked slowly.

'What? No. I just wanted to ask you a few more questions about the remains we found on your land.'

It took Tom a minute to process that and Dave sat there quietly while he did so. He'd seen people like this before and he knew he needed to give Tom time to catch up. Head injuries could be buggers of things.

'Oh right, the bones. Up on the reserve.' Tom nodded.

'Yeah, they're the ones. I've found out there was a family living on the reserve way back in the early 1900s. Apparently, they were squatting and, once the Taylors acquired a long-term lease for the reserve area, they were shifted on. Do you know anything about that?'

Tom shook his head. 'That'd go back to my grandparents' day. Adelia and Baxter. But I don't remember ever hearing them talk about anything like that. We got that lease back in 1932. I think the paperwork is in my office somewhere. But Granda Baxter lobbied the government to get the lease. I know he and Grandma had to work hard to convince them.'

'What's so special about that piece of land?'

'Well, nothing really, other than it's a large piece of land with a public road running through it. There's enough area there to run sheep on and there's fresh water. I guess that was the main thing he wanted—underground water is precious out here because we don't get a lot of rain, so run-off into dams doesn't work well for us. Places where there is constant underground water, no matter how much you pump out, are like gold. Granda Baxter said he wanted to be able to have the use of it for as long as he was alive, if not longer, so he set about getting it.' Tom paused. 'That was Granda Baxter all over. If he wanted something, he went and got it. One of the reasons Shandona is as big as it is. He kept acquiring land. Every time a piece came on the market, he bought it. Sometimes it wasn't even on the market and he bought it.'

'How did that work?'

'I guess he just turned up at the neighbours and offered them money. They said yes or no.'

Dave nodded. 'Smart man.'

'He certainly left our family in a good position.' Tom scrunched the bedsheets up again and looked around the room as if searching for answers.

'So you can't remember the name of the family who were camped on the reserve then?'

Tom thought for a while. 'No. They would've all been gone by the time I was born. And I don't remember anyone talking about anything like that. But I guess people came and went back then, didn't they? There were lots of people walking the roads and looking for work during the Depression. I remember Grandma Adelia telling me about having to turn people away. They always gave if they could but it was a hard time and they had barely any food for themselves. Sometimes they had to keep the chooks in the cellar and guard the pigs and dairy cow so people didn't steal them. Different times back then.'

'Certainly,' Dave agreed. 'Tell me a bit more about your Granda Baxter.'

Tom shrugged. 'What's to tell? One of life's gentlemen. He and Grandma always had humbug lollies sitting in a wooden bowl next to their chairs in the sitting room. Grandma worked as hard as he did during the day and cooked for the whole family as well. They lived with my parents until they died. Made for a full house but it was fun when we went over there. My family lived in the overseer's cottage until they all moved out and retired. Grandma

Adelia died first, then Granda Baxter. After that, my mum died unexpectedly, and Dad didn't want to be out here on his own, so he retired. Moved to Adelaide.'

'Baxter was always around? For as long as you can remember?'

'Sure was. He had a lot of time for us grandkids. I loved spending time with him.' Tom was beginning to look tired. 'Has someone called Pip?' he asked.

Chapter 25

Chelsea was holding Aria's hand as she recognised the tall, solid figure walking towards her down the hospital corridor and smiled.

'Hello, Detective,' she said.

'Call me Dave, please. We're all pretty laidback out here. Hello, Aria.'

Chelsea dipped her head in acknowledgement as Aria said, 'We're going to see Papa.'

'I think he'll be very pleased to see you,' Dave said.

'Have you been in to see Dad?' Chelsea asked.

'I have. He seems in good spirits, despite everything.'

Chelsea felt a sense of relief—as if a weight had been lifted from her shoulders. 'I haven't seen him yet. The doctor told me to head home until he woke up, so I did.'

'And the doctor will be back today?'

'I imagine so. I spoke with him last night and there are a few things that have to happen before they take him to Adelaide for surgery on his ankle.'

Dave nodded. 'Well, I hope he mends quickly. He did seem slightly confused when I left, but I'm sure it's just the knock to the head.'

Chelsea narrowed her eyes. 'Confused?' She turned to Aria. 'Do you want to run on ahead, honey? Papa is in that room just there. She pointed and Aria skipped away. When they heard Tom say, 'Well, hello there, young lady', Dave continued to talk.

'He was asking if anyone had called your mother.'

'Oh.' Chelsea felt her shoulders slump again. 'I see. There's been a bit of that recently.'

'Do you want to sit?' Dave asked, indicating the chairs lining the corridor.

Undecided, Chelsea rubbed her right thumb over her left hand. 'No, look, I'd better get in and see him. Thanks.' She started to move away but turned back quickly. 'Oh, is there any news on the bones?' she asked. 'Is that why you were here?'

'Sort of. I wanted to ask Tom about a family that used to squat up on the reserve back in the early 1900s. I know he wasn't born back then, but often there are family stories passed down. I thought he might know something.'

'Sounds interesting,' Chelsea said. 'I love hearing old timers' stories or reading old diaries. I think their lives were much more colourful than ours today, where we're stuck on computer screens and always discontent.'

Dave grinned. 'Some of the best times I've ever had have been spent around campfires, telling stories. I had a mate who was a travelling minister—he's dead now, but he used to tell the best stories. All true, but he made them sound like they couldn't be!

'Anyway, back to the bones, that was all I was after—any information on the squatter's family.'

'I don't know anything about them, but I'll have a look and see what's in Dad's office when I get home. I know Great-Granda Baxter used to keep diaries, but I have no idea where they are, or even if they're still around.'

'Do you think the bones have something to do with my great-grandparents?'

'Who knows. The time frames might fit but, at the end of the day, I don't have any family members to compare any DNA we might be able to get from the bones, because I don't know who he is.' He shrugged. 'It's a bit difficult—with bones that old we'd usually leave them undisturbed in the ground, but we didn't know how old they were. Following through on a case like this is more for my own sense of satisfaction than anything else.'

Chelsea processed the information then asked, 'If the person was murdered, would you be able to tell from analysing the bones?'

Dave held out his hands in a 'who knows' gesture. 'It's so tricky. Unless there is a clear bullet wound through the skull or something, it'd be hard to say it was murder. For me it's about identifying the person rather than how they died.'

Chelsea nodded. 'Well, I'll certainly have a look when I get back home and see what I can come up with for you.'

'Just quickly,' Dave said, 'do you remember your great-grandfather well?'

'Baxter?'

He nodded.

'A little bit. I was about six when he died. He loved to play the piano—the one we have at home is the one he bought. I can remember how the notes used to sing when he played, and his hands were arthritic by then, so I can only imagine what his playing must have sounded like when he was younger.

'He used to tell us stories. Dale and I,' she clarified. 'We'd sit on his knee—or I would, and Dale'd sit at his feet—and he'd tell us stories of the olden days. About his team of Clydesdale horses and the others he used for mustering. There's a photo somewhere . . .' She wrinkled her brow, thinking hard. 'I'm not sure where, but I remember it quite clearly—more than him maybe, because the photo has been around all my life and he hasn't, of course. It's a black and white shot of Great-Granda Baxter sitting on a really tall horse. He was wearing a huge hat and had a rifle slung through the saddle. He was a very imposing figure, but he was always so gentle with his animals and us.'

'Those stories would be worth a mint if you could write them down,' Dave told her.

'If I could remember them! I'll have to put my thinking cap on. It'd be good to be able to tell Aria some of them.'

'Absolutely. Guess you'd better get in there and see Tom, then. Give me a yell if you find anything. Like I said, it's more for my own satisfaction than anything else.'

Chelsea gathered up her handbag and nodded. 'I'll let you know.'

Dave left the hospital, his heard whirling. No one had mentioned Oscar. So what Kim had found was indeed odd. But what did it mean?

❧

'Hi, Dad.' Aria was sitting on her father's bed, eating chocolates when Chelsea finally walked in. 'Oh, you're lucky Aria. Where did they come from?'

'The nurse brought them,' Tom said. 'And we're sharing them, aren't we?'

Aria nodded, her mouth full.

Tom shut his eyes, then opened them again, studying her for a moment.

She pulled a chair up to the side of the bed and sat down. 'How are you feeling?'

'Bit groggy.' He shut his eyes again but held out another sweet to Aria.

Chelsea handed Aria a book from her handbag. 'Can you please sit near the window for a little while?' she asked. 'I need to talk to Papa about something important.'

Aria gave Tom a chocolaty kiss and climbed down from the bed, taking the picture book with her.

With Aria settled, Chelsea reached over and took her dad's hand in hers and held it. His face twitched a bit at her touch, but he didn't move. Keeping her voice low and steady, she said, 'I've spoken to the doctor and he says you need to go to Adelaide for an operation.' She told him everything Ryan had said to her. Continuing to rub his hand, she took a breath and went on. 'I hope you don't mind, but I've been worried about you, so I spoke to him about your memory. I was a little concerned you'd been under so much pressure since Mum died that it was affecting your memory.' She paused, waiting for the angry response.

It didn't come.

She continued. 'Ryan—that's the doctor—is going to talk to you about this and, if you agree, he'll order some tests to be run when you get down to the city.' This time she squeezed his hand. 'Dad . . .' she paused and took another deep breath. 'Dad, I'd like to stay here, if it's all right with you. Live on Shandona.'

Again, there was no answer.

'I saw the birth certificates for the babies too. You've been through so much. So much stuff I didn't even know about. Do you . . . do you think we could put all of that behind us and not have any secrets again?' Her throat closed over as she said the last part of her rehearsed speech: 'I really want a relationship with you, Dad.'

There was nothing more to say, so she didn't. She just sat and watched his face, wondering at the memories and emotions flittering behind his closed eyes. The lifeless babies? Had he held them in his arms before giving them to the nurse to prepare for burial? Or had he and her mum bathed and dressed them themselves, then handed them to the funeral director? Was he remembering the breakdown in relations between his wife and his daughter? Had he automatically sided with Pip, or had he tried to stand up for Chelsea? What other scenes from his life that she knew nothing about were passing through his mind?

None of it mattered, Chelsea decided. She'd said what she wanted to say and now it was up to him. All she hoped was that she hadn't overburdened him. She didn't want to exhaust him. Or scare him.

She was so lost in thought, she didn't realise he was squeezing her hand gently. Holding her breath, she looked at her dad and, even though his eyes were still shut, he was smiling.

∾

It was just about dark when the doctor arrived at the ward and Aria was getting tired and cranky.

Chelsea had begun to worry she wasn't going to make it home in time to have dinner with Lily, when he pushed open the door and came in with a large grin.

'I heard from the nurses that you were awake and chatty, Mr Taylor. And you've got visitors! That's nice. How are you feeling?'

'Not too bad.' Tom's voice was gruff and Chelsea could still see the redness around his eyes from the tears that had slipped out earlier. Although of course they weren't tears, only his eyes watering from all the medication, according to him!

'Great! Let me have a look . . .' He pushed the sheets aside so he could see Tom's ankle, and Chelsea gasped. It was held together with what looked like a gadget from outer space. The pins encompassed the whole ankle and at certain points looked like they pierced the skin to hold the bones in place. His skin was a deep purple—the sort of colour Chelsea imagined a dead person's skin would be as they decomposed.

'Oh my God, what a mess!' she said involuntarily, then wished she hadn't spoken as Aria looked up from the iPad she was playing on and saw it too.

'Yucky,' she said, wrinkling her nose up.

'Oh no, this isn't too bad. I've seen much, much worse. The swelling has gone down a little, but I think we've got a couple more days before you'll be close to seeing the inside of an operating theatre, Tom.' He examined the ankle a little more then stood up. 'So how about I organise a transportation ambulance to take you to Adelaide over the next couple of days? What do you think?'

'If that's what you reckon, doc.'

'Sure is.' Ryan pulled Tom's chart from the end of his bed and wrote a few notes before asking how the pain was.

'About a seven.'

'I'll write up some more meds. These ones might make you a bit drowsy too, so if you come in and your father is asleep,' he said to Chelsea, 'that's why.'

She nodded.

'Now, Mr Taylor, Chelsea and I had a chat yesterday . . .'

'I know,' Tom spoke up in a strong voice. 'She told me today. And you do what you gotta do. I've not been wanting to admit there's something amiss with me, but I know there is. You organise what you need to and I'll do it.'

Chelsea's eyebrows shot up and she leaned forwards. 'Really? You've known and not said anything?'

Tom shrugged. 'Didn't want anyone to think I was going mad. Didn't think anyone would've noticed.'

'Cal has,' Chelsea said softly.

Her dad looked down at the sheets and twisted them in his hands.

'Mr Taylor, can you tell me what's been happening?'

Tom told him about a few incidents she knew nothing about. Chelsea felt as though someone was squeezing her heart. Where was the strong man who had tossed her into the air when she was small? Held the reins of a horse in his hands and been able to throw a sheep?

'He's an old sixty-three,' she thought. She listened to Ryan tell her dad there was certainly something going on with his memory, but they needed to do tests to find out what it was.

'I'll organise for you to see a neurologist in Adelaide. They'll make a hospital visit, okay?'

Tom nodded and seemed exhausted with the effort.

'Righty-o, I'd better get on with my rounds. Nice to see you both.'

'I've got to get going too, Dad. Aria needs to go home and I'm having dinner with Lily.'

'Run along then, both of you. I'm ready for a sleep anyway. Tell Cal I want to see him.'

'Will do. And I'll see you in the morning, Dad. Coming Aria? Say goodbye to Papa.'

The little girl gave him a kiss and handed him her toy bear that she'd been playing with. 'You keep Pandy tonight, Papa,' she said. 'So you don't get scared.'

Tom took the bear and cuddled it. 'Thank you, Aria. I need Pandy tonight.'

She touched his hand and he grabbed hers, giving it a squeeze.

Ryan held the door open and they walked down the corridor together.

'Are you happy with that outcome?' the doctor asked Chelsea.

'He took it a lot better than I expected.'

Ryan stopped and leaned against the wall. 'Sometimes it's a relief to be told there's something wrong. Dementia patients, before they're diagnosed, often feel like they're going mad—that's the way they describe it. Now I'm not saying that's where this is headed, just that talking about it is a relief.'

Chelsea nodded.

'Good, well, I'd better be off.'

'So you're not from here?' Chelsea asked as they walked together towards the hospital entrance.

'No, Port Augusta. I've got to say, though, it's always nice to come here and get away from the busyness of the hospital there. I enjoy staying at the pub and having a few counter meals. This is my third time back and I'm just beginning to meet some of the locals. Almost like coming home now.'

'Don't your family find it hard while you're away?'

'No family, just me.' He grinned. 'Makes it easier to do this job.'

She smiled. 'I can't see that being a doctor is at all easy.'

'It has its moments. What do you do, Chelsea?'

'I've just retired as a concert pianist.' Suddenly it felt right to say that. There was no need to hide that she wasn't working anymore; she'd just retired. Anyone was allowed to do that. 'I've been away from Barker for a while, and when I came home this time, it felt right to stay. And I guess Dad might need me as time goes on.'

'He might. Are you the only child?'

'Yeah.' She stopped. 'It's just Dad and me. And Aria.' She smiled as she stopped at the front door and Aria said, 'Yes, and me!'

'I guess that makes three of us now,' Chelsea said.

'I guess it does, and it'll be nice for you all to be together.'

Chapter 26

Dave pulled a beer from the fridge and waved it at Jack.

'If you're offering,' Jack answered.

'So, fill me in.' Dave handed him the stubby and poured Kim a wine. 'Any breakthroughs?'

'My biggest breakthrough,' Kim said, 'is I've convinced Jack to try online dating.'

Dave looked at Jack in surprise. 'Really? I thought you were deadset against that.'

Jack took a long pull of his beer and shrugged. 'Guess beggars can't be choosers, can they?'

'You're not a beggar, don't be stupid,' Kim said. 'And there's nothing wrong with online dating. I know plenty of people who've tried it and found lovely partners.'

'Like who?' Dave wanted to know. He kept a straight face as he copped a severe glare from Kim.

'Oh, you know, friends I knew before I met you.'

A smile spread across Jack's face. 'Really?' he asked. 'Maybe I should ask to meet them. I'm beginning to think I've been set up here.'

'Not at all,' Kim said quickly, but a rosy blush was spreading from her neck towards her face.

'My wife seems to have hoodwinked you, Jack. But I wouldn't worry, she does it to everyone. If she thinks it's worth a try, you might as well have a go.' He started to say: 'After all, what have you got to lo—' when Kim stepped on his foot.

'I've looked at a couple of them,' Jack confessed, 'but the questionnaires . . . I mean, really, who cares what my favourite colour is? How's that going to find me the perfect partner?' He took another swig of beer and thumped the bottle down heavily on the table.

'Who knows? They must put all the answers into a computer and wait for them to spit out matches.'

'I guess if it works, it'll be a story to tell the grandkids.' Jack sounded despondent.

'Absolutely. Now instead of wallowing in self-pity, do you want to hear about the bones?'

Jack straightened up and Kim leaned forwards.

'You've got news?'

'I do. The man in the grave was murdered.'

Kim gasped and clutched her hands to her chest. 'Really, how?'

Dave gave her a little pat on the shoulder. 'Settle down there. We in the police force don't usually get excited about murders.'

'What's the drum?' Jack asked.

'Not only did he have a cracked skull, there was a shotgun hole found in one of his ribs.'

The kitchen was quiet as they all took in the news.

'It must be one of the hawker travellers, yeah?' Jack said. 'The family that was squatting.'

'Could be. I ran into Chelsea at the hospital today and she said her great-grandfather, Baxter, used to write diaries. I asked her to have a look and see if she could find them. Hopefully there might be the name of a family or something in there we can use.'

Kim twirled her wineglass around on the bench, a frown on her face. 'What I want to know is, who is this Baxter?'

Sitting at the kitchen table, Dave crossed his legs and leaned back in the chair. 'From everything Tom and Chelsea are telling me, he's Tom's grandfather. He's the one they all remember.'

'I'd love to get hold of Leo's birth certificate and see who's named on there as his father. I think it'll be Oscar.'

Jack took another swig of beer. 'I didn't think there were allowed to be scandals back in those days. Wasn't everyone a God-fearing Christian who knew they'd face Judgement Day if they sinned?'

Dave laughed. 'There might've been more scandals back then than there are today. Did I ever tell you about my great-great-grandmother?'

Kim looked at him curiously. 'Nope, what about her?'

'On my mother's side. She was a feisty old stick by all accounts. Living way out in the middle of nowhere, raising four kids. Husband used to come and go a bit, but she kept the farm running. Had all the kids working, doing their bit.

'Apparently, even though she was married, there was always another man in the background. Now whether she was having an affair with him for years, I don't know, but one day she got sick of the husband disappearing all the time, so she turfed him out. Told him not to come back.'

Jack was listening wide-eyed. 'Turfed him out? Were they allowed to do that?'

'Pretty unusual for the woman to do it, but those women out in the bush, living in nothing but a humpy, they were tough, no-nonsense. If they felt someone wasn't pulling their weight, they got told!'

'There are a few people who could learn that today,' Kim said wryly.

'Anyway,' Dave continued, 'it didn't take long, once this bloke left, for the new one to move in. They didn't marry or anything, just moved him right on in. Like I said, he'd been hanging around for years, so you'd think they had a pretty good understanding of each other, but the minute they got together, Granny decided she didn't like him as much as she thought she did and got rid of him too. The story goes that she chased him out of the house with a hot poker!'

'Good Lord,' Kim said with a giggle.

'Here's the best bit,' Dave said with a cheeky grin. 'He didn't have any clothes on!'

'He wasn't keeping up to her standards?' Jack asked with a snort. 'I don't reckon I'd want a hot poker near my dick,' he added with a pained look on his face.

'His hot poker couldn't have been working the way she wanted it to,' Kim said with another snort of laughter. She put her hand on Dave's shoulder and opened her mouth to say something else, but Dave quietened her with a shake of his head.

He was almost certain she was about to say, 'Good thing yours works,' but with Jack in the room that would be like talking in front of the children. He wanted to laugh but decided that would only encourage her.

His phone vibrated in his pocket and he took it out to look at the screen. Frowning, he slid the green answer bar across and said, 'G'day, Dean. How's things, mate?'

Kim's eyes widened at the mention of Dean's name.

Dave got up and wandered outside to the patio so he could continue the call in private. 'How're you coping, mate?'

'It's something different,' Dean said in a shaky voice.

Dave leaned against the patio wall and took a sip of beer. 'Tell me about it?' he invited.

'Geez, Dave,' his voice broke off. Then he cleared his throat and sounded stronger when he continued, 'Actually, I don't want to talk about it. I'm ringing about something else.'

Staying silent, Dave waited.

'Would you come home?'

'What do you mean, come home?' Dave asked slowly.

'Not forever. Just to see us. There's unfinished business here, don't you think?'

Dave blew out a breath and stared at the stars. 'There's a lot of unfinished business in lots of people's lives, Dean. I'm not sure what me coming home would achieve.' He didn't want to be forced to admit to his family that, after all this time, he was still angry with his father and brothers. More at his father, but Dave had always thought his brothers had been quite happy to see the back of him as well.

'I'm going to ask you to think about Mum,' Dean said. 'Don't worry about me or the farm. It's Mum who needs to see you. And to meet Kim. I mean we'd all love to meet her and to see you both.' There was a long silence before Dean spoke again. 'Dave, when my arm was in the auger, I didn't feel any pain. I knew what was happening and I was frightened—shit scared. But no pain. All I thought about was Mandy and making things right with her. My kids and you and Adam. For some reason our family has brooded over history that wasn't of our making.

'Dad caused all of this breakdown. And we're partly to blame for that by keeping it going. Wouldn't it be better to fix this before it goes any further? Before it's too late to fix things? Like Mum said to you the other day, she's not getting any younger.'

The stars in the dark sky calmed Dave. This was what he'd fought the whole time he'd been living in South Australia. The black mist of fear swirled around him when he thought about going home. He loved his mum for sure, and he'd love to see her. But the hurt and devastation caused by his dad kicking him off the farm with nothing wasn't that easy to get past. With Kim's coaching, he'd talked a little about it, but he was a policeman. He'd been taught how to prevent feelings from affecting the way he operated, so he'd buried it and didn't think about Wind Valley Farm and his family unless it was absolutely necessary.

'Dave?'

Clearing his throat, he said, 'I'm here. Just thinking.'

'Do you have any holidays coming up?'

'I'll have to check with Kim,' he stalled. 'I think she had plans to go and see her sister.' Even as he said it, he knew she'd be on a plane to Perth in a heartbeat if it meant he was going to see his family.

He could hear her saying, 'For someone who is so smart, you can be so stupid at times. You've got to face up to things, Dave. If you let them go they only get worse, until they reach crisis point, and when you get there, you usually can't fix the problem.'

'Well, look, I just wanted to talk to you about it. Having a near-death experience changes the way you look at things. Nothing material matters anymore. The only things I care about are the people I love: Mandy, the kids, Mum. You.'

'Me?'

'You're my brother. At the end of the day we're blood. I don't like what Dad did to you, but back then I wasn't strong enough to stand up to him, or even see the need. I'd been programmed by him to agree with most things he did. I've got to make up for that.

'The past few weeks while I've been lying here in hospital, I've been replaying the night that changed everything. The one when you left. Course, I never knew anything about you going until after the buck's night. I came home and the first thing I saw was Mum passed out on the floor. And you wouldn't have known about that until later because you'd already left. Dad said you'd gone and I didn't understand what he meant. I thought you'd gone to get help, but when the ambulance arrived, he said you'd left the farm. Then I got angry because I couldn't believe you'd do that, right before my wedding.

'It was when Mum was able to tell me what happened that I realised it wasn't your fault. I need to apologise to you for not standing up in all this time—for you.' He took a breath. 'Material things don't matter,' he repeated. 'But you're not material. You're my brother and I want to sort out all of this shit so I can have you as my friend.'

Chapter 27

Chelsea raised her glass of wine to Lily, who responded with her glass of lemon, lime and bitters.

'Here's to new beginnings,' Chelsea said with a smile.

'Yes, new beginnings. I can't believe you're going to stay here for good now. Aria and Alecia will be in the same class at school! I never expected anything like that to happen. Is she asleep?'

'Ha! Me neither. Never in a million years did I think I'd ever come back to Barker to live. And, yes, when I looked in on her she was snoring. Poor little thing. These past few days have been a bit unsettling for her.'

Lily put down her glass and looked at Chelsea. 'So, spill. Tell me everything.'

Chelsea smiled and took another sip of wine. 'There's so much.'

'I've got all night. Tell me about Aria's dad—how did you meet him?'

'That's a short story.' Chelsea explained why she'd started working on cruise ships then said, 'In the staff quarters of the ship, it's a bit like a social world in itself. While all the passengers are upstairs, on the decks, drinking and eating and having a good time, well, we do the same below. I met a few of the other musicians and they were all really nice. We did some gigs together—I played the piano for some of the singers and also performed solo. None of us had any family around, so we became each other's family while we were on the boat. Jazzy—she was a jazz singer of course— was there to save money so she could build a house in the English countryside. It was her fifth tour.

'Then there was Gray, who was a comedian. Totally hilarious. I'd steal into his shows on the top decks if there was room. He'd have the crowd in stiches. I don't know how comedians tell jokes and make people laugh without laughing themselves. He was driven, wanted to have a TV series of his own.'

'So everyone had a reason for being there?'

'Absolutely, it was a stepping stone.' She took another mouthful of wine and swirled it around in her mouth. 'Mine was to pretend I was still somebody. I still mattered in the world of music.'

'Oh, Chels, you've always been somebody. Your music never defined who you were. It was part of you, but not everything about you.' Lily leaned forwards, distress on her face.

Chelsea shrugged. 'I don't see it that way. Anyway, not only was Gray funny, he was smooth and addictive.

He always knew the right things to say to make you feel good. I was still smarting from not being able to play as a concert pianist anymore and he sort of took me under his wing on the first cruise. But on the second one, well, that was different.

'We already knew each other, and it didn't take long for us to become an item.' She smiled sadly. 'He was everything I ever wanted in a man: good-looking, funny, caring. I know, I know,' she said at Lily's raised eyebrows. 'Sounds too good to be true. And he was.

'I didn't know I was pregnant until after I got off the ship. The thing was, he'd never made any plans for us to catch up. I had his phone number, but he had to go back to England to see his mum and dad and I had . . . Well, not much to do until the next cruise.

'After a month I missed him so much I decided to fly to England to see him.'

'Oh, Chels,' Lily said, her face full of sadness.

Through gritted teeth, Chelsea said, 'Yep. Everything that is running through your head right now happened. He had a wife and two littlies.

'He never expected me to come over. I managed to track him down to where he lived, through Facebook and a few Google searches. I planned to turn up at the front door to surprise him. I was waiting to cross the road and knock on his door when his wife came out, with the girls all wrapped up in winter coats and scarves.' She swallowed. 'I turned and walked away then. I was absolutely devastated.

'But, do you know,' Chelsea's tone changed to upbeat, 'I don't care. I wouldn't change anything because Aria is the best thing that's ever happened to me. One day I'm sure she'll want to find her dad. And I've promised myself I'll never lie to her, so the minute she asks I'll tell her.'

Lily reached across and held her friend's hand. 'What a roller-coaster of a life you've been on! Makes mine sound incredibly boring.'

'Tell me about you. And the hubs and kids.'

'Oh, I don't know, what's to tell? I got married, stayed in the same town, had the two kids. I deal with day-to-day shitty nappies, teething, the occasional sex when I feel like it. It's everything I dreamed about growing up.'

Chelsea laughed. 'Do you love your life?'

'I do,' Lily answered simply. 'Look, we travelled before we got married. Went to South Africa and America. And I'm sure we'll do more, once the kids have grown, but right now I don't want to change a thing. Well, perhaps the youngest could sleep through the night, that'd be a bonus.' She laughed. 'Little bugger is going to be a night owl like his father.' She picked at the salad in front of her. 'Now you've decided to stay here, what are you going to do?'

'Workwise?' Chelsea asked, spearing a piece of chicken.

'Yeah.'

'To be honest, I have no idea. Dad will need some looking after and I have some savings. I'll need to go back to Sydney and sell my flat, but I can do that when there's time. It's not urgent.'

'Oh yeah, what happened with Tom?'

Chelsea filled her in, finishing with: 'It'll depend on what the neurologist says. I don't suppose it'll be a quick diagnosis. Unless they do a scan and find something.'

'It mightn't be dementia, Chels. My grandma has MCI. Mild cognitive impairment. It's when the person has the symptoms of dementia, but it's not bad enough to disrupt daily life. Sometimes it goes on to become dementia, but other times it doesn't. So far, touch wood,' she tapped her head, 'it hasn't progressed.'

Chelsea thought about that. If there was significant memory loss it probably didn't matter what the condition was called. She sighed. 'Well, no matter what the disorder is, it's going to be a bit of a slog until we know what we're dealing with. At the moment, not knowing what is exactly wrong is like playing with invisible balls. We're not sure about anything! And,' she paused before smiling coyly, 'I'd rather play with balls I can see if you know what I mean!'

Lily snorted with laughter then cocked her head to the side. 'Sooo, was he happy you were staying?'

'Put it this way, he didn't say no and he smiled. Dad has never been big on emotions.' They ate quietly for a little while, then Chelsea said, 'Hey, can I ask you something?'

'What's that?'

'Why don't you drink?'

Lily kept eating, then put her fork down. 'Don't you remember?'

'Remember what?'

'I was the vollie ambo on call when your brother died. I was still a junior, at eighteen, but I was there.'

'I remember,' Chelsea said, corrected herself, then: 'I heard you were there.'

'I saw what alcohol could do to people. To friends. Jason's never got over it. Shane and Kelly, well, they seem like they're able to function, but you can always sense a deep sadness inside them.

'I never want to be in a situation where alcohol makes me do something I'll regret. Just the way it is.

'Oh, and don't worry, I *know* how much of a wowser this town reckons I am, but do I look like I care? Not one iota.' She smiled widely. 'Happy to be known as everyone's designated driver!'

'I saw Jason the night of the pageant.' Chelsea picked up her wineglass and twirled it between her fingers. 'He didn't look good.'

'He's had so many DD charges, it's a wonder he's still got his licence. It's crazy that one mistake you made when you were young can stuff up your whole life. Dale's death was an absolute tragedy and no one could have foreseen something like that happening, but the devastation his death caused goes on forever. Do you know what I mean? Like you guys, you'll never stop grieving for him, and no parent should ever bury their child. Jason lives with the knowledge he killed his friend every single day of his life.'

Chelsea swallowed hard and put down her glass. 'I miss my brother,' she said. 'Jason wasn't to blame. It was an accident. The coroner's report said so.'

Lily leaned forwards and reached out to Chelsea. 'I know that. Maybe, if you're staying, it would be a nice thing to go and see him.'

'Maybe.'

Sensing the mood had become a little heavy, Lily changed the subject. 'Now speaking of balls you can see, tell me about this gorgeous bloke who's working for your dad . . .' She wiggled her eyebrows at Chelsea.

Chelsea snorted. 'What are you talking about?'

'Cal.'

'I know who you mean and, yeah, he's around. But . . .' Chelsea made her tone casual.

'And exceptionally gorgeous, wouldn't you say?'

'Hmm, I'd agree with that.'

'And?'

'And nothing. I don't need a bloke. I have a child to raise.'

'But he's gorgeous!'

'That doesn't mean I'm about to jump him in some darkened corner of the hay shed.'

'Maybe you should. I saw your face when I mentioned his name. You're keen!'

'Lily!'

Her friend laughed. 'I'll be keeping an eye on you two!'

'Nothing to see.' Chelsea tried not to sound regretful. 'Invisible balls!'

Lily wiggled her eyebrows suggestively but, to Chelsea's relief, she changed the subject.

'What's this I hear about an excavation going on here?' she said. 'What's the goss about that? A murder, no less!'

'Oh my God, Lily. Have you turned into the biggest gossip? There's nothing to say it was a murder!'

'I haven't been able to gossip with anyone for years, so humour me.'

'Right. So you mean the skeleton? That's really weird, isn't it? The rain washed a heap of dirt away and exposed this skeleton, so Dave Burrows, the detective, is trying to find out who it is.'

'But how did the bones get there in the first place?'

Chelsea laughed. 'Geez, I don't know. Maybe someone buried them?'

'How strange though. To be buried there for so long without anyone knowing.'

'Dave was saying it's going to be hard to identify them. There was one piece of evidence that might help though.'

'What's that?' Lily's eyes were glowing. 'You do realise this is one of the most exciting things to happen around here since, like, forever!'

'I must have you wrong, Lily Jackson. I never thought I'd see you getting excited over someone else's misfortune.'

'Oops, sorry.' Lily dropped her eyes and tried to look apologetic.

'Not working, Lils! But, here, this is what they found with the skeleton.' She took out her phone and found Dave's text message with the photo of the brooch.

Taking the phone, her friend examined the picture, enlarging it and shifting the screen so she could see all of it. 'Stunning.'

There was a knock on the door and Cal, covered in dust, stuck his head in.

Both women swung around, and Chelsea smiled and gave a small wave. 'Hi.'

'Oh bugger, sorry, didn't realise you had company. I saw the lights on and just wanted to know how Tom's going.'

Lily got up. 'Don't go, Cal. We've just about finished here, haven't we, Chels? We can catch up tomorrow when you're back in town.'

'You're welcome to stay,' Chelsea said, getting up too. 'I won't be long talking to Cal.'

'No, no, I'll leave you two to it,' she grinned at Chelsea. 'Besides, hubs will be wondering where I am—it's past ten and since I had kids I don't do late nights!' She hugged Chels. 'We've got loads of time now you're staying. I'm so glad we had tonight though. Cleared the air with so many things.'

'But not your wedding.'

Lily shrugged. 'You didn't get the invite. What more do I need to know? I've got my old friend back now. See you tomorrow, okay?'

Chelsea waved her goodbye and turned to Cal, exhaustion beginning to set in. 'How was your day?' she asked, indicating for him to sit down.

'I won't sit,' he said. 'Bit dirty. Just finished digging out the top dam with the dozer.'

'What, you've only just finished work?'

He nodded. 'Wanted to get that dam done so I can start on the next one tomorrow. How's things at the hospital?'

Chelsea told him what Ryan had said, then added on the bit Lily had told her about MCI and a possible prognosis. 'But they've got to run the tests.'

'You're right. Doesn't matter what they call the bloody thing, what matters is he's probably got some kind of memory loss. Shit.' Cal rubbed his hands over his jeans. 'I was really hoping I'd been imagining things.'

'Dad was actually relieved, if you can believe that. He thought he was going mad.'

'Yeah, right.' Cal's voice was soft and distressed. Chelsea moved from her chair to stand next to him.

'It'll be okay,' she said. 'Whatever happens. I haven't told you yet, but I've decided to stay. Aria can go to school here. I'll be here to help.'

Cal looked at her. 'You're staying?'

'Yeah. Aria and I are staying.'

Chapter 28

When she finally climbed into bed that night, Chelsea was exhausted.

Even though she needed sleep, she couldn't relax. Cal's reaction to the news about her dad had made her sad. And she was regretful too. After all, she'd lost so many years of her dad's life. But she'd decided it was all about the future rather than the past now. She was determined to make the best of every day she had in front of her.

Getting up and turning the light on, she pulled out one of the photo albums from the box her dad had given her. Starting to flick through it, she recognised old photos of her and Dale when they were younger. She found a photo of herself, dressed up for the pageant on Pinto. She smiled and thought she must show Aria.

The next album had photos of Gran and Papa, and there was even one of Great-Granda Baxter. He was in the lounge room, dressed smartly in a suit. She wondered what the event was. Maybe Sunday church.

Seeing the photo reminded her she was supposed to be finding Baxter's diaries for Dave. She finished flicking through the photo album without seeing anything remarkable then went into her dad's office. She opened cupboards and looked through them without finding anything other than old paperwork.

Knowing the cellar was empty, she wasn't sure where else to look, until she remembered the books without titles on the spines in the sitting room.

The ladder was in the same spot it had always been, just behind the door in her mum's office. Setting it up next to the bookcase, she carefully climbed up and pulled out as many as she could carry, then stepped back down the ladder again. She piled the books one on top of the other on the coffee table and then opened the first one.

A musty smell greeted her, and she saw beautiful cursive writing filling the pages. As she read, she realised it was an invoice book rather than a diary. She was disappointed because she thought she recognised the writing as Baxter's. She'd seen it at various times throughout her life, although in the examples she'd seen when she was little, the letters were shakier and more fragile than the bold, strong handwriting here.

Sold to Hunters Co-op, four goats at one pound per head.
Sold to Hunters Co-op ten mutton at one pound per head.

Putting the book down, she picked up the next one. It was the same handwriting but this time the pages were full of handwriting and she knew she'd found what she was looking for.

It was common to keep a diary back in Baxter's day. It was the way people kept records. She'd seen Great-Granda Baxter writing in a diary, and then her grandfather as well. Two different lots of diaries for two different generations.

As she flicked through, there didn't seem to be many details of daily life, rather the mundane information of farming activities, rainfall and other information about Shandona. The next one was the same, and the one after that.

She put them back on the shelf and gathered a few more. These were different. The writing seemed older.

I am struggling with the work I have to do, with three little ones at my feet. Milking cows, churning the butter, cooking cakes. I don't want to be stuck in the kitchen just because I am a woman. I was raised to be able to work in the paddocks, work the sheep. I can handle a horse better than any man, yet here I've been assigned to the house. It is frustrating and demoralising.

Chelsea ran her hands across the page, wondering whose writing it was. Her gran's? She didn't remember her writing often, more her knitting and crocheting, and she wasn't much of an outdoors worker. She'd go on picnics or a drive around Shandona with Papa, but not be out in the paddock every day. In fact, Gran loved the kitchen. In Chelsea's mind her sponges and scones were legendary.

These must be her great-grandmother's diaries. But she could see no mention of Baxter as she scanned the pages.

He is angry today. My normal ways of keeping him content are not working. Womanly wiles usually do. My mother always taught me that the way to a man's heart is through one of two things. The first is his stomach; she never told me about the second directly but handed me a book titled The Sex Factor. *It told of the whole act and was clearly written by a man.*

I was shocked when I first read it. After all, having slept my whole life next to my mother, the thought of an act such as that was quite confronting. However, I've learned about the uses of sex and calming him is one of them.

I suspect tonight there will be violence and all I can hope for is the children will not be awake.

Chelsea's eyes widened as she continued to read.

It's hot today and I wished I didn't have to wear long sleeves. Of course I do, because the bruises are a deep purple colour now. I want him to stop. But every time he loses another gambling match, it is me he takes it out on. Not his own weak nature. He disgusts me.

Looking for a date, she continued to read, absorbed in the horrible life of this woman, who had poured her soul out onto the pages.

I am with child again. I do not want another baby.

That was the last entry.

Grabbing the next diary with a sense of urgency, Chelsea opened the cover.

Being in love with the wrong man must somehow run in my family. My sister, Agnes, confided in me recently she has a lover. I, of course, was shocked, for she has children and a husband. However, I couldn't judge. That is the Lord's job and who am I to do his work for him. However, there is a man I love, though he does not know it, and it is not my husband.

This man has been my friend for years and I have only recently understood how much I care for him. He calls in here regularly, when he returns from his hunting trips.

When he arrived last time, he had a family with him—not his, but one he was helping.

Perhaps that's why I love him so; he wants to help everyone, including me. I don't think I'll ever forget his anger when I told him about the bruises on my thighs. He swore he would make it stop, but I don't see the point. Nothing will change.

The desperation in the woman's words tore at Chelsea and she got up and paced the room. It couldn't have been her great-grandmother who wrote these entries. She and Baxter were in love; everyone could see it. Baxter's desolation when Adelia died had been devastating for the family to watch—her mum had talked about it for years afterwards. It had been true love.

She'd always adored the stories her mum had told her of Baxter's romantic gestures towards her great-grandmother. He'd pick flowers from the paddocks and bring them home for her. He'd leave little love notes around the house, and every night he would bring her a cup of tea in bed, then they would read the Bible together.

Who was this nameless woman?

None of what she was reading made any sense. Then she had an idea. Racing over to the antique writing desk against the wall, she began searching for letters her great-grandmother had written.

Frantically flicking through the envelopes and hymn books, she finally came across a card: *To my darling Baxter, with every ounce of love I hold, Adelia.*

Chelsea wasn't a handwriting expert by any stretch, but at a glance she could see this was the same writing.

'Oh my God, she had another life! No, no, no.' Chelsea's brain was racing. 'No, not another life, another husband. Other than Baxter.' She glanced around wildly and her eyes fell on the plastic folder.

Spreading all the certificates around, she examined each one carefully. There was Dale's birth and death certificate, along with the two other children. Her parents' marriage certificate, and registers of births and marriages going back three generations. Carefully she picked up the paper-thin marriage certificate for her great-grandmother, Adelia. It was handwritten, and she marvelled at the beautiful writing. Loopy cursive that had long ago stopped being taught in schools—every letter was the exactly the same height and width.

'Beautiful,' she muttered, tracing the words.

Then she saw it.

Oscar and Adelia.

'That's not right,' she said out loud. 'It was Baxter and Adelia.' She looked up at the piano that had come from Great-Granda Baxter. 'It was Baxter and Adelia,' she repeated. But as she said it, she realised her first reaction was right. Great-Grandma Adelia had been married before.

She flicked back through the papers and re-read everything carefully. Baxter's name didn't appear anywhere. And Leo's birth certificate said that his father's name was Oscar.

But who was Oscar? Chelsea didn't know, but the one thing she was sure of was that Baxter wasn't her dad's real grandfather.

Chapter 29

Chelsea laid out the diaries and certificates in front of Dave. They were sitting in his office at the Barker Police Station after Chelsea had dropped Aria off for a play date with Alecia and Lily.

'It's all in here,' she said. 'Read this bit.' She pointed to a page and Dave started reading.

The baby died in birth today. She was born too early and there was nothing to be done. I don't care. I've been unravelling ever since I found out I was with child again. Perhaps I am going mad, but I don't care, not about the birth, nor the death. I'm just pleased the child didn't live. I couldn't cope with another baby. Three is more than we can feed, especially during this awful Depression.

Of course, he hit me when he found out. Told me I was good for nothing. 'Can't even birth a child. What you were put here on earth to do!' he screamed at me.

I hate him. I hate him.

I will have to bury the baby somewhere. Maybe the reserve area. It is pretty and peaceful. Although not our land yet, there is the possibility it will be in time.

Although a few weeks ago when I last passed by, there was a family of squatters camped there. I have overheard Oscar lamenting the fact, although he hasn't done anything to move them on. That's not surprising as he's very weak. I saw a woman with a small child—she had a friendly face. It would be nice to talk to another woman, especially a mother, because I have to wonder if I am the only woman who feels the way I do.

There is a heavy cloud descending upon my shoulders, like the fog which sits on the hills during the autumn mornings. I don't want to get out of bed each day. Any extra money I manage to earn by selling the goats or cheese I make, he takes to the local hotel and gambles with it.

He is not a man but a coward.

Dave re-read the diary entry. 'So we have reference to the body of a female baby but not to the man. I'm guessing you have information on him too.'

Chelsea took the diary back and turned to another page. 'It's horrific. I can't believe this has happened in my family,' she said quickly. 'Here,' she thrust the book back at him and Dave began to read again.

It happened without me even knowing it was going to happen. He came at me again, wanting to satisfy his needs. Usually I am compliant, but not this time. This time I fought

*him with every ounce of strength I had. But he still took
what he thought was rightfully his. It wasn't his to take!
When he'd finished, he walked away without even seeing
if I was all right! I pulled the gun out from under the bed.
I'd had it hidden there for the past two days, unsure what
I was going to do with it but feeling I needed it.*

There was nothing else written. Perhaps it was clear what
had happened, or maybe it wasn't. There was no way of
knowing for sure. But Dave felt fairly certain. He could see
it happening—a woman at the end of her tether, a woman
who'd been continually beaten and raped, expected to work
within the house and do as she was told. He could imagine
her reaching down slowly as Oscar walked away, taking
out the gun and lining it up with his chest. The noise of
the shot. Oscar falling backwards, cracking his head as he
fell. Perhaps she screamed, or perhaps she walked over and
stood looking down at him silently, without regret.

No one would ever know. As much as Dave abhorred
violence, he somehow felt that this woman was justified in
what she did. Well, perhaps not justified; it was her only
option in the 1930s. Oscar would've kept on doing what
he had been if she hadn't stopped him. Thank God today's
society was starting to talk about domestic violence more
openly so that women were able to find help and get out
of these kinds of desperate situations.

'What do we do now?' Chelsea asked.

'That's a really good question. We can take some DNA
from you and Tom and see if it matches. When it's a few

generations down, it will never be one hundred percent correct, but it'll be in the eighties at least. So you'll know if the man in the grave was Oscar, Tom's grandfather. Do you want to do that?'

'Well, yeah, I guess. I don't know about Dad, I'm really not sure whether to hit him with this or not. It's . . .' Her voice broke off. 'It's a lot to take in.'

'Have a think about it. Now we're pretty certain we know who the bones belong to, there is no rush to do anything.'

Chelsea thanked Dave and walked out into the bright sunlight, slipping her sunglasses back on, before heading towards the hospital. She kept shaking her head, unable to believe the skeleton in the closet she'd discovered. Or rather on the reserve.

There were still a few unanswered questions though—whose brooch was it, and how did Baxter slip into the family unnoticed? Or for that matter, how did Oscar disappear without anyone noticing? Surely his gambling buddies must have realised he wasn't attending their games.

Still deep in thought, she ran into Ryan at the hospital entrance.

'You're looking serious,' he said. 'Everything okay?'

'Fine, fine. Well, not really, but nothing's wrong.'

Ryan chuckled softly. 'Do you often talk in riddles?'

Laughing, Chelsea said, 'I guess that sounded very odd. I've discovered a family secret and it's a fairly big one. I'm trying to wrap my head around it.'

'Sounds intriguing.'

Blinking, she was lost for words. 'It is. It really is!'

'I'd love to hear about it some time, but I'm in the process of organising a transfer for Tom. He'll be going to Adelaide tomorrow.' He kept walking.

'That's great.' She said to his departing back.

She started on again, only to bump into Cal. 'Oh, hey,' she said. 'Been in to see Dad?'

'Yeah. Just dropped in quickly. Thought I'd see you in there.'

Chelsea saw his eyes drop to her mouth, then come back to her face. 'I had to go to the police station first. You'll never believe what I found out last night. I've worked out who the bones are!' she said quickly.

'Really? Who? How'd you do that?' The questions came thick and fast.

'My great-grandfather and his baby girl.'

Cal's breath came out with a whoosh. 'That's not small shit. How the hell did you work that out?'

Chelsea couldn't help herself. She laughed. Then stopped. 'Oh my God,' she said.

'What?'

'I . . .' She looked up at him. 'I don't know, I feel . . . I don't know, I'm just pleased I've decided to stay.'

Cal stared at her and she took a shaky breath as a flash of longing passed over his face. She reached out and put a hand on his chest, not breaking eye contact.

The door opened and two nurses chatting loudly to each other walked in and the moment was gone.

Stepping back, Cal said, 'That's got to be nothing but good.' He smiled at her. 'Let's have a drink tonight and you can tell me about it, okay?' He patted her shoulder in a brotherly way and jogged down the steps, leaving Chelsea wondering what was actually happening between them.

❧

'Hey, Dad,' Chelsea said cautiously after she'd established his memory was clear today. 'I want you to look at a couple of things I've found and tell me if you remember anything about them, okay?'

She opened a photo album and turned to a page with the picture of a couple in a wedding dress. 'Do you know these two?'

Tom slipped his glasses on and peered at the photo. 'Hmm, she looks like Adelia,' he said, taking the album from her. 'But that's not Baxter.' He flicked over the page and looked at another wedding photo. It was the same again: Adelia and Oscar.

'I've found out that Adelia was married to a guy called Oscar before she was with Baxter, Dad. Oscar was a horrible man, but Baxter was lovely. And after she got rid of Oscar, she was really happy.'

Tom stilled. 'The skeleton?'

Chelsea nodded. Today her dad's mind was as sharp as ever.

'I always thought . . .' He broke off.

Chelsea held her breath.

'I always thought there was something not quite right. They lived as if they had a secret—oh, we all loved them, adored them really. But they protected their privacy fiercely. Now it all makes sense.' Looking back down at the photos, he asked how she'd worked it out.

After she explained it all to him, she said, 'I can leave the diaries with you. Read them if you want to, but they're not pleasant reading.'

'Well, then,' her father said noncommittally.

'And Ryan said you're going to Adelaide tomorrow. I'm going to pick up Aria on my way home today and we'll pack up and meet you down there.' She bent down and kissed him. 'I'll see you in Adelaide, okay?'

Tom grabbed her hand. 'Thank you for coming home, Chelsea. It means the world to me.'

❧

There was one more thing Chelsea wanted to do before she left Barker.

Jason was in his father's sheep yards drafting lambs into different pens. One mob was larger than the other when she pulled up. He glanced up to see who'd arrived and froze. The lambs kept running, but Jason seemed to forget to use the drafting gate. Finally he stopped the sheep and put the block in. As he walked towards her, he wiped his brow nervously.

'Hope I'm not interrupting,' Chelsea said.

Jason didn't reply.

'I wanted to come and see you. To talk about . . . Dale.'

'I'm sorry,' Jason said, tears forming in the corners of his eyes. 'I see what happened every night. I dream about it every night. I'm so, so sorry. He was my *friend*.' His voice broke and the despair was etched deeply in his face.

Putting her hand on his shoulder, she smiled gently at him. 'I know. He was lots of people's friend. And lots of people miss him. I do. You do. Shane and Kelly would too, I'm sure.'

'Everything your dad has been through . . .'

Chelsea shook her head. 'That's got nothing to do with it. What happened to our family happened. None of us likes it, but we can't change it. You didn't kill Dale. It was an accident. No one's fault. You've got to let it go. You're the one who's still alive, so you have to live your life. Dale would've wanted you to.

'I've got to go to Adelaide tomorrow with Dad. You probably heard he had an accident. When I come back, you and I are going to catch up. We're going to talk, laugh about the old days and learn to live again, okay? Both of us need to learn to live.' She pulled him into a hug and felt his tears on her shirt.

❧

Chelsea picked up Aria from Lily's and brought her back to Shandona. After a day without her doggy friend, the little girl's first port of call was to see Scout. Her laughter as she let him off the chain and threw the stick for him was blissful.

'Mummy,' she called.

'Yes, honey?'

'Are kittens and dogs friends?'

Chelsea raised her eyebrows at the question. 'Why do you want to know?'

'I want to know if Scout and my kitten will play together.'

At that moment Cal arrived.

Forgetting her question, Aria flew across the lawn and threw herself at him. Chelsea loved the way he hugged her and asked what she'd done when she stayed at Hec and Colleen's and then how her day with Alecia had been.

Aria chatted nineteen to the dozen until she finally fell asleep on Cal's lap.

'Do you want me to carry her to bed?' he whispered.

'Would you?'

He nodded and gently put his hand under her small body and gathered her into his arms. Aria gave a low sleepy murmur. When he placed her on her bed she snored loudly.

Chelsea wanted to laugh, but held it in, glancing at Cal with amused eyes. She pulled up the sheets and tucked them in before kissing her daughter goodnight.

In the kitchen Cal poured Chelsea a glass of wine. 'Sounds like she's had a great time with her friends.'

'It sure does. But I think I'm going to have to get her a kitten! She fell in love with Sooty at Colleen's.' Chelsea grimaced. 'Dad hates cats! She's so exhausted I'll think she'll sleep for a year. Goodness knows what she's been doing!'

'Didn't you listen?' Cal asked. 'When she was with Colleen and Hec, they milked the dairy cow and played with the kitten. She'd helped make cakes—'

'Yeah, yeah, I heard!' Chelsea held his gaze as she smiled at him.

'And with Alecia today they painted their fingernails and braided their hair!' Cal winked at her, then asked, 'How are you feeling?' He handed her the wine.

'Spun out!' Chelsea laughed. 'Too many emotions to put names to. I feel like I've sorted out so much, but who knows what tomorrow will bring.'

'Shouldn't worry about tomorrow just yet. There's still a few more hours before the clock ticks over.'

'By the way, I was talking to my friend Tori today and she's going to come and visit. You'll like her.' She smiled at him. 'Come on, let's sit on the verandah so we don't wake Aria.' She walked outside and breathed in the cool, fresh air. A welcome change from the daytime heat. The landscape was quiet except for the crickets, and the moon bathed the land in a soft glow.

She felt Cal place his hands on her shoulders and turned to face him.

'Speaking of liking,' he said, 'Chels, I really like you.'

'I really like you too,' she answered.

'Do you . . . I mean, did my story . . .'

Chelsea put her finger on his lips. 'Shh. We've both made mistakes, but not with each other. We've got a fresh start, haven't we?'

Cal gathered her close to him and groaned quietly. 'Oh, I hope so.'

❧

Later, Chelsea tried to imagine what that night would've been like for Adelia. Did she send a message to Baxter to tell him to come? How did he know what had happened? Did he turn up to help her?

She imagined the night bathed in pale moonlight; two figures out in the dark. A woman in heavy skirts and a man in overalls. They had shovels and were digging on the edge of a hill. The tinny noise of steel on earth was echoing through the valley.

On the ground alongside them was a large man-sized bundle wrapped in hessian.

The two worked together silently until the hole was large enough and deep enough. Between them they rolled the bundle into the grave. Then the woman picked up a box, knelt next to the grave and, leaning over, let it drop to the bottom of the hole. She didn't stand until the man put his hands on her shoulders. The two stood together, their arms around each other, and Chelsea could hear them talking.

'How did you know to come back this time?' the woman asked.

'I felt it. I knew you needed me.'

'Our connection,' she said.

'I don't understand it, but I know what it feels like.'

'How do we explain this?' She pointed at the grave.

'We don't. Unless someone asks. It's the Depression, my love. People are walking away all the time. You woke up one morning and he was gone. I can't imagine anyone will ask any questions.'

The woman was agitated. 'But what if someone finds this? Digs them up?'

'I will make sure no one ever knows about it. You know the government is offering peppercorn leases for this type of land. I'll secure it. There will be no reason for anyone to know they are buried here. Trust me.'

'You know I do, Baxter. You know I do.'

'From here on in, your children are mine. I will raise them as if they were mine and love them the same way. You can do whatever you like—work the paddocks or stay at home. I want—*need*—you to be happy. I want us to be happy together.' Baxter bent down and kissed her.

'I will be just so long as I'm with you. Come on, let's finish this up,' Adelia said, taking the shovel in her hand again. 'Oh wait.' She fished around in her pocket and drew something out. 'I never could understand how something so beautiful could come from someone so awful,' she said.

Chelsea could see a piece of jewellery spiralling downwards. It caught in the moonlight and two ropes twisted together glinted.

She nodded. Yes, she thought. It could have happened that way.

Chapter 30

'Hey Joan, can you give me a hand for a minute?' Dave called out. He was looking at the Qantas website but wasn't sure how to book flights to Perth. Joan had a much better understanding of websites than he did.

'Where are you going?' she asked when she saw what was on the screen. 'Planning a second honeymoon?'

'No,' Dave answered grimly. He still wasn't really sure how he felt about the decision he'd made. 'Going to Perth to see the family. Can you please help me book the tickets? For some reason it won't let me use my frequent flyer points.'

Joan grabbed the mouse, clicked a few buttons. Fifteen minutes later he had the printed e-tickets in his hand and was walking out of the station towards his house.

'Oh my God, are you serious?' Kim squealed when he held them up to show her. She flung herself at him and hugged him tightly. 'You won't regret this,' she told him. 'Not one little bit.'

'I'll have to get Jack to look after everything here,' Dave said, frowning.

'He'll be fine. You've taught him so well. Whatever comes up he'll be able to cope with it, and if worse comes to worst, I'm sure you'll be able to help him over the phone.' She kissed him. 'Now call your mother.'

In the office, Dave picked up his phone and scrolled through the contacts, looking for Dean's number. He wanted to tell him first.

'G'day, it's me,' he said when Dean answered.

'Been thinking?'

'Yeah. Kim and I are booked on a flight Monday week. I've got a few things to tidy up here and then we'll be over.'

Silence, and then Dave heard the muffled sob. 'I'm real glad,' Dean said in a tight voice. 'Real glad. Mum's here, so she knows too.'

Dave cleared his throat. 'Good. Righty-o, I'll be in contact a bit later.'

'See ya, mate.'

Dave walked to the window, shoved his hands in his pockets and looked out. He rocked on his heels.

His grandfather had been a constant source of inspiration to him when he'd been growing up and he still remembered many of the pieces of advice he'd been given.

'Face your fears, son. Don't let them get the better of you. A man always stands up tall and faces them head on.'

Dave knew that was what he needed to do now. Face his fears, head back to Perth and hug his mother.

Epilogue

It was a cold, bleak day, with only a handful of people standing around a grave in the Barker cemetery.

A small coffin containing the remains of Oscar Taylor and the unnamed baby girl was laid to rest, far away from the graves of Adelia and Baxter.

Chelsea read a short Bible verse and Tom, still on crutches, said a few words, before the minister signalled for the coffin to be lowered into the ground.

Cal was holding Aria's hand, and on the other side of the grave were Lily, Jason, Jack, Dave and Kim.

Chelsea had been surprised to see how much clearer Jason's face looked. Perhaps her healing words had made a difference to him.

'Come on,' Aria complained. 'I'm so cold.'

'It's not that bad,' Cal said, taking off his coat and wrapping her in it. 'You're being soft.'

Aria pouted. 'I am not.'

Grinning, Cal picked her up. 'You just wanted my jacket, didn't you?'

'Who, me?' The pout changed to an innocent look. Chelsea smiled at the interaction. She was lucky. So lucky.

'I need a cup of tea,' Tom said.

'You all go on,' Chelsea said. 'I'll catch you up.'

The small group wandered back to their cars while Chelsea picked a path over to her mum's grave. She traced the words on the headstone with her finger, then sighed and leaned against it.

'Sorry, Mum,' she whispered. 'I guess I failed you there for a while. But I think I'm back on track. I'm home. Looking after Dad. He needs a bit of help at the moment. He's been forgetting things and the neurologist seems to think that some of his medication could be causing the memory loss. We've got a few more trials to get through before we see if that's the case. If it's not, well . . . But I'm not going to worry about that just yet.' She looked around her. 'I'm surprised. I didn't think I'd ever want to live here, but I do. So I'm staying. Aria loves it here too. And then there's Cal.' She turned and looked down at the grave. 'Yeah, did you hear that? Cal and I?' She laughed a little as she felt her stomach flip. 'Yeah, the "we" astounded me too, I can tell you.'

There was another blast of bitter wind and she shoved her hands in her pockets. 'I wish you could've seen Aria though. She looks like her father, but sometimes I see your expressions on her face. I think Dad does too.'

'Come on, Chelsea!'

She turned at the sound of her name and saw Cal waving her over.

'Guess I've got to go. Oh, one other piece of news. I've taken a job at the school teaching piano. Can you believe that?' She laughed loudly at the irony of it and knew her mum would probably be laughing wherever she was too.

Chelsea kissed the headstone. 'Love you, Mum.' And she turned and ran over to her family.

Acknowledgements

Firstly, I need to tell everyone that Allen & Unwin is the best publishing house in the world, and, Annette, I'm incredibly grateful for the understanding you've shown towards me over the past few months. Since my spinal surgery in January, writing has been a bit of a battle, but hopefully we're on the up and up from here.

My heartfelt thanks to all the wonderful people at Allen & Unwin—in particular Tom, Christa, Tami and Andrew. To Annette, I'm beyond thrilled to be under your banner. I can't tell you how much I appreciate your professionalism and guidance. Thank you for caring about my books as much as I do.

A very special thanks to Dave Byrne, who is continually on the end of the phone, email and messaging to answer my weird questions about investigations. Without you, Detective Dave wouldn't be who he is.

As always, colossal appreciation to Gaby Naher from The Naher Agency. No better agent exists.

To my beautiful kids, Rochelle and Hayden, one who is no longer a kid and one who is nearly not. Bear with me; just because you're off on your own adventures doesn't mean I won't worry or cry. You've been my world. You'll always be my world and I love you as much as is humanly possible.

To Amy Milne, you've always been such a special person within the book sphere for me and now we've taken it further. Here's to continued dealings!

It's always hard to find the words to let my special crew know how much I love and appreciate them. I'm a lucky girl to have such wonderful loyal friends. You all mean the world to me. To the people who know me best, you are everything I hold dear: Aaron and Cal, Catherine, Emma and Pete, Garry, Heather, Jan and Pete, Robyn, Tiffany.

Last year, I went home for Christmas, which I've only done three times in the last twenty-five years. When you're a farmer, leaving animals during the summer months just isn't possible, so heading to South Australia to celebrate Christmas was off the list for a long time. But not last year.

Finally, finally, with an L-plater in the car to help me drive, we set off across the Nullarbor, the anticipation of finally 'heading home' hanging in the air. Perhaps this is why I felt the need to write about Chelsea 'going home'. Every one of my senses seemed heightened as I drove the back roads to Mum and Dad's. I felt every emotion there was to feel—happiness, sadness, numbness.

All the little memories came back: how heavy the blankets were—never had doonas when I was a kid, just the heavy woollen blankets and bedspreads. How the mozzies attacked at dusk and as soon as I went to bed. Locals mixing me up with my sister—we do look very similar!

Where the River Runs is very much inspired by the emotions of me going home. I hope Chelsea's story adds a bit of spice and adventure among the excitement and sensation of a homecoming.

With love,

Fleur x